TOUCHING THE FIRE

▼ ▲ ▼

TOUCHING
THE FIRE

Buffalo Dancers, the Sky Bundle,
and Other Tales

Roger Welsch

University of Nebraska Press
Lincoln and London

© 1992 by Roger Welsch
Manufactured in the United States of America

♾ The paper in this book meets the minimum requirements of American National Standard for Information Sciences—Permanence of Paper for Printed Library Materials, ANSI Z39.48-1984.

First Bison Books printing: 1997
Most recent printing indicated by the last digit below:
10 9   8   7   6   5   4   3   2   1

Library of Congress Cataloging-in-Publication Data
Welsch, Roger L.
Touching the fire: buffalo dancers, the sky bundle, and other tales /
Roger Welsch.
p. cm.
ISBN 0-8032-9798-X (pbk.: alk. paper)
1. Indians of North America—Fiction.   I. Title.
PS3573.E4944T68   1998
813′.54—dc21
97-17729   CIP

Reprinted from the original 1992 edition by Villard Books, New York.

In memory of my brother,
Buddy Gilpin

Philosophers are forever trying to explain visions, but visions are a part of everyday life; the problem for philosophers, therefore, is to explain everyday life.

GEORGE SCHWELLE, *Visions*

ACKNOWLEDGMENTS

▼ ▲ ▼

I am forever indebted to my wonderful wife and in-house editor, Linda Welsch, for going through all this agony once again. My son Chris, daughter Joyce, and friends Mick Maun and Dave Ratliff read my text carefully. They were unmerciful in their insistence that things be right and cogent; I hated them for that then, but I am grateful now.

Thanks to the *NebraskaLand* magazine editors for letting me lift parts of an essay I did for them many years ago and transplant them to this book. And to John Carter for his help and support.

Most of all, of course, I owe thanks to my Native American friends for what they have given me in this life as well as in this book. I cannot list them all; many of them are gone—Clyde Sheridan, Buddy Gilpin, Richard Fool Bull, Oliver Saunsoci, Frank La Flesche, Elizabeth Stabler, and John Turner, for example. But for starters, for those who are still living, thanks to Calvin Iron Shell, Shirley Cayou, Frank Sheridan, Louis Sheridan, the Stabler Family,, Bill Canby, Louis LaRose, Rayna Greene, Dennis Hastings, Clydia Nahwooksi and Reaves Nahwooks, Walter Echo Hawk, Bob Peregoy, Robert Campbell, the Saunsocis, the family of Clyde and Lillian Sheridan (especially Matthew, Dewey, and Ago), Wayne Webster and all of the Wind Clan members, and all of my kin in the Gilpin Family.

Perhaps to make it clear how profound my debt is, I should note that in fact I owe thanks to the thousands and thousands of Omaha, Lakota, and Pawnee who have every right to hate but love nonetheless and have let me be where I had no right to intrude. All of us who love America, which includes me—in spades—owe gratitude to the Native American Church of America and the Native American Rights Fund, who fight the worst to preserve the best.

CONTENTS

▼ ▲ ▼

I magine Golgotha in the hands of a group of radical Muslims who close it to Christian pilgrims and erect a mocking parody of the Crucifixion on its crest. Imagine the Wailing Wall held by a Christian fundamentalist sect that decides to dismantle it and scatter its blocks irretrievably. What if Israeli guerrillas occupied the Kaaba in Mecca and set to rebuilding its shelter into a temple?

The inevitable results of that sort of desecration of holy sites, structures, and objects would be fury and despair, war and death, enmity enduring for millennia, perhaps forever. Desecration of that magnitude is unthinkable, of course. But that has been the usual and accepted historical plight for the most sacred objects of America's native populations.

The Sun Dance was the center of Brule Lakota life, not simply a ritual reflection of how life works but the very fuel that keeps it humming along; the Sun Dance was declared a criminal activity in 1881 by federal legislation.

For the Omaha, the Sacred Pole was the purest and most complete expression of everything and everyone Omaha, which for them of course meant everything human. It was known to them as the Venerable Old Man or the Ultimate Omaha. Its last keeper surrendered it in the 19th century and it lay in a New England museum's vault for nearly a hundred years.

Pawnee holy sites—Pahuk, for example, the sacred hill on which the Council of the Animals meets and decides the fate of man and beast alike—were the landmarks of their cosmos and religion, not simply their geography. In 1875 the Pawnee were removed from their ancestral Nebraska land and today not a single acre is theirs.

Where have the *good* people been while such horrors have been going on? Well, it isn't all that simple, good people against bad people. Archaeologists insist that they are not desecrating Omaha graves; they are salvaging information that is likely to be even more valuable to future generations of Omaha than to the Germans, Czechs, and Norwegians who now farm what a century ago was Omaha land. Collectors preserve timeless art that would probably otherwise deteriorate in its native contexts; yes, the *objets d'art* also have a religious importance, but is Michelangelo's *Pietà* essentially art or icon? What good to anyone are pots buried six feet under the surface of the ground? Why should a Baptist with the name Rassmussen care that he is building his cattle feedlot on a hill where the Pawnee believed the bear, elk, and buffalo held councils? After all, the Pawnee are gone now, and for that matter, so too are the bear, elk, and buffalo.

It is hard for someone who believes absolutely that his faith and its symbols and artifacts are the true and only legitimate belief system to have much sympathy for people who not only deny the "truth" but also embrace an error. It is even harder when the people, beliefs, and artifacts are from an ignored, nearly forgotten past. It is perhaps impossible when that past has little presence and doubtful promise.

So articles of Native American faith, from songs and prayers to totems and sacred bundles, have been bought and stolen from the people who consider them to be gifts from the gods, or to be the very gods themselves. Now the bundles, recordings, images, and carvings rest safely in controlled-environment vaults, cases, and rooms—safe, but dead.

Some hope these sacred objects are dead, at any rate! The understanding of the original and rightful owners is that the immense and dangerous powers of some of these sacred objects never dies, and if not propitiated, properly maintained, or kept within a context of mitigating ritual, these powers are capable of wreaking frightful damage. The consequences are believed to fall not only on those guilty of violating the sanctity of the holy objects but on the innocent as well. In the last decade thieves have stolen divine objects that Native Americans maintain govern the laws of nature. Tearfully, those who know how to care for these objects predict the imminent and inevitable death of the earth as a result of the thefts.

Are such fears less reasonable than those of any number of majority religions that foresee similar doom on other schedules of sin? Less credible than the predictions of atheists that the world will be destroyed by religious wars?

Reckless disregard for Native American religious belief angers me, but I believe that eventually the power of these ancient beliefs—often not merely idle speculation but bodies of empirical knowledge—have a strength well beyond whatever damage desecrators can inflict on them.

So, these seven stories from the Nehawkas' Sacred Sky Bundle, its rise and fall and resurrection, are not to my mind tales of despair. I was once talking about old medicine ways with a Brule Lakota, Richard Fool Bull. His knowledge about plants and their uses in physiological and medical practices was remarkable. I asked him, "Mr. Fool Bull, are you teaching what you know to others? Are you writing it down someplace so it won't be forgotten?"

Fool Bull shook his head and laughed at me. "No, my friend," he said. "There is no one of my people ready or willing right now to learn all this. But it will not be forgotten. If everyone today, right now, forgot that aspirin from the inner bark of the willow eases a headache, would that mean that aspirin would no longer cure a headache? Of course not! Truth may sleep, my friend, but it never dies."

The truths of the Sun Dance, the Sacred Pole, and Pahuk did not die either. Though they have slept briefly in law books, mu-

seums, and exile, they persist in the spirit—not only in the spirit
of the people of the tribes but within the spirit of the greater
humanity. Laws to the contrary, there has probably never been a
year since 1881 when some defiant group, some faithful handful of
Lakota have not celebrated the four-day sacrifice of the Sun Dance.
Perhaps it was the very act of repression that steeled the resolve of
the faithful.

After an absence of almost exactly a century, the Venerable
One, the Sacred Pole of the Omaha, has returned to the soil of His
people, even refreshed by His rest, to a people reinvigorated
through the struggle to regain Him. As it turns out, the museum
people who held the Pole for so long came to think of themselves as
caretakers rather than owners and transformed the return of the
Pole from litigation into celebration.

The Pawnee have recently emerged victorious from a long, painful battle to regain the dead excavated and stolen from sacred
resting places, and have reburied them, thus reclaiming Pawnee
land through the unlikely agency of the spirits of their dead. Now
the Nebraska homeland, long forgotten as a Pawnee legacy, is again
thought of within tribal leadership as *their* land.

The struggles of the New World's tribes are anything but finished. For every small victory, for every Sacred Pole or Sun Dance,
there is a new assault against the truths of the tribesmen. Sacred
objects are stolen as art, and eternal rituals are diluted by well-
meaning white men or venal tribal members. Tribes fade and approach extinction, sometimes only through the ostensibly
benevolent forces of brotherhood, sometimes before the firebrand
of religious, political, and economic intolerance.

The Native American Church, one of the dominant forces in
North American Indian spiritual life in the twentieth century, is at
this very moment under massive assault from the courts. This

fundamentally Christian church—almost puritanically Christian, in fact—uses a sacred cactus in its prayer services, much as the Holy Communion of other Christian churches uses alcohol in the form of wine. It would be absurd, of course, to suggest that Communion is an abuse of alcohol, and it is equally foolish to assert that the use of peyote within the prayerful context of the Native American Church is drug abuse. In all-night prayer ceremonies, in a context of song, prayer, witnessing, and devotion, the role of the sacred herb is almost insignificant.

So why not dispense with the controversy by no longer using the cactus in prayer services? Well, why not eliminate the images of cannibalism and vampirism from Christian rites? The premise is silly, of course. The worshipful context of Communion transforms wine with its alcohol into something that is not only beyond sin but contrary to sin. That is the way it is with the sacred herb of the Native American Church, too, and yet there are those who work to deny Native Americans the same agency for their prayers.

Some elders who are adherents of the peyote cult have told me that they welcome the attacks because they firmly believe that truth prospers precisely when it is under attack. Faith attacked is faith defended.

I would never be so arrogant as to contradict Richard Fool Bull, nor even to try to improve on his wisdom, but it does increasingly seem that not only does truth sleep but never die, neither can it be killed. Like a willow, it falls to the ground, apparently having lost the battle against the tornado, but then sends up a hundred new shoots along its prostrate trunk. If misguided legislation and judicial injustice force the Native American Church underground, it will thrive as it has not been able to do for a century in the rich soil of the white man's world.

Hardly recognizing the processes of the present within Native

American spiritual life and sacred objects, non-Indians can scarcely be expected to understand their past. The Sun Dance has been forever. The history of the Sacred Pole survives in a couple of lines of hazy legend recorded by nineteenth-century anthropologists— the very ones who destroyed the tradition. The Pawnee cannot be faulted for having forgotten the stories of their land, the land having been taken from them almost a century and a half ago.

That doesn't mean there are no stories. Indeed, the humble artifacts and spare accounts that are left are only the most scant and superficial expressions of events that were soul-shaking—even soul-shattering—for those who were there at the time. Imagine, insofar as anyone can, what long-forgotten events must have brought the Sacred Pole to the Omaha, how its power was revealed to them, what the Venerable One has seen and where He has gone with the Omaha. The stories must still be there, for they are the truth. And the truth may sleep, but it never dies.

The Mandan tribe of the Upper Missouri Valley offers a dramatic example of a body of lost information and wisdom. The Mandan were a tall, light-skinned people; those who argue for early and deep pre-Columbian exploration of the continent suggest the Mandan as evidence of surviving Norse genes where archaeological evidence is lacking. What did the Mandan know about the medicinal uses of Plains plants? What did they know about the ways of the gods and of man? Did their folktales or songs contain valuable historical memories of Viking visitors? What could the Mandan have taught us?

We'll never know, because war and disease crushed the Mandan during the nineteenth century. As a people, as a culture, they are gone. Aside from a few drawings and the brief accounts of travelers, we know little of them. Are their songs and stories dead, too? Can it be that Fool Bull was wrong and the Mandan truths *are* dead? No, the Mandan's stories are still alive in *our* spirits. Are the visions and dreams of the Mandan dead simply because we do not know the complete historical and geographical facts of the Mandan? Of course not.

Is any philosophical or literary truth dead or invalid simply because we do not know precisely or with absolute certainty its historical facts? What a ridiculous thought! I can hear Richard Fool Bull's laughter now!

The accounts that follow are those of the Nehawka Sky Bundle, a sacred bundle whose origins are lost in time, found again in my imagination. The paths of the Nehawka people, their songs, their ways, their dances, and their Sacred Bundle are the stories of the Sun Dance, the Sacred Pole, Pahuk, and the Mandan. This is the spirit of a Plains Indian tribe and its spiritual artifacts. There is no factual history of such things. Such things are spared factual histories by virtue of their own power. Such things live best and strongest within the heart, within the imagination of those who love them.

When you read the narratives from the Sacred Sky Bundle of the Nehawka, you will learn little of the conventional historical nonsense of important names and important dates, both of which are rarely of any importance at all. You will instead understand a good deal about the life and spirit of sacred processes like the Sun Dance, the Sacred Pole, Pahuk, and the lost ways of the Mandan.

Fool Bull would argue that we learn too much these days, that we need to learn less and understand more. That, in fact, is how I met Fool Bull. He was visiting a friend of mine and they were talking about where he might find some juniper heartwood that he needed for the beautiful Lakota love flutes he made. My friend was sorting through her mind for anyone at all who could help Fool Bull find the rare wood he needed. She was at the end of her wits. She began listing out loud anyone who might have any way of getting the large trees he needed. When she mentioned my name, Fool Bull said abruptly, "Yes, he's the one. Call him. He has my wood."

My friend knew that I lived in a suburban ranch-style house with virtually no trees anywhere close to it besides the six- and eight-foot saplings I had recently planted. She tried to explain to Fool Bull that she didn't want to disturb me, considering the obvious fact that there was almost no chance that I would have access to juniper trees of any size at all.

"No," Fool Bull insisted. "He has the wood. Call him."

She called me, introducing her request with a long apology. She told me that she had tried in vain to convince Fool Bull not to bother me, that she obviously knew that I had no way to get the wood.

What she did not know, and could not have known, as Fool Bull could not have known, was that the school where I was teaching was about to raze one of its old buildings, and that that building was surrounded by trees, and that I had gotten permission to harvest the trees. The previous day some friends and I had felled thirty very large trees and with a truck moved the massive trunks to my yard.

They were juniper trees. There was no way she or Fool Bull could have known that I was the one person in our city of 150,000 who had two dozen juniper trunks, piled up with no particular purpose. At least, no purpose known to me.

The next day my friend brought Fool Bull to my home. I watched his face for the amazement that was sure to overwhelm him when he realized his incredible luck. But there was no amazement. He shook my hand, moved quickly to the pile of logs, and began pointing. "Yes, I want about six foot of this one, and yes, four feet from this one and this one. And this one. And if you can get at it, this one. And that should about do it."

"Aren't you surprised that I have all of this wood precisely on the morning when you are looking for it?" I finally asked.

He looked at me with surprise. He was not surprised that I had the wood. He was surprised that I didn't understand that he knew I had the wood. "The reason we are here," he explained patiently, "is because I knew you had the wood for me. It wouldn't have made sense to come here for wood if I hadn't known that you had it."

"But I mean that it's quite a coincidence, you calling the one person who has a huge supply of red-cedar heartwood."

"It's no coincidence," he said seriously. "Before we called, I knew you had the wood. The only reason we even bothered to call was because she insisted on it." He pointed to our mutual friend. "Think about it a moment. It would be crazy to think that this is luck, wouldn't it? How could I possibly guess that you had this wood? No one can guess such things. But we can *know* such things."

"How did you learn to know like this?" I asked.

"That's the problem with education. They educate you out of that kind of knowing in white man's schools. We are all born with the ability to know these things but there are ways we can forget them. Wonderful events happen around us all the time. The spirits talk to us. They laugh at us. They tell us things and give us things. Just watch and listen. They are there."

Among the native peoples of the northern Plains a common name for God is the Great Mysterious. No noun, just two adjectives. The great, mysterious what? Just the Great Mysterious. That is enough to know, Richard Fool Bull told me, and maybe even too much, since so few have understood even the little we have been given.

All across the Plains, Native Americans avoid saying anything at all about the Sun Dance, peyote cult ceremonies, or sacred bundles; no one can predict what the white man, his governments, and his churches will do next to insult or injure Native American ways.

There is more to the silence around sacred objects and words than that. Much more than that. The Omaha are reluctant to talk among themselves, yet with others, about the Sacred Pole. Not only is its power enormous, but the rituals, songs, words, and prayers that once protected those who had to deal with that power have been lost. No one can be sure anymore what the consequences are of dealing with such a strong and sacred object.

One of the reasons within Christian tradition that the Lord's name is not to be taken in vain—probably the most important reason, originally—is because no one can be sure what the results will be of evoking those unknown and crushing forces. To speak directly of rituals and names and objects connected with the Powers, the Thunderers, or the Great Mysterious is risky business, too risky to be done lightly. It is better in such matters to tell stories about the way the world used to be, to talk of Coyote and Rabbit and avoid dealing with the Powers altogether, to speak obliquely about things we do not understand, if at all. When one wants to see the face of the sun, it is best to poke a hole in a piece of paper, project its image on a wall, turn your back to the reality of the great fire, and see only its reflection in shadow. So it is too with sacred ways and objects.

When I was adopted into the Omaha tribe in September 1967, I spent the night after the evening ceremony sitting outside in the cool night with my new brother, Buddy Gilpin, as he told me the implications, complications, and responsibilities of my new relationship with life. I had not been given an honorary name, as I had thought; I had been transformed, he explained, made a full-blood Omaha.

And a member of a tribal clan.

As bearer of a clan name, Tenuga Gahi, there were foods I could never again eat and substances I could not touch, precautions I had to take in order not to offend the powers that affect the weather. The prohibitions were manifold and apparently arbitrary; Buddy even laughed at some of them. Obviously, some were lethal and others only inconvenient.

I listened to Buddy's instructions, and listened intently, as a white man. I asked Buddy about the nature of these prohibitions. Were they like the Catholic practice of not eating meat on Friday? Or like voluntary sacrifices during Lent? Or the Jewish avoidance of pork? Did my new name bring with it symbolic gestures, obligations, or requirements?

Buddy sat under the starlit night in silence for a quarter or half hour, considering my questions. We could hear the drums of peyote meetings and the choral ornamentations of coyotes from the reservation's wooded hills. I sat in silence, waiting for my new brother to find his words. "These ideas are . . ." he said slowly, deliberately. "They are like fire. If you put your hand in fire, on purpose or accidentally, no matter how good your heart or how quick your mind, no matter, your hand will be burned. Fire is fire and cannot be otherwise. Fire is good and fire is the heart of our home, but fire must be fire. The ways of the Powers are like touching the fire."

"You have seen the ways of the Omaha at a campfire during powwow," he said. "White people chase their children away from the fire to protect them, to keep them from being burned. Of course that doesn't work. The child must play in the fire to learn that it is light, then bright, then warm, then hot, then painful, and finally dangerous. An Omaha woman watches her child approach the fire for the first time. She lets him see its magic and feel its warmth. She rises slowly as he gets too close and shields his eyes from the heat. She gets closer as he picks up a stick from the fire and begins to play with it, drawing smoke designs in the air, as all children do. Then she watches him burn himself with his glowing stick. He cries. She comforts him and kisses his burn and cries with him at his pain. She knows he has learned about touching the fire."

Since then I have had plenty of reason to remember and witness the truth of my brother's words. The Powers are wonderful, generous, sometimes even funny. But they are also potent and must be approached with caution. One does not speak of them lightly. I am not even sure if it is safe for me to tell you about the specific nature of my clan prohibitions and requirements. One of us, you or I, might be getting too close to the fire, through the light and warmth and heat and, realizing too late, past the boundary where pain begins. Maybe we are touching the fire. I don't know. But better safe than sorry.

The narratives of the Nehawka Sky Bundle are not the traditional or historical legends of any one particular people or one particular holy object; they are accounts of all Native American peoples and sacred artifacts, not *a* people or *one* sacred artifact. The truth is here, but in such a way that we are spared the jeopardy that accompanies any dabbling with immense, dangerous forces. In these stories we can see against the darkened wall the image of the sun's surface and feel its warmth against our backs; we can sit at the campfire and see its magic and know its comfort; we can speak of the power and wonder of sacred objects—without touching the fire.

▼▲▼

The Story of the Winter
the People
Came Home Again

In the old days, the native people of what would eventually be called North America kept track of the passage of years with winter counts. They named each year after whatever remarkable event had happened that year, usually during the winter months. Arriving at a name for the year was the task of the elders of each tribe, but the remarkable circumstances of any year were well enough known to everyone in the community that there was rarely any debate or surprise.

Early ethnologists recorded many winter counts. Often the native people themselves forgot the rationale for the names. In other cases, the names were so obscure that not even tribal traditionalists and historians could imagine what the names meant. Some historians, like Clarence Edgley, theorized that the names were originally nonsense terms, or that the winter count names had been so confused in the passage of time that they no longer made any sense. What could possibly be the meaning of a phrase like "The Winter of the Buffalo Rain" or "The Winter So Hard, Black Deer Became Elk" after all?

The tradition of winter counts faded away in the late nineteenth century, but a few Native American traditionalists fought to keep the custom alive, much the same as they worked for generations to remember and repeat the customs of the Buffalo Dance and Sky Bundle. The year of the Sacred Sky Bundle's return, not long after the Jefferson Medal was returned to Elk's grave, was the year that Quintan "Moose" Man-Elk became an apprentice to Elder Buddy Foster to learn the ways of the Sky Bundle and formally convened a panel of elders to reestablish a tribal winter count among the Turtle Creek Nehawka.

The panel had to consider many things. Though more happens

in a year now than when the Turtle Creek Nehawka first came to the Plains, the Committee of the Nehawka Winter Count remembered the previous year well, and told its story. It was no surprise to anyone in the Turtle Creek community that the first year of the New Winter Count, the year the white man called 2001 A.D., was called "The Winter the People Came Home Again."

That is certainly not the way the events of the winter started. A year that ended with such joy among the people could scarcely have started less auspiciously. In fact, Quintan "Moose" Man-Elk was pretty much in a state of despair when everything started to break loose, just before the quarterly hearing of the State Humanities and Arts Council at the capitol. Everything had been going so well—there was every indication that the Densmore Museum in Boston was prepared to return the Sacred Nehawka Sky Bundle to the tribe. After a century, the most sacred object of the Nehawkas was going to return to its rightful home. On one condition: that a proper and safe repository be constructed for it. A museum, in other words. Moose Man-Elk understood the necessity of that prerequisite, but he also knew that his people did not have the resources to build a museum, since they hadn't even been able to scrape up the money to build a cinder-block toilet at the town baseball diamond that summer.

Efforts to raise money from the legislature, from the Midwestern Archaeological Foundation, and from private donors had failed. The Sky Bundle was so close, yet so far. This hearing with the arts and humanities folks might be the last hope, Man-Elk knew. The Nehawkas' position with humanities and arts funds was not strong, because Clarence Edgley sat on the panel. Clarence Edgley was one of the few obstacles, maybe even the *only* obstacle, certainly the most difficult obstacle the Nehawkas faced in this struggle. Moose Man-Elk knew that Edgley would be a tough opponent of

the Nehawka, because he had proven himself to be a tough opponent of the Nehawka many times in the past. Aging and slight,
Edgley was nonetheless clever and powerful, not a man to be un-
derestimated. He could be very determined.

Jeff Blanchard and Champ Svoboda could tell you about that.
They once drove out to the campsite of the Seventh Dragoons to
deliver a cold six-pack to their buddy Jim Kacek. At the cattle gate
leading down to the pasture where the Dragoons were camped,
they met Clarence Edgley, dressed in his military outfit festooned
with epaulets, fringe, and tassels, carrying a muzzle-loader.

On weekends and during vacations from his longtime position as
director of the Midwestern Archaeological Foundation Museum,
Edgley spent time with the Dragoons, who did everything they
could—too much, some thought—to reproduce the life and ways of
nineteenth-century Indian fighters. The Dragoons were frequently
invited to participate in local parades because they were so colorful,
dressed in nineteenth-century clothing, carrying nineteenth-
century weapons, and speaking nineteenth-century military language.

"Stand and identify yourself or prepare to die!"

"Oh, lay off the soldier crap, Edgley. If you want to shoot someone, join the National Guard." They certainly weren't going to put
up with bullying from that wienie, Clarence Edgley.

"I'm telling you right now, you drive past that cattle gate and I'm
going to fire."

"Screw you, Edgley," Blanchard snarled and popped the clutch
on his pickup, throwing gravel behind him and at Clarence Edgley
in front of him. It's hard to say who was more surprised, Edgley or
Blanchard and Svoboda, when Edgley raised his muzzle-loader,
squeezed the trigger, and blew a hole the size of a grapefruit in the
tailgate of Blanchard's Ford.

Jeff and Champ turned their truck around with the intent of kicking the bejesus out of Edgley, no matter how old and skinny he was. He had shot Blanchard's pickup truck, which was almost like shooting a man's dog. Almost instantly sixteen Dragoons ran out, all carrying rifles and sidearms, ready to defend the camp. Even Jim Kacek, the guy they were bringing the beer for, leveled his weapon at them. When Jeff and Champ got back to the Town Tavern to report the encounter, they were still more stunned than frightened. "Imagine shooting at two buddies bringing cold beer into camp!" Champ sputtered, and he never bought beer for Jim Kacek again.

Other would-be visitors to Dragoon encampments experienced the same reception. The Dragoons did nothing to discourage their reputation as men who took their hobby seriously. "When we are out there on maneuvers, we *are* Dragoons, and if you don't understand nineteenth-century military life, you'd better stay away from the camp."

Thing is, you don't just drive into a Seventh Dragoon encampment like that, Edgley later explained to his troops, and they all agreed he had done the right thing. Small wonder that Clarence Edgley was not only the commanding officer of the Seventh Dragoons but was the only commanding officer the Dragoons had ever known. Everyone said Clarence Edgley was born two hundred years too late. His world was the world of the frontier, of exploration, of savage, nomadic tribes, of French trappers and traders, of Indian fighters, of docile women, and of men making, not kneeling to, law.

The day of the hearing Quintan Man-Elk met with the other members of his committee in the hallway outside the hearing room. There was Silver Mapateet and her husband Luke and Moose Man-Elk's uncle Buddy Foster. Moose knew that Silver and Luke had a reputation for being politically passionate, even rash. He knew that as a political elder and tribal religious leader Buddy Foster enjoyed enormous respect outside the reservation, even among white people, but his age and his difficulty in concealing the emotional pain this matter of the Sky Bundle had caused him made it difficult for him to make his case before a panel like this. He also knew that his own reputation as an easygoing joker considerably diminished his capacity to be taken seriously. The Nehawka presentation team was not strong. Its chances of bringing home money to build a Sky Bundle Museum were not good.

"My friends and cousins, I appreciate you being here to help us ask for money to build a Sky Bundle Museum. I have been working on my speech for the past three weeks but there is nothing here." He tapped the package of paper in his left hand. "I can't find the words to tell these people what the Sky Bundle means to us."

The three nodded and looked at the marble floor. Quintan Man-Elk had talked with each of them during the previous three weeks. Not one of them had an idea how to proceed. Their pessimism was even deeper than his.

"You know, I really hoped there would be a sign. A sky sign. Wind, rain, clouds. I know it sounds like old superstitions"—now his friends and relatives were shaking their heads—"but I really thought the Sky Bundle would send a message of some sort. I thought maybe there would be a storm. Maybe someone would see a cloud that looked like a sign. Maybe a wind would ruffle my papers one of these past few days and I would say 'Mary, close the window' and she would say, 'The window isn't open' and I would know it was a sign. Nothing like that happened. I hoped maybe the sky would send a flood to keep Clarence Edgley from getting to this hearing, but nothing of the sort has happened."

"Perhaps . . ." Buddy Foster started.

Moose Man-Elk reached out and touched his great-uncle's arm. "I know what you are going to say, Uncle, and you may be right. Maybe we are not supposed to have the Sky Bundle again. Perhaps we are being punished by the Powers for losing it in the first place. Maybe the sign is that there are no signs."

The four stood in silence a moment in the great, echoing hallway. "But I think we have to try to regain what is ours. Are you with me? Do we try?"

His compatriots nodded, but without enthusiasm. "Who knows," tried Silver Mapateet. "It may not be as hard as we think it is going to be. Maybe our request will blow right on through. Even if it doesn't, this can be our opportunity to see which way the wind is blowing." The other three sensed the terrible pun at once and looked at her in surprise, wondering if she realized how close she had come to saying offensive, almost blasphemous words about the Sky Bundle.

She suddenly realized that she might have committed a terrible gaffe. "I didn't mean . . ."

Her husband Luke—not really a Nehawka but close enough— tried to control himself but blew out a laugh like a sneeze. "That's terrible, Silver!"

Old Buddy Foster—a holy man, after all—chuckled, "Didn't your name used to be 'Big Blow'? Maybe that's the sign."

"It was 'Bigelow,' " Luke said, still choking back laughter. "And a *windy* old goat like you shouldn't try to *cloud* the issue over."

"And you call Silver's jokes terrible?" Quintan laughed. "When this all *blows* over, if Clarence Edgley doesn't *rain* on our parade, maybe there'll be a *Silver* lining. We'll buy a bottle of cheap wine and celebrate. After all, any *port* in a *storm*."

"If we didn't have bad *Luke* we'd have no *Luke* at all."

"No *Moose* is good *Moose*."

"The *sky*'s the limit."

"I'm laughing so hard I'm going to wet my pants!"

"Or *break wind*!"

The wretched puns tumbled one on the other, each speaker straining to outdo the others, each new effort met with groans, which only encouraged the next exchange. Tears running down his face, Quintan Man-Elk stopped to catch his breath and realized that it was the first time he had laughed, the first time he had felt good in three weeks. Buddy Foster slumped onto one of the marble benches along the wall, racked with laughter. Silver poked Luke in the shoulder. "What a blessing," Moose Man-Elk thought, "that we can have this moment of laughter during such hard times, times that seem to have so little promise."

Then it occurred to him what was happening. These were not innocent jokes between old acquaintances. This was the sign he'd been waiting for. Of course! This was not the Powers or the Thunderers speaking with the great forces of earth and sky. This was Coyote, the Trickster, at work. Coyote, who laughs when he should cry and cries when he should laugh, would speak in just this way. Coyote would border on the edge of blasphemy, at the rim of decency, at the margins of madness. No, this was not just laughter; this was a clue. A clue to the course the Nehawka should follow this afternoon at the hearing.

Quintan "Moose" Man-Elk knew precisely what this peculiar, almost inappropriate moment meant. "Time to go," he said with a smile. "It's going to be a *breeze*." And they laughed again. Then they put on their solemn "Indian faces" and entered the hearing room.

Clarence Edgley was seated at the end of the long table on the raised platform. He was lost in thought. He was thinking what a waste of time this was and how much he wished he were with his comrades of the Dragoons.

Clarence Edgley probably couldn't analyze his feelings for Indians. He had grown up in a community near the Turtle Creek Reservation of the Nehawka Indian tribe, and that proximity had given him a special contempt for Indians. As a boy he had had Nehawka friends and had gone to powwows and Buffalo Dances in the oak arbor in the squalid town of Turtle Creek. He went to school with Nehawkas. He was strangely drawn to the Turtle Creek Nehawka and at the same time repulsed by them. He hated their indolence and yet admired their accommodation to the hard life of the reservation. He envied the athletic abilities of his Indian schoolmates and yet he would never have traded his intellectual and social superiority for a spot on the school's football team. He had been drawn to the Indians' pride in their past but knew that the death of all those things they held sacred was a gift to them from his own people. Most of all, deep within him, he resented that despite that long history and hard life, his young companions showed no envy of his own life and heritage.

The bottom line is that Clarence Edgley was attracted to the American Indian but resented the undeniable fact that Indians had become the principal threat to the preservation of the West's past. It was quite enough for Edgley that Indians threatened the social, scholarly, and legal structure of the pioneers' America; increasingly they threatened the substance of the past—its artifacts, its museums, its reality.

Edgley made a career . . . no, a mission . . . no, a *crusade* of holding the figurative fort against all too real Indians. He didn't hate Indians, but he knew them well enough not to trust them. He had devoted his life to protecting museum collections around the country from raids by modern, three-piece-suit Indians who decided they wanted back what their ancestors had thrown away or sold—the Sky Bundle being a perfect example.

He was uneasy about the spooky side of the whole issue, a fact he admitted only to his Dragoons. The bones of the dead Indians had caused him some discomfort, but the Sky Bundle with its uncertain origin and unexplained contents—a corroded nugget of native copper, a dead parakeet, for example—was another issue. The Nehawka had warned him quietly but firmly of the Bundle's powers and that abuse of the Bundle might carry with it terrible consequences. He had tried to dismiss the threats as superstitious nonsense—"nothing but skins, feathers, rocks, and seashells," he had said again and again. Yet every time he had occasion to look at the Bundle on display or in the storage cases, he had to turn his eyes. Something troubled him when he looked at the Bundle directly. He would be relieved if he could get rid of the thing, but as long as its loss to him constituted a victory for the Nehawkas, he would take his chances.

And there was the theft of the Jefferson Peace Medal by the Nehawka Buffalo Dancers, a crime for which the Indians had not fully paid. It was a transgression Edgley had not forgotten and for which he had made them pay in a hundred small ways over the intervening years.

Nor had the matter of the Sky Bundle gone well for Edgley so far. As director of the Midwest Archaeological Foundation Museum and the state's chief preservation officer, Edgley should have handled all such transactions, but the Indians bypassed Edgley, and even the curators of the Densmore Museum, where the Bundle had been stored for a century, going instead to the grand old museum's directors—"wimps who received the Indians like long-lost buddies," Edgley later growled.

The Densmore board of directors wined and dined the Nehawka delegation from Turtle Creek, took the Indians on a tour of the collection so they could see if there was anything else they might like to take home with them, and then announced that they were proud to have been caretakers—"caretakers!"—of the Sky Bundle this past century and were now proud to return it to its rightful home. As soon as he heard the news, Edgley called up Clark Franklin, director of the Densmore, to offer sympathy and to insist that the transfer of the Sky Bundle be stopped immediately.

"Well, Clarence, frankly I am in agreement with my directors on the return of the Sky Bundle, and on what basis do you want to interfere with the transfer?" Clark Franklin asked.

"Because we can't even be sure the bundle belongs to the Turtle Creek Nehawka. You know for yourself that none of the stuff in it is indigenous to the Plains—an Atlantic clam shell, a wad of native copper, a smear of cypress ash, a few corn chips, a fragment of mastodon tooth, a *parakeet*, for God's sake. The Turtle Creek people probably stole the Bundle from some other tribe two hundred years ago. If anything, we should hold it until we hear the claims of other tribes." Edgley liked that idea: it smelled of the chance of delay.

"Edgley, the Sky Bundle belongs with the Turtle Creek people because that's where we got it. And that's where it's going to go."

"Where the hell are they going to keep something as fragile as that mess of old skins and feathers, Clark? It'll fall apart in a matter of months. We must keep it for future study. If the Bundle is lost or destroyed, no one will suffer more than the Nehawkas themselves."

"The Bundle belongs to those people, Clarence, and maybe it's time for it to fall apart. We've studied the living hell out of it: we've measured it, photographed it, weighed it, analyzed it. Besides, we are working to protect the Bundle. It doesn't go back to Turtle Creek until they have an appropriate repository for it. If you're so concerned about the welfare of the Sky Bundle, why don't you work with the Turtle Creekers to build a museum for it?"

So, not two weeks after the Densmore announced its intentions, Nehawka tribal elders were knocking at Edgley's door, and the legislature's, asking for money to build a museum of their own, where they could care for the Sky Bundle and other historical artifacts. It was easy enough for Edgley to deny the tribe museum funds. "We have insufficient funds to care for our own collections, yet to dole out money to non-professionals to build and maintain storefront museums," Edgley wrote the Turtle Creek tribal elders in denying them funds. "Perhaps you could place the Sky Bundle within the state historical collection and thus ensure its proper and respectful care in the future."

He argued the same point—a valid point—before the legislature's budget committee when the Nehawka representatives appeared there seeking funds for the Sky Bundle Museum. Without the blessing of the state's preservation officer, the request from Turtle Creek for state museum monies had little chance. If the Nehawkas couldn't get the Bundle back until they had a suitable museum, then he would do whatever he could to keep them from getting that museum. Clarence Edgley sensed he was on the verge of victory again, for the first time in a long time. He would preserve the Sky Bundle for future generations of Nehawkas, whether they liked it or not.

Today was the day the Turtle Creek Sky Bundle Museum Committee was scheduled to present its case for museum funding to the State Humanities and Arts Council. Clarence Edgley, as state preservation officer, was a permanent member of that distinguished panel. Normally, he was bored by the proceedings of that committee, endless requests for literature programs and art exhibits, constant whining for money to pay for projects communities were not willing to pay for themselves, but today he looked forward to that point on the long agenda when the Turtle Creek people would stand before the committee and ask for money for their Sky Bundle

Museum. Edgley knew that he could count on the other members
of the panel to defer to him on any issues of history or anthropology.
With any luck at all, he could have a unanimous vote against the
Turtle Creek Nehawkas' proposed home for the Sky Bundle.

The Indians had bushwhacked him often enough in the past that
he knew better than to be prematurely confident, but he simply *had*
to smile when he saw the Indian representatives file into the hearing room. He couldn't believe his good fortune. The four Indians
who would be presenting their case were Buddy Foster—doddering
and too emotional about such issues as the Sky Bundle to do anything but embarrass his allies; Silver Mapateet—a radical agitator
who offended every white person who came within range of her
razor tongue; her husband, Luke Mapateet—a pretend-Indian
white man whose unsavory record wasn't going to win many votes
from the Council, a man with so little self-respect that instead of
giving his wife his name, he had taken hers; and—this was the best
part—Quintan Man-Elk, the reservation clown, a roly-poly oaf
devoid of any savoir faire whatsoever. Small wonder that Man-Elk's
nickname was "Moose." Edgley almost relished the next hour.
This might be fun.

"Dr. Edgley, are you going to vote on the city of Kearney's
application for $2,500 to fund a folk-artist-in-the-schools pro-
gram?" Edgley was startled out of his thoughts by the glass-cutting
voice of Saundra Basely, chair of the council.

He didn't want to cast a dissenting vote that would prolong the
meeting. He wanted to get down the agenda to the Turtle Creek
petition but, lost in his thoughts, he didn't know how the discussion or vote was going at this point. "Madam Chair, I'll have to go
with the majority on this one, though there is plenty of merit with
the minority opinion."

"Thank you, Dr. Edgley. Then the vote is unanimous." Edgley
was so quickly back in his thoughts that he didn't even notice

which way the vote had gone. "Would the representative of the Turtle Creek Museum Committee like to present that group's petition for museum funding?" Saundra Basely asked.

When Quintan Man-Elk hoisted his huge frame from his chair in the back of the room and began to move forward, Edgley had to clamp his jaw so hard to keep from smiling that he was afraid he was going to hurt himself. The Turtle Creekers were actually sending up the reservation clown to request the museum funding!

Man-Elk didn't even amount to much as an Indian, in Edgley's opinion. One of the few customs Edgley appreciated within Indian culture was that they kept their distance. In conversations, meetings, social events, Edgley could usually be sure that he wouldn't have some damned Indian hanging all over him. One of the things he had always hated about people at such meetings—including white people—is that they wanted to be buddies. It wasn't enough to talk business and make the right social gestures and then move on. When you enjoy some power, Clarence Edgley had found, people want to rub shoulders with you by actually rubbing shoulders with you.

Not Indians. They shook hands fleetingly and with no grasp at all, so you could be rid of them without delay. Except Quintan Man-Elk. The one tradition Man-Elk should have learned from his Indian ancestors, he had apparently missed. Man-Elk had the insufferable habit of shaking Edgley's hand and then not letting go. Edgley had to stand there holding Man-Elk's hand while Man-Elk talked on and on for fifteen minutes or so about whatever scheme he was up to. Sometimes he would add his second hamlike hand to the clasp and Edgley would stand there, his arm like an ax held by a woodsman, and for reasons Edgley could never understand, Man-Elk managed to get an invitation to damned near every social and political function Edgley attended. It was maddening.

There was no sense in trying to escape Quintan Man-Elk's distinctly un-Indian handshake by force. Man-Elk stood maybe six-foot-four and weighed at least three hundred pounds; when they stood together, Edgley's hand trapped in Man-Elk's, Man-Elk loomed over Edgley. The only reason Edgley went to social gatherings was because he had people to talk to, important people, powerful people, and these quarter-hour imprisonments in Man-Elk's clutches were costly to him and his ambitions. No escape strategies worked.

Once Edgley tried to avoid Man-Elk's handshake by not raising his hand when Quintan offered his. Unabashed, Quintan threw his huge arm over Edgley's shoulder and stood there talking with him chest to nose, shaking Edgley's fragile frame in his bear hug whenever he made a particularly important point. Never again did Edgley avoid Man-Elk's offer of a handshake.

And now here was Moose Man-Elk, sitting in front of him, asking for money. He hoped Man-Elk took his time presenting his case. In the eighteen years Clarence Edgley had been on the Humanities and Arts Council, he had never listened so attentively or so thoroughly enjoyed himself while reviewing grant applications. He eased his thin frame back in the big, soft leather chair, put his hands behind his head, and watched Quintan Man-Elk sort through his papers and begin his presentation.

"Ladies and geraniums, er, ladies and germs—" Man-Elk started, and then laughed at his own joke "—I mean 'gentlemen.' Just a little joke. I sure appreciate you listening to what we have to say. Actually, all we are trying to do is even up the bum deal we made on selling you white folks Manhattan Island. We got twenty-four dollars worth of beads for New York when we should have asked for at least forty-eight dollars worth of beads."

Other council members chuckled uneasily. Edgley's smile did not change but he felt a growing, glowing warmth in his gut.

Man-Elk continued, "Seriously, folks, we people up at Turtle Creek are always asking for money and things. We don't call it 'welfare' on the reservation; we call it 'Indianfare.' Anyway, this time we are asking for something extra special. We want money for a museum.

"And that's why my relatives here . . ." Man-Elk gestured back to the Turtle Creek committee members in the back row, ". . . are glad that our old friend Clarence Edgley is on your committee today. He knows about museums. He knows about Indians."

Edgley eased his chair forward and looked at Man-Elk, although Man-Elk did not look at him.

"We Nehawka people are used to being in museums but are not used to having one. The last time I was in Clare Edgley's museum I noticed everyone was wearing tags that said 'Visitor.' I looked down at mine, and you know what it said? It said 'Artifact.' I thought that was pretty good." Again there was uneasy laughter from the members of the committee.

"But now we people at Turtle Creek want a museum. Clare says he don't have money to help us, and the legislature don't have money neither. So we have come to you. You got money for people pasting stuff together and making piles of cement and teaching kids how to play the dulcimer, so we figures you must have some extra money for us poor Indians up at Turtle Creek.

"Clare, I heard you at the annual museum meeting and you did a report on a place called Old Sewerage Village Museum, where they recreate eighteenth-century life back in Massachusetts, right?" Edgley nodded and chuckled at Man-Elk's malapropism, knowing that the rest of the panel, no matter how modest their museum experience, would recognize that this boob was out of his element.

"That's 'Old Sturbridge Village,' Moose," he chuckled.

"Whatever. And Clare, you even said that this is the direction of the modern museum, this lived-in history—"

"Living history," Edgley corrected.

"Right. Thanks, Clare. Living history. That's where people who ain't really the real folks pretend to be what they're not, so other people will understand what the people they're not were. See, at Old Steerage Village, people who are really alive now, and who may be university history students or even lawyers, dress up and pretend they're farmers in 1775 or something so other university history students and lawyers can come and see what they would have been like if they'd been alive two hundred years ago. I don't have that quite right, do I, Clare?"

Edgley snorted. Man-Elk looked at him. "You're close, Moose," Edgley said. "Living history museums are reenactments that focus on process rather than item. The idea is that with the use of relatively inexpensive reproductions, or in some cases actual artifacts, we can demonstrate the processes of farm life, industry, village life, whatever, so the modern museum visitor can see not only what the objects of the past are, but how they were used. From buildings to tools, animals to resources. In its highest development, the interpreters take on the character of the people they are representing, so-called 'first-person' interpretation. The visitor walks into a seventeenth-century Pilgrim home at the Plimoth Plantation Museum, for example, and sees people in period clothing, using period tools to prepare period foods. If you ask the interpreter, 'What did the Pilgrims do for tableware?' the museum worker takes on the role of a Pilgrim and answers, 'Why, sir, we eat with our fingers as a proper person does. What do you do?' First-person interpretation, living history museology is a difficult method, but it can be effective if done well."

"Thanks, Clare," Man-Elk answered, pointing his forefinger

directly at Edgley, who was glad Man-Elk wasn't close enough to throw his arm over Edgley's shoulders. "And these museums don't have to be real old-time stuff, do they?"

"No." Edgley's uneasiness had grown to suspicion.

Man-Elk continued: "Some living history museums depict fairly recent life, material culture traditions that are gone or exotic or unusual or distant even if not particularly old. I think these museums are useful in helping people understand each other. Sometimes we can live right side by side and still not know how the other person lives. I wonder how many of you have ever been in an Indian home, and for sure, I don't get many invitations to fancy white folks' homes."

"Madam Chair, I suggest we move on with this petition. We have a good many items on our agenda," Edgley said with a nod toward Man-Elk. Chairwoman Basely smiled and waved to Man-Elk to continue his presentation.

"Thanks, Edge," Man-Elk said, with unlikely gratitude. "That's what we want up at Turtle Creek. A living cultural museum. Not one that just shows history, but one that shares culture, brings people together, encourages understanding, builds bridges."

Clarence Edgley looked at Man-Elk's face. There was no clue there of what he was up to, but Edgley knew it wasn't good. Nothing in the previous struggles over a museum for the Sky Bundle had contained any mention of a living history museum or living cultural dimension.

"Moose, since most of the rituals and processes associated with the Sky Bundle have been long forgotten, I fail to see . . ."

"Edge, no one's saying anything about the Bundle," said Man-Elk. "You convinced us about our goof with that project. We've pretty much put that on the back burner, or maybe back tipi fire! Edge, we are talking here . . ." Man-Elk paused dramatically, looked from one end of the panel to the other, stopping with Edgley. "We are talking here . . . the Turtle Creek Wache Museum."

Edgley sat bolt upright. He knew that word, *wache*. It meant "white man," but was used by the Turtle Creekers as a modest insult, like "honky" or "gringo." " 'Wache' means 'white man,' " added Quintan Man-Elk. "We want to build . . ." Man-Elk paused and surveyed the panel with his eyes again, ". . . the Turtle Creek Plains White Folks Museum."

There was a confused rustle in the audience as well as on the panel. Edgley was not the only one who had expected a petition for a funding of a museum for the Sky Bundle. Man-Elk continued, unruffled by the stir: "The Turtle Creek Reservation lies on a central point for many Indian travelers, visitors to powwows, ceremonials, Buffalo Dances, Sun Dances—spiritual, cultural, historical meetings of all sorts. We get Indian visitors up at Turtle Creek from all over. Hundreds, thousands every year.

"One of the things we talk about is the mystery of how white people live in their houses. We see things on television, but we know that what we see on television soap operas and sitcoms is not the way white people really live. And we want to know. White people want us Indians to live like white people but, you know, we Indians don't really have any way of knowing how that is.

"So what we want to do is to build us a ranch-style suburban home, just like all the white people have, and put white folks' furniture in it, and white folks' clothes, and a white folks' car, and staff it with real white folks who will live in that white folks' house just like white folks. Then, during museum hours, Indians can go through the house and see the old man sitting there in his lounge chair watching an NFL game and drinking Budweiser right out of the can, and the kids will be at the kitchen table doing homework, and the wife can be out there in the kitchen whipping up cake mixes and casseroles, or whatever the hell it is that white women cook on a Saturday afternoon. It sure isn't fry bread, right, Clare?"

Edgley nodded. He was speechless.

Quintan Man-Elk continued with his presentation, obviously warming to his subject: "And we want to have a little gift shop behind the house where Indian folks can buy samples of wind chimes and stuff the white guy makes in his shop out in the garage, and whatever it is that the kids make in their crafts classes over at the Y, and actually sample the food that the white woman cooks in her kitchen. You know, like red Jell-O with bananas in it and grilled cheese sandwiches and fluffy rice.

"I can't think of anything that would go further toward helping us understand you people and help us achieve the kind of life you enjoy and so generously want for us. I've been to Doc Edgley's house. Remember, Doc? After a historical society meeting, when you invited all of us to come over for drinks?" Boy, did Edgley remember.

"I saw the coyote skin on the wall." Man-Elk used the city pronunciation of three syllables, Edgley knew, just to gall him. "I saw a big jar full of old green pennies and Doc Edgley's silver medal for outstanding service to the Midwestern Archaeological Foundation Museum. I saw a lamp made out of beautiful smooth wood— cypress, I think—and the pretty blue songbirds in a cage. I saw ears of squaw corn tied onto the front door real pretty. And the ivory chess set. I saw all the things white people like in their houses but I didn't understand any of it.

"The Turtle Creek Plains White Folks Museum would help Indian people understand such things. Why do white people gather strange birds, bits of metal, bone, and wood, and skins together? Why would anyone put them in special places and pay special attention to them? What do these curious things mean to white people? I think if we Indian people understand that, we might find that we are in some ways closer together, closer to being cousins, even brothers, than we Indians know. I think this museum would bridge that gap in understanding."

Wilbur Olson, an English department medievalist who Edgley could count on to embrace every half-baked cause for every bunch of dark-skinned beggars who came around, said, "You know, I think Mr. Man-Elk has something here. I was skeptical when he began, but I think he really has hit on an important idea."

"Wilbur, I know you mean well," Edgley groaned. "But these people have no capacity to develop, maintain, or staff such a museum. It's a ridiculous idea. If the Indians want to know how we live, they don't need to build a museum. They can see it all around them."

"But that's the point, Clare," Man-Elk interrupted. "Too many Indians get the wrong idea. You can work with us. You have the staff, you have the research anthropologists, you have the skills. You and I can work hand in hand to build this museum so it's right. You said at the legislature that our efforts to build a museum for the Sky Bundle were 'an exercise in the past,' and that we should start thinking of the future. We respect you, Edge, and we are hoping that you will work with us at every step on this project."

Edgley shivered. The prospect of spending more than ten minutes of the rest of his life with this big bozo made his stomach churn. He saw his museum budget going up in smoke, as well as his plans for a new Pioneers and Progress exhibit.

"I think Dr. Olson is right," said Saundra Basely. "I think this is a uniquely charming exercise in brotherhood."

Edgley looked sideways down the panel. He saw heads nodding. He saw smiles. He saw agreement. He saw his world crumbling. He knew enough about Indians to see the hand of Coyote in this.

He was about to become a museological ally with Quintan Man-Elk. He sensed a motion coming, a motion to build this asinine museum.

"I move—" said Saundra Basely, and Clarence Edgley blurted, so loud that he startled even himself, "Madam Chair, with all respect, I would like to ask for a point of professional privilege here. I believe that I am the senior member of this panel, certainly in matters of museums and anthropology . . ." He looked up and down the panel to be sure that he had agreement on that point. "And I would like to suggest that while Mr. Man-Elk's proposal has merit, we have here a problem of priorities.

"The problem of the Turtle Creek Sky Bundle is quite separate, of course, from the matters dealt with by this committee. The matter is part of the responsibility of the State Museums Board and the Legislative Finance Committee, but since I serve on both this and the Museums Board, perhaps I can be, as our distinguished chairlady suggests, a bridge here. I suggest that this committee, instead of setting off in an untried, questionable, even hasty direction, endorse the Turtle Creek Reservation's pending request for a museum to house their Sky Bundle. I have had my own doubts about the feasibility of that project but this new proposal suggests to me that the people of Turtle Creek are perhaps more sophisticated in such matters than I had suspected." The vote was unanimous, money was allocated, support was offered, legislators in attendance assured speedy action, other old business was quickly disposed of, the meeting dismissed, and the room emptied. Edgley was the last to leave.

He dreaded the prospect of leaving through the only door of the boardroom and encountering Man-Elk and his compatriots laughing at him in triumph, but he sensed no alternative. He left the boardroom and entered the open hall.

Man-Elk, the Mapateets, and Foster were sitting on a low bench along the wall. He hurried past them. They paid no attention to him. They were bent over, huddled together, hugging each other, simultaneously crying and laughing. Even in his haste Edgley heard Silver Mapateet crying, "I can't believe it, ten years ago the Buffalo Dancers brought home the Jefferson Peace Medal and now the Sky Bundle is coming home, too," and Moose Man-Elk choking out, "We are all coming home, Silver. At last, we Nehawkas are all coming home."

No wonder there was so little question about what the year should be called in the New Nehawka Winter Count. Man-Elk and the Turtle Creek elders consulted tribal records and the memories of the tradition keepers and found there was already a "Winter the People Came Home," so they decided it was fitting that this year, known to the white man as 2001 A.D., be known as "The Winter the People Came Home Again."

The Story of
LaVoi Antler and the
Jefferson Peace Medal

LaVoi Antler lay in the dark, staring toward the ceiling. He thought about the Jefferson Peace Medal, a silver medallion given to his Nehawka tribe almost two centuries earlier. He thought about Clarence Edgley. He tried to forget the angry words he had heard that day. He listened instead to Elizabeth's deep breathing. She pressed her back against his right side, as if gathering in his warmth. His right hand rested on her hip. He knew her so well: if he turned toward her, she would press back toward him for a moment, even in her sleep; if he rolled away from her, she would gather him in with her arms and squeeze his back to her breast, never fully waking. She said that at night she did with her body what she did with her mind during the day — giving comfort to him and seeking comfort from him, clinging to him, depending on him for warmth and protection.

The thought made Antler hate Clarence Edgley. Well, that wasn't quite it either. He didn't hate Edgley nearly as much as he hated Edgley for reminding him that he wasn't always comfortable with himself. The previous day Edgley had reminded Antler of what he had so often thought without Edgley's prompting, that he had betrayed his people, the Turtle Creek Nehawka. One of his own brothers had not spoken to him for the ten years he had been married to Liz, maintaining, Antler heard by rumor, that his marriage to a white woman had hastened the death of their mother and weakened the blood of The People, as the Nehawkas called themselves.

Antler knew well that the Turtle Creek people were losing their tribal vitality quickly enough by their own attrition, by killing themselves with cheap wine, homemade drugs, and guns. By forgetting their traditional ways. Now young men and women of the

Turtle Creek sub-tribe were marrying into other tribes or, like Antler, non-Indians. What Antler resented most of all was the reinforcement he had given to the racist Hollywood crap embraced by people like Edgley, that Indian men had a particular attraction to white women and, it followed implicitly, a distaste for Indian women. Maybe it was just as bad for the ways of the Nehawkas when their young men became lawyers like Antler and lived in suburban houses in the part of town called "Fox Hollow," and married white girls they met in college.

Sleep still eluding him, Antler recalled how, as a young man, he had flirted with Indian girls on the reservation, had kissed them in play, felt their firm softness. His first experiences with sex had been with Indian girls, and an Indian woman. Elizabeth still felt uneasy about the way he stared at the women dancing the round dances at the annual powwow. Antler dismissed her uneasiness by explaining that all men, whatever their origins, watched powwow dancers that way, and she could scarcely argue with him because the grace and dignity of dancing Nehawka women is obvious.

Some tribal members envied their brother Antler his white wife, he knew from their talk, but others—he could see in their eyes— resented him. Worst of all, now he had been married to her for twenty years and doubts still haunted him about the racial, tribal, cultural implications of his choice of a wife. He hated his thoughts, thoughts he never shared with Elizabeth, and thoughts of which Edgley had reminded him at the legislative hearing that morning.

LaVoi Antler enjoyed a peculiar position as lobbyist and legal representative for the Turtle Creek Nehawka in that he was also a member of the tribe. His hereditary membership gave his arguments as a lobbyist credibility but it also erased any advantage he might have gained from an attorney's usual objectivity. Antler grew up as a Nehawka, speaking the language, eating the food, understanding his role in the processes of life in accordance with how his family and community understood their roles. It wasn't hard for him to be a Nehawka and a lawyer because the logic of his people not only permitted, but even encouraged other paths to knowledge.

What *was* hard for LaVoi Antler was to be a lawyer and a Nehawka. Without reason, without logic, the legal system of which he was an officer, the white man's world within which and through which he moved constantly was not so tolerant of alternative thinking. He had grown up within the Holy Indian Church, sitting up all night, praying with his relatives and tribesmen, singing the powerful songs, exhausted from the long trial of sitting all night around the sacred fire—there is nothing to lean against in a tipi!—ingesting the sacred but difficult peyote cactus and retching from the impact of the herb on his system and the confusion of the visions in his head. It would have been painful enough for Antler to have his profound faith in his people's religion dismissed by his colleagues but worse, increasingly, the ways of the Holy Indian Church were opposed in law and declared illegal—just like the Pawnee Sun Dance and the Lakota Ghost Dance. As an agent and officer of the courts, he found that he was increasingly forbidden to follow his faith and his people's religion.

And he had eventually, painfully, decided to separate himself for the moment at least from the church, not simply because he was concerned about his professional and ethical obligations but because he feared that as a visible figure from the mainstream white culture—Indian or not, Nehawka or not—he might inadvertently bring to his tribe's religious practices the attention of hostile zealots. Again Antler's guts growled and he had to relax each part of his body, muscle by muscle.

He felt Elizabeth stir beside him. He wished he could share the refuge of her sleep. He would, he had once told Elizabeth, rather defend a serial murderer because then he could stand apart from the results of the legal actions, removed from the families of the victims—at least to some degree—and could successfully convince himself that he was serving the noble goals of America's legal system by providing a legitimate defense even to people he despised. When he served as tribal attorney, however, he represented himself, his parents, and his children, insofar as only half of their blood was Norwegian, half Turtle Creek Nehawka.

So it would have been easier, perhaps, to be at the legislative hearing representing the Bleaker County Pork Producers, which he had done with some success, or the Coalition Against the Death Penalty, a cause that had received less enthusiasm in this culturally and politically conservative area. The Turtle Creek Nehawka, on the other hand, had no one else whom they could trust, and they did trust Antler because he was a Turtle Creeker.

Antler liked to believe that he had been instrumental in previous struggles of the Indian peoples of the state. He was especially proud of his role in taking from Edgley and his institution, the Midwestern Archaeological Foundation, the bones of Nehawka people stored on its shelves. That legal struggle had turned into an ugly war, and Edgley and Antler had looked at each other across a lot of hearing rooms and courtrooms in the battles that had determined the war's outcome.

Antler looked at the pale light of the alarm clock beside the bed. Two A.M. Tomorrow was certain to be a miserable, exhausting day. He could not rip his mind away from the events of the day and the events of the past that had led to today. Antler recalled how during the trial Edgley argued that medical science needed the forensic evidence provided by Indian remains exhumed by archaeologists; Antler countered that modern diseases require modern evidence, European ailments call for European bone samples, modern dietary deficiencies can scarcely be analyzed through samples of pre-frontier remains.

Edgley raised the torch of knowledge and argued that a society should not destroy information, that without the data gained by archaeologists at their digs, the grandchildren of living Turtle Creekers would never be able to understand their own past. Antler had left the court silent on that occasion by pointing out that not a single significant cultural analysis based on the museum's holdings had been published in the century and a quarter the Nehawka bones had been collected—inventories, but no analyses. He concluded that it was not reasonable to think that the dignity of the future is in any way assured by contempt for the present and past.

Edgley countered that as science moves forward, we can never know what new techniques science might develop to provide analyses. DNA analysis, he argued, would soon make it possible for scientists to determine more from those bones in the cardboard boxes than anyone in the courtroom could imagine. Antler countered by asking, again quietly, if time and mismanagement had not compromised the bones on the shelves beyond analysis, and if, left in the ground, the graves of the Turtle Creek people might not be of more value to these projected analytical systems a century or so down the line.

Clarence Edgley never compromised his position or backed down, even when it appeared that he had lost the debate; he invented new barriers. He sought advantage. He fought with the fury of a man who represented science in a bloody battle with superstition. He knew that to be an effective scholar, he would have to be a successful politician. He firmly believed that his was the position of the long view, not the whim of the moment. Edgley honestly felt, Antler granted, that he was injuring the living few only to serve the future many.

He had once told Antler over a glass of good Scotch, "Sometimes we have to put aside ethics and do what's right." Edgley laughed, but LaVoi Antler couldn't tell if he was laughing at the joke or at him.

The legislature passed the reburial bill by an overwhelming majority, one that surprised even Antler. Edgley would have to return the remains of dead Nehawka to their respective tribes and subtribes, but Edgley was not done: he took the issue to the state's supreme court and argued that the dead have no rights, that Nehawka bones on museum shelves are nothing more than mineral deposits. Antler reminded the judge that America put great importance on the return of the dead from Vietnam and Libya, and had held a grand ceremonial reburial for one of Custer's soldiers found at the edge of the Little Bighorn battleground only the year before.

Antler's most telling point was that Edgley's museum, like so many other American museums, dug, analyzed, and exhibited Indian remains but never German, never English, never Greek, never Italian, never Irish remains. Only Indians. "As flattered as I am that our bones contain so much more information than yours, Dr. Edgley, I think it is time for you to devote study to the remains of your own people and leave ours at rest."

The judge took less than an hour to reach an opinion: Edgley would have to return Turtle Creek remains and burial goods to the people of Turtle Creek for ceremonial reburial. Other museums in the state would have six months to inventory their holdings of human remains and burial goods and do the same.

Edgley had lost again, but it was clear to Antler that he was not getting any more accustomed to losing. "You got me again, LaVoi," he smiled. "It's going to be tougher the next time."

"Next time?" Antler asked.

"Next time," Edgley insisted.

Antler almost laughed aloud. God, if he didn't get to sleep soon . . .

Edgley's "next time" was the next fall, when he convinced several state senators to introduce yet another bill, limiting the scope of the burial remains and goods laws to *future* excavations and leaving the dead who had been dug up in the past in the cardboard boxes on the museum's shelves. Edgley and the museum staff, some with obvious reluctance, appeared before the legislative hearing in support of the bill and used the same arguments that Edgley had used in vain before. Antler and an even larger list of witnesses than had appeared at the trial paraded before the legislative committee, shooting down each argument as Antler had done before.

Antler explained to the panel of lawmakers that he had known Edgley most of his life, that many years before they had attended the same small college as undergraduates, and that this was Edgley's style. He did not always present arguments he believed in, even though he almost certainly believed in the ultimate good of his position; he was providing straws that dissenting legislators might grasp, chimeras that might blur the truth even in the face of clear contradiction, tones that might set off harmonics in a hostile heart. Edgley presented all possible options every time, even though they might have been rejected in previous argument. "The truth remains the same," Edgley argued. "It is the minds of the judges that we hope will change." Edgley's cooperative senators introduced a clause modifying the "bone bill," as the press labeled it, so that "articles clearly of foreign, non-indigenous manufacture among burial goods not be surrendered to families or tribes for reinterment."

Antler knew what Edgley wanted and wished that he had been more specific in helping the legislative committee formulate the bill. Edgley did not want to surrender for reburial the Jefferson

Peace Medal that a presidential delegation had given the Turtle Creek Nehawka in 1802. It was one of Edgley's debating tactics. He had a history of avoiding saying precisely what he wanted and he had been successful in that strategy of frayed margins; dim silhouettes, he once told Antler, are tough targets. "Sometimes, if they're not sure what it is that you want, they'll give it to you by mistake," he said.

Antler was sure this was not Edgley's best strategy this time, because now Antler could attack the fuzzy edges and avoid the clear core of the issue, an Edgley tactic turned against him. In press releases Antler argued that just as Americans today are buried with diamond rings from South Africa, silk from the Orient, and gold from Australia, his ancestor Elk was buried with the Jefferson Medal.

For a moment, in one press release from the museum office, Edgley tried to develop a tension between what he represented to be the ignorance of Indian superstition and the undeniable superiority of Western learning. "This is not a matter of sentiment; it is a matter of science," Edgley insisted.

In a private conversation with Edgley at a legislature reception, Antler dismissed that contention with a question: "For the interest of several groups of Indian anthropologists who want to investigate the curious burial customs of white folks, would you be willing to share with us the location of the graves of your parents and grandparents?" Edgley expressed indignation at Antler's lack of sensitivity and snapped that perhaps they should reserve further discussion for the legislative hearing.

Edgley's elusiveness was frustrating, but Antler knew him well and knew that if he could only be patient Edgley would back off once again. In their years of contention, Antler had also learned not to attack Clarence Edgley personally. Given some time, Edgley would say something stupid, something that would defeat his own case. He had done it again and again. Just about the time his board or his staff or his wife rescued him from some fix or another, Edgley would say something dumb and be right back in the news and in the frying pan.

With this thought, Antler's stomach growled so loudly he was afraid it might awaken Elizabeth. She rustled, pushed against him again with her firm back, and breathed deeply again, in sleep.

Antler enjoyed legislative hearings. In the courts, judges could be painfully firm in enforcing prohibitions against extra-chamber bickering, but in legislative hearings the politicking outside the chambers was even more telling than the brief appearances before the committees. In such encounters with Edgley, Antler always thought of himself as Crazy Horse, leading four or five bedraggled warriors on limping mounts in full flight before a cavalry unit of sixty eager soldiers thirsty for Indian blood, not noticing until it was too late the hundreds of well-armed, freshly mounted, hardened Nehawka warriors waiting just over the crest of the hills to either side of them. The cavalry never learned to suspect the easy bait, and neither apparently would Edgley.

Antler heard the big clock in the front room chime three. He *had* to get to sleep. Instead, he thought again about the hearing, and how the supporters of the bill to change the burial bill had spoken first, arguing that if the bones of the dead and perhaps some pottery or flint goods were to be reburied, those burial items that were clearly foreign to Nehawka culture—trade axes, rifles, and especially the Jefferson Peace Medal—should not be returned.

Edgley appeared in a dark blue suit, dressed, as the phrase goes, for success. He took the stand, nodded, and smiled at each of the legislators before him. "Clarence, would you like to make a statement or do you prefer to answer questions?" asked Senator Jerome Barnard, chairman of the committee.

"I'd like to make a statement, if that is acceptable to you and the distinguished members of the committee, Jerry—er, Senator Barnard," Edgley responded.

"We are here to hear what you have to say, Clarence."

"Thank you so much, Senator. Chairman Barnard, distinguished senators." He looked at each of them in turn and spoke their names, as if to remind them that they were old friends, from the same traditions, serving the same constituents. "Loren, Betsy, Robert, Bill, Twila. We are all on the same side here today. There are no bad guys in this issue. It is simply a matter of how we are going to do the best for the past, the present, and the future of our great state and our good people." Edgley had looked to his left, behind him in the large, crowded hearing room, toward where the Indian representatives and LaVoi Antler were seated. Again Antler's stomach growled as he remembered the moment.

"No one sympathizes more than I do with our Indian brothers," Edgley continued. "I understand their fear and uneasiness in this matter of archaeological collections and research. Not everyone in mainstream America understands the complexities and rewards of such scholarly research, after all. It would not be fair for us to expect a people who only four or five generations ago were living in earth lodges and hunting buffalo to accept without question the necessity of archaeological excavation and preservation.

"On the other hand, while we can understand and sympathize with the Nehawka's fear, born of generations of superstition, no educated person can expect museums and science to operate within the same restrictions that govern primitive tribes in which people still dance in feathers and bells." Several of the legislative panel members smiled at that, and Edgley paused and smiled back at them. Edgley reminded them, after all, that he himself had been adopted into the Winnebago tribe and enjoyed a little Indian fry bread and corn soup now and then himself.

Lying there beside Elizabeth twelve hours later, Antler still felt his face grow hot and the perspiration blossom on his forehead. The family that had adopted Edgley almost twenty years ago had done so out of kindness and the sincere belief that he was among them as a friend, when he had in fact used the occasion to gather information he would later use against them in a land acquisition dispute. Edgley had not returned to the Winnebago reservation since, and it was a good thing: some young men from the tribe had threatened castration.

"But enough of theory and speculation and superstition and predictions. Let's talk about the specifics of this issue," Edgley said with confidence. "Let me show you precisely what we are talking about here, my friends. Let me show you what it is that my friends the Nehawkas propose to destroy if you should somehow fail to pass our bill defining more carefully and more closely what it is that should be thrown away and reburied forever."

Edgley had dramatically put on a pair of white cotton gloves and carefully unfolded a black velvet envelope he took from his pocket. As if it were a religious relic, he took out the Jefferson Medal and held it up before the hearing committee. "The Philadelphia mint struck this medal," he said, "sometime in the late eighteenth century, when Washington and Franklin were still alive. Jefferson put it in the hands of an official legate, who carried it by riverboat and canoe and then horseback to the Nehawka tribe village on the Turtle Creek. There the leader of the expedition, Hugh Farley Barnard, great-great-great-grandfather of our own *Senator* Jerome Barnard of District 16, distinguished chairman of this distinguished committee, presented it to the Turtle Creek leader Elk. For reasons only Indians would understand, they buried the Medal with Elk about twenty years later, and it lay there, lost in the ground, for a century and a quarter, until a team of archaeologists from our own Midwestern Archaeological Foundation Museum discovered it again in 1948. Since then it has been safely on deposit in our archives, where it is preserved, studied, appreciated, protected.

"We cannot," he continued, "surrender this historical prize again to the earth, no matter what these people say. Few of them speak the language of Elk; they wear jeans and tank tops, three-piece suits and silk ties"—he turned slightly and smiled at Antler—"they no longer even know the religion of their ancestors, and yet they argue that they want to destroy this priceless artifact in the name of that religion.

"This medal is more than 10.3 ounces of silver; it is a precious artifact that we can use to instruct our children about our past."

Sure, Antler thought to himself at the time of the hearing, and thought to himself again as he lay in bed reviewing the day's events. The Medal can instruct our children all right. It teaches them that what the white man gives for all eternity he is perfectly willing to steal from your grave before the flowers on it wilt.

"Why, I ask myself, do the Turtle Creek people want the Medal?" Edgley said, as if sharing a secret with the committee. "I think I know why they want it, my friends and honored members of the legislature. They know that the Medal is valuable. There are only six other Jefferson Medals in existence. One sold three years ago at auction for just over $125,000. The Turtle Creekers and their lawyer LaVoi Antler see an easy windfall for the tribe in this piece of precious metal, forgetting the heritage it represents."

Tears came to Antler's eyes. Even as he lay in bed hours after Edgley had spoken these words, he was embarrassed. He knew that he could not be an effective spokesman for the Turtle Creekers if he wept at the outrage of such insults. He had seen tribal elders cry, at moments when tears were appropriate, but he had also watched them stand stolid and stoic in circumstances that would have driven most men to explosions of rage. And here was Edgley, cynically dismissing profound Turtle Creek concerns about tribe, tradition, religion, and honor as petty greed.

Of all the peoples on this earth, the Turtle Creek band of the Nehawka knew the value of heritage. It was about all the white man had left them, the memory of tribal traditions they carried in their minds. Antler choked back his anger and pain and wondered if this had been how his people felt when church officials carried off the children to missionary school or when soldiers raped the women in the villages, or worse, when the women gave themselves to the soldiers in the forts for whiskey, or trinkets, or food for their children.

Antler wondered if it had been so bad in the old days, when those who strayed from tribal ways knew that those ways were strong enough that should they ever want to return, they could. Now every loss was permanent.

"Golly," Edgley said, smiling with boundless charm, sweeping his glance across the panel of legislators before him, "isn't it enough that Indian braves carried off our women? Now they want our history, too!" Edgley chuckled to make it clear that he intended his remarks to be, of course, only an innocent joke.

Antler clenched his fists angrily at the memory of Edgley's words, prompting Elizabeth to mumble from her sleep, "Are you okay, honey?"

"I'm fine, Liz. Go back to sleep." He patted her hip gently. She pushed against him and was again breathing rhythmically.

When his turn had come on the stand at the legislative hearing, Antler had wondered if he could make it through his prepared statement; he was sick to his stomach from anger and he hated Edgley for destroying his composure. He had learned at hundreds of tribal council meetings that you can destroy your own arguments with anger. He sensed all too well the disadvantages of being a lawyer in the capital city and, at the same time, an Indian from Turtle Creek.

On the stand he told the legislators that Turtle Creekers had not thrown the Medal away but had deposited it in the ground with Elk. The tribe had understood then, as it does to this day, that in Elk's grave it was safe. How could these people, among whom graves were considered sacred sites, have known that grave robbing is acceptable within white culture? Antler read passages from the peace declaration that had accompanied the Medal: that it would symbolize "as long as the grass should grow and the rivers flow" the peace between the Turtle Creek Nehawka and the United States government, a promise, Antler noted, that had been broken while Elk was still wearing the Medal on his breast.

Antler argued as calmly as he could that the Medal had been a gift and the Nehawka could not understand how someone could take away a gift, given freely by the United States government, as if it were only the loan of a garden rake or a cup of sugar. "We do not understand it to this day," Antler said, and the room was dead quiet.

The Medal was a symbol, Antler explained, and its theft carried with it a powerful symbolic message for the Turtle Creek people and all other Indians who heard the story. He told the legislative panel that his clients, his people, understood that the few ounces of silver in the Medal had a value, perhaps $75, and an antique value, perhaps $125,000, but for the Turtle Creek people it had an even greater value. It was, he told the legislative panel with as much control and yet as much passion as he could, the funeral talisman of a tribal hero and a symbol of the integrity of a promise made by the United States government and the Turtle Creek band, a promise the tribe had kept with careful precision for nearly a century and a half. The Medal, according to tribal tradition, had once been a part of the Sacred Sky Bundle. It was not only valuable; to the Nehawka people it was therefore also holy.

"Excuse me, Senator Barnard," Edgley had interrupted from his seat toward the rear of the hearing room. "There is no evidence whatsoever that the Medal was ever a part of the Sky Bundle."

"Mr. Antler, is that true?" asked Senator Barnard.

"Senator, our traditional stories about Black Deer, who later became Elk, the first Keeper of the Sky Bundle, state that during a part of his term as caretaker, the Medal was included in the Bundle," Antler responded.

"Folktales?" asked the senator almost incredulously.

"Yessir, folktales, but we believe that our folktales are like biblical stories—perhaps not supported immediately and obviously by physical evidence, and yet even more true than historical fact. It is not simply a matter of superstition, as Clarence Edgley suggests, but of carefully preserved oral histories that, where there is physical evidence, have proven to be remarkably accurate.

"It is true," Antler told the senators, "that my people believe that the medal in Mr. Edgley's hands gives us peace and its absence has given us turmoil, and that may sound like superstition in this day of the computer and space shuttle, but then perhaps the belief of my people is true: since the Medal was stolen from Elk's grave, our tribe has known no peace. My people had dreams of the day that our dead would come back to us, a dream we have now realized. Now we dream of a day when the Sacred Sky Bundle will come back to us. And all of its parts, including the Jefferson Medal."

"Mr. Antler, Clarence Edgley is of the opinion that if this precious historical artifact from our state's history should be returned to the Nehawka tribe . . . if so many beautiful, significant artifacts like it should be returned, there is reason to believe that the Nehawka people will destroy them by burying them. Do you have information or an opinion regarding that suggestion?"

"Yessir," Antler admitted. "The Nehawka tribe has not made a secret of its intent to return the Jefferson Medal and other burial goods to where they belong, the graves of the dead where they were originally buried, where the Nehawka people intend them to rest."

"Thank you, Mr. Antler," Senator Barnard said without looking at him. Antler looked along the panel of senators. Not one of them was looking at him. At the close of the hearing Antler was confident that he had done his best—probably the best that anyone could have done—and now here, in bed with Elizabeth, he could only hope that the justice of the matter would win over its politics. He could only hope.

Antler awoke the next morning with the same thought on his mind. "Didn't sleep?" Elizabeth asked him at breakfast, running her fingers through his hair to remind him that he hadn't brushed it himself.

"No, not until after three o'clock."

"Oh, honey, that's going to make it a long, tough day. The hearing?"

"The hearing. And that bastard Clarence Edgley."

"Don't let him get on your nerves. You know you're on the right side on this one."

"Yes, I know, but still, who knows how the legislature will vote, and there's more to it than that."

"Did he pull the Indian-violation-of-our-sacred-womanhood routine again?"

"Yeah, well, sort of."

" 'Fate worse than death,' right?"

"You ought to know."

She kissed him and laughed reassuringly but the joke was not, somehow, as funny as it had once been. He looked at her, thinking how beautiful she was even in full morning rumple. Why should she, with her blue eyes and auburn hair, care about Edgley's slurs against his people?

Antler hadn't been in his office two hours when his secretary came in with a paper in her hand and a look of pain on her face. "Bad news, LaVoi. Just in from the capitol."

He knew before he looked at the cover page what the bad news was: the legislature had granted the museum its variance on the burial goods law, and Edgley could keep the Peace Medal. Close vote, hard debate, good hearts, but Senator Barnard called in some overdue debts and he and his ancestral pride carried the revision of the burial goods law to adoption.

The defeat hurt Antler but the worst was yet to come—telling his clients of their loss. His friends. His relatives. He called Elizabeth to tell her he was going up to the reservation after work. "You lost the Medal?" she asked.

"Well, I'd like to think that *I* didn't lose the Medal, but the legislature says Edgley gets to keep it."

"I'm sorry, LaVoi. Do you want me and the kids to go up to Turtle Creek with you? Are you going to be all right on the highway after not getting any sleep last night?"

"No, you stay here. It's going to be tough enough as it is. Let me try to sort everything out with the tribal council tonight and maybe the situation will cool off enough that we can still go together to the powwow next month, okay? I'll be okay driving. I have enough things on my mind that I probably won't sleep again tonight anyway."

"Okay. I'll have your clothes ready and your dishes packed. Is there anything else you'll need?"

At any Indian gathering there is certain to be food, and everyone is expected to join in the meal by way of fellowship. Everyone is also expected to bring along dishes. There would be food and fellowship on the Turtle Creek Nehawka Reservation, even in the face of the defeat the legislature had dealt to the people that afternoon.

"I don't look forward to eating at the meeting but I suppose I better put the best face on things by staying for the meal. Put out the beaded necktie Buddy Foster gave me. Maybe if I wear that they won't burn me alive for losing the Medal."

"I thought you said *you* didn't lose the Medal," Elizabeth said, offering a scrap of cheer.

That evening Elizabeth greeted him with a kiss, handed him a sandwich and thermos of coffee for the two-hour drive from the capital to the reservation, read some of the mail to him as he changed clothes (he learned the next day that she read only the good news to him), and sent him out the door with a warm kiss. "I love you, LaVoi, and we'll beat Edgley yet," she said.

"What you mean, 'we,' white woman," he smiled, lifting her chin for another kiss.

On the drive to the reservation Antler tried to concentrate on the road and the spring scenery. As seems to be the case with western Indian reservations, the Turtle Creek Reservation was on scenic land, another phrase for land that is suitable for little more than looking at. Scenic land is what Indians usually got in treaty settlements. All he could think of, however, was how much he dreaded breaking the bad news to the tribe.

As he entered the dusty streets of the village of Turtle Creek, he slowed down. The streets of the reservation town were always crawling with kids and dogs. He drove by shattered houses and stores. The only business left in town was the post office. Nothing seemed to change in Turtle Creek. Except maybe the burned-out hulk of a wrecked automobile impaled on the school's bicycle rack. That was new. It hadn't been there when he was in town a couple weeks earlier.

And yet the derelict car wasn't a new feature of the reservation town either. The only place Antler had ever seen the curious highway sign reading DO NOT DRIVE ON RIMS ON HIGHWAY was on the Turtle Creek Reservation. "DWI" the Nehawka called it. "Driving While Indian."

Antler waved to three old men sitting on the filthy remnants of a sofa on the front porch of the abandoned Nehawka Crafts Shoppe. They raised their brown-bagged bottles by way of a friendly if bleary toast. Antler never brought alcohol onto the reservation. Too bad, he laughed bitterly to himself; tonight he could use a drink.

He parked outside the tribal building and walked to the front door, past the loafers sitting on the benches outside. "Aho, Cousins," Antler said to two young men, drunk but not yet oblivious. Another of the white man's gifts to his primitive people. "Ho, Antler," they answered.

Inside the tribal headquarters building he made his way through the lobby to the tribal council offices and into the council meeting room. A couple dozen people had already entered the council chambers and taken seats in preparation for the meeting. On the reservation, everything moves in the rhythm of "Indian time." "Indian time" usually means that most people will be late, but there are always those who show up an hour or so early, too.

Several of the men nodded at Antler in recognition. Antler said, "Aho, Uncle," to one of the older men, who smiled and answered, "Ho, Nephew." They were not related but were demonstrating respect. Antler settled down in a folding chair near the back of the room and began to shift into his Indian mode. He tried to slow down his metabolism, to think like a Nehawka, to relax and enjoy being among friends on Turtle Creek land again. He could feel a warm cultural cover come over him, "the blanket," as Indians called a native Nehawka's return to the reservation.

In another hour the room was full of people, and children were careening around, running into chairs and adults, knocking each other down. Some babies were already crying, tired of the meeting even though it had not yet started. While Antler loved being on the reservation and loved living in the white man's world, it was hard on occasions like this to move from one culture to the other and back. If the meeting started right now, at eight o'clock, it wouldn't be over until at least ten, and then there was the long, drawn-out process of the meal, and another couple of hours to drive home. He wouldn't be in bed beside Elizabeth until two or three in the morning.

Finally, about a quarter after eight, the tribal council members filed in from their offices. When Antler was a boy, the tribal council had consisted only of old men, but now there were young men—especially veterans—and two women. Antler thought that was good for the tribe; the women and the young had been good council members and they remained popular on the reservation, a rare circumstance because factionalism—an inevitable result of pure democracy—had always torn at the political and social fabric of the tribe.

As usual, the meeting opened with a long prayer in Nehawka. Antler was eager for the meeting to move along but it was so good to hear the language again that he forgot his impatience. The tribal secretary, Claire Danreaux, who had graduated from high school with Antler, read the minutes of the last meeting and asked for approval. Antler raised his hand and quietly said, "I move for approval of the minutes of the last meeting," and Claire said with a glance at him and a grin of recognition, "Mr. Antler moves for approval of the minutes." The old business of paving the parking lot behind the tribal building passed without discussion, and, mercifully, the only new business was a motion from the floor to invite the Pawnee tribe from Oklahoma as special guests to the annual powwow coming up in July.

"Are there any announcements?" asked John Edward Rouliere, council chairman.

Antler raised his hand to the level of his chin, as if in hope that John Edward would not recognize him. "LaVoi," said John Edward. Antler rose slowly and cleared his throat. "Tribesmen, friends, relatives, I represented the tribe at the legislative hearings this past week in the matter of the Jefferson Peace Medal. I want to thank my grandfather, Mr. Buddy Foster, and Mrs. Red Shirt for their testimony at that meeting." He glanced at Mr. Foster and Alma Red Shirt, both sitting at the tribal council bench in the front of the room. He paused while the audience applauded their contribution.

"I received news this morning that the legislature has voted to permit the museum to keep the Medal. I am sorry." Antler sat down. For a moment there wasn't a sound, and then he could hear around him a growing murmur of voices, some in English, some Nehawka, some angry, some sad, most confused.

"LaVoi," said John Edward, "would you be willing to explain the problem in more detail for those who might not understand?"

"Sure, Mr. Chairman, if I can. I haven't had a chance to find out many of the details myself. I'm not sure I understand what I have read."

"I'd sure as hell like to ask you something, LaVoi," said Dennis

Flint Hand. "How long does Whitey think we are going to put up with this shit? The federal government gave the Medal to us and it is ours. It is not theirs, and we want it back. It was once a part of the most sacred object of the Nehawka people, the Sky Bundle. They stole the Sky Bundle, and now they've stolen the Peace Medal. Peace Medal! What a joke! They stole it from Elk's grave, and now they say they are going to keep it and we can go straight to hell. What kind of justice is that? Some of us are tired of talk. The Jefferson Medal and the Sacred Bundle will be ours again, and Whitey better get used to the idea."

"Cousin, the legislators think they are saving the Medal for all of us by letting the museum keep it. They don't understand that the Medal is more than metal, more than money."

"Well, they better figure it out pretty quick. I don't know how long the lid is going to stay on the trouble around here. There are a lot of us who are ready to go to the museum and take what's ours, whether the legislature likes it or not."

"I understand your anger," said LaVoi. "I just hope you'll give us a little more time to continue the legal process. The situation is not yet hopeless, but it will be if someone from Turtle Creek gets too hot and gives Clarence Edgley and the museum people an excuse to put the Medal away in a vault someplace."

"Grandson, I worry about the Turtle Creek people," said Buddy Foster. "We have survived without our Peace Medal, but without it we have not been in peace. We cannot live much longer without peace. We cannot live much longer without that which is rightfully ours. Do the white men understand that? Is it that they *want* to destroy the Turtle Creek people?"

"No, Grandfather," said Antler. "They do not want to destroy us. They do not understand what the Medal is."

"But they have the papers. They made the Medal. They told us it was a gift and that it meant peace. How can they now not understand?"

"Grandfather, I cannot explain how the white man thinks."

"LaVoi, would you pass along to the legislative committee the disappointment of the tribal council and all members of the tribe?"

"Yes, Mr. Chairman, and I will also request that the committee and the legislature reconsider our request."

The meeting broke up in angry confusion and on the drive home Antler worried that some of the angrier young men might do something that would make further discussion with the legislature more complicated. In a way he was glad he had something to worry about: as tired as he was, he might have fallen asleep behind the wheel of his car if his mind were not chewing away at the problem.

Liz hated these nights when LaVoi drove to the reservation and back. The reservation was a dangerous place to drive at any rate, with cars always breaking down along the shoulder of the road and people walking God knows where. During the day, the hilly and twisting landscape demanded a driver's attention and made for good driving, but at night, well, you could never tell what was sitting just over the next hill. Thank God, Liz thought, he would have the weekend to recover. His visits "home" to Turtle Creek always wore him out and this mess with the Jefferson Medal didn't make things easier. She was glad when she heard the garage door opening and Antler's car driving in. She was asleep by the time he slipped in at her side.

It was good that Antler had had the calm of a weekend with Liz because, as if Mondays were not already problem enough, the sheriff's car pulled up the long, curved driveway behind Antler's just as he was about to leave for the office. "How you doin', Larry? Did you finally find out about my past as an ax murderer?" Antler laughed as he walked back to the sheriff's car.

The sheriff, Larry Bradley, Antler's friend since he had been a boy on the reservation and in occasional trouble, unfolded from the driver's seat. He leaned easily against the top of the car and smiled, but he didn't laugh. "It's not quite that serious, LaVoi, but it ain't funny either."

"Uh-oh, what's the problem?"

"Would you mind if I asked you a few questions?"

"Of course not, but you know if it involves a client I'm not going to be able to say anything. You know that, Larry."

"Right. Well, can you tell me what you were doing Friday evening?"

"I was up at the tribal council meeting at the reservation."

"Can you tell me who else was there?"

"It's a public meeting, Larry, and the tribe keeps good records. I think you'll be able to find a complete and official list of everyone in attendance. I know that John Edward Rouliere, the chairman, will be glad to make that list available to you."

"What did you do after the meeting?"

"I came home. I got here about three in the morning." With the questions so obviously focusing on himself, Antler knew that he should end the conversation, but he was curious enough about what the sheriff had in mind that he thought he would play along with him a little longer.

"What did you do on Saturday?"

"Took the kids skating; watched the Atlanta 500 on ESPN in the afternoon—Darrell Waltrip won." Antler added verifying details so that Larry would not have to ask the embarrassing questions himself. "In the evening I watched a couple of boxing matches on television—Michael Carbajal and . . . I forget the name of the other guy. Sunday morning I watched Kuralt on *Sunday Morning*, then David Brinkley. Sat in the family room all morning long. It's my Sunday ritual. I hear some folks go to church. In the afternoon I pruned trees—that's the brush, piled right there. Last night Liz and I played Nintendo with the kids. Now, would you mind telling me what this is all about?"

"I can't really do that, LaVoi," the sheriff said.

"Now look, Larry, I tried to make this as easy as I could for you . . ."

"I know, I know, but . . ."

"I don't think it's too much to ask that you give me some clues. Since you asked about the tribal council meeting, I suspect it has something to do with the tribe, right?"

"Yes, I'm sorry to say that it does."

"The Medal?"

"The Medal. Someone stole it from the museum over the weekend and we think it was your people."

"I sure as hell hope it was, Larry. It'd be a shame to have that Medal fall into the hands of anyone else, don't you think?"

"That's not for me to say, LaVoi. It's a theft, and that's all that counts."

"What makes you think Indians stole it?"

"I can't tell you that, LaVoi."

"Sheriff, you know I am the tribe's legal representative and you're going to have to give me all this information sooner or later anyway. Why don't we work together on this? You know I didn't advise them to steal it, and I would like to head off any trouble for the tribe before it gets serious. You know that too."

"Well, what we know is that on Saturday afternoon there were a bunch of Indian kids running around in the museum. As we piece the evidence together, one of them left a top latch open on a window in the library and the thieves came in through that window sometime during the weekend, probably Saturday or Sunday night."

"Weren't there white kids running around the museum, too? As I recall, the place is always full of kids on Saturdays."

"Sure, LaVoi, but since the Indians have been making such a fuss about the Medal, we figure it was Indian kids that jammed the latch on the window."

"You'd play hell proving that in court, Larry. No judge would admit such speculation as testimony."

"There's more. The Medal is the only thing missing out of the museum."

"That doesn't mean Indians stole it. If you were a thief, what would you steal from the museum? Clarence Edgley has been yelling about the Medal being worth $125,000 and the papers have been printing his claims. If you were a thief and ran across this little piece of information, the first thing you would think about is slipping into the museum, pocketing the Medal, and running out. Easiest thing in the world. Edgley has been inviting a robbery. You don't have to be an Indian to figure that one out."

"Now, don't go blaming the victim, here, LaVoi."

"No, Sheriff, I'm not, but I think you should be a little slower in accusing the Indians."

"We're investigating and we are open to any suggestions."

"Okay, well . . . I'm not very eager to do this, since I was at Turtle Creek last Friday, but I'm going up to the reservation again this Friday for a Buffalo Dance and I'll see what I can find out. If the Nehawka have the Medal, Larry, I guarantee you that I will do what I can to get it back to the museum. I'm not saying they took it—I don't know a thing about it—but if they did, I'll do what I can to try to work it out. I expect you to do what you can to calm down Edgley and give me a little room on this, okay?"

"Right. I'd appreciate anything you can do. Thanks for the help. I hate to see this kind of trouble. You know I do."

"I know, Larry." Antler watched the sheriff back out of the driveway and then turned to Elizabeth, who had been listening to the exchange from the door. He shrugged his shoulders and forced a smile. She waved, sighed, and shook her head in answer.

Antler knew from experience there would be no sense in writing to the reservation. No one ever wrote back. He also knew there would be little reason to try to do any nosing around by telephone. If someone on the reservation had stolen the Medal, no one would be willing to talk about it, even with another Turtle Creeker. If he were there, someone might tell him about it, but not if he asked.

All week the newspapers were full of stories about the theft of the Medal. Edgley made it clear that he believed the Indians had stolen it and promised to demand the most severe punishment possible for the thieves, including the children who had abetted the theft. Edgley put as much pressure as he could on the sheriff to make arrests soon. Antler knew that Larry was fair and honest, but he could not be immune to political pressures like Edgley's.

John Edward Rouliere called Antler on Thursday and reported that the sheriff had been on the reservation asking questions and had gone over to Dennis Flint Hand's house. "I want you to make it clear to the sheriff that he is treading mighty thin ice, coming onto the reservation and interrogating tribal members."

"I will talk with Larry at once. Did Dennis tell him anything?" Antler asked John Edward.

"Yeah, he told him to get the hell out of there and leave his family alone."

"That's good advice, John Edward. Spread the word around the reservation that no one is to talk with the sheriff unless they talk with me first. Larry's a good man but he's under a lot of pressure to get that Medal back for Clarence Edgley. He may not be as careful as he would be otherwise. Don't get ugly. Don't even be rude. Just tell Bradley he'll have to talk with me before he talks with any tribal members, okay?"

"Okay, Cousin. Are you coming up to the Buffalo Dance Friday?"

"Yes, I'll be there."

"Liz and the kids coming?"

"I think Liz will but the kids are spending a couple days with their grandparents."

"We miss them, you know, Cousin. They are going to grow up white if they don't learn how to live like a Nehawka."

"I know, Cousin, but I also know that the first time I try to force them to come with me to the reservation, they'll do whatever they can to stay away. You know how kids are, John Edward."

"Yes, LaVoi, but it is tougher to be a Nehawka when you are only *half* Nehawka, and when you grow up away from home." Antler was struck again by the Indian convention that no matter where you live, or for however long, the reservation is always *home*.

"See you Friday, Cousin."

Antler left work a couple hours early on Friday, thinking that if he could spend a little more time on the reservation, he might have a better chance of learning something about the whereabouts of the Medal. He left the office about three; picked up Liz, who had fixed some food and drink for the trip; changed into jeans, a beaded bolo tie, and a tweed sports coat; and drove north toward the Turtle Creek reservation. About the time they reached the southern limits of the hilly Turtle Creek land, however, it began to rain, which complicated matters for Antler because no one with whom he could discuss the matter would be standing around outside.

He drove the short length of Turtle Creek's shabby main street to the south side of the powwow grounds, to Buddy Foster's little house. He and Liz ran through the rain from his car to the porch

door, where Buddy's wife Naomi was already waiting to greet them.
"Come in, LaVoi, come in, Liz. Have some coffee. That'll warm
you up. Grandpa is in the front room watching his soap opera."

They took the coffee from Naomi and stepped into the front
room, where Buddy was dozing on the couch in front of the television set. "Aho, Grandson, Granddaughter," he mumbled, struggling to sit upright on the soft furniture. Although many called
Buddy "Grandfather," he was actually only sixty or sixty-five years
old—not exactly ancient. A hard life and health problems had
weakened him even in middle age, but he was still a spiritually
strong man; his moral courage and his lifelong struggle to maintain
Nehawka customs and language and to recover the Sacred Sky
Bundle from the Densmore Museum had earned him universal
respect on the Turtle Creek Reservation.

Buddy Foster enjoyed respect from many non-Indians too. Wes-
leyan College in Rising City had given him an honorary Doctorate
of Humane Letters a few years before, noting that he was one of
the best anthropologists around, having spent a lifetime collecting
the old ways from tribal elders, salvaging information about the Sky
Bundle from those who remembered, giving new strength to the
Buffalo Dancers by lending his prestige to their membership, in-
sisting that the Old Ways of the Sacred Bundle could live quite
comfortably beside new ways like the Native American Church and
even computers. It was Buddy Foster who was spearheading the
struggle to regain possession of the Sacred Sky Bundle for the
Nehawka people.

"And here is our tribe's spiritual leader watching *All My Children*," laughed Antler.

"Well, last week you said you cannot explain how a white man
thinks, so I watch this stuff hoping maybe I will find out something," Buddy Foster laughed.

For almost two hours Antler talked with Naomi and Buddy and the dozen or so visitors who dropped by, shaking the rain from their hair and clothes, having seen Antler's car parked by the house and wanting to welcome him "home." It would have been impolite to ask directly about the Medal, because among the Nehawka one simply doesn't ask questions, so Antler did not bring up the subject and no one mentioned the Medal. Not one word.

Antler was uneasy. The loss of the Medal in the legislature and then its theft should have been the most important topic of conversation among the Turtle Creekers, but from today's conversation you wouldn't have known there was such a thing as a Jefferson Medal. In Antler's opinion, everyone was trying too hard to avoid the subject. About six o'clock everyone walked through the gentle rain from Buddy Foster's place to the tribal hall—actually the old school gymnasium—where a large crowd had gathered. An unusually large crowd, even for a Buffalo Dance, LaVoi whispered to Liz.

For an hour or so men smoked and chatted, women passed around babies swathed to cradle boards, and children ran unrestrained in and out and around the hall. John Edward opened the meeting almost precisely at seven, another surprise, and quickly dispensed with the evening's business. He announced that the powwow plans were moving along nicely and an impressive contingent of guests would be present, from Miss Indian America to the tribal council chairmen of the Pawnee and Osage tribes, possibly the governor, some state senators for sure, and . . . John Edward paused dramatically and looked around the large room, where now nearly three hundred people had assembled . . . the county sheriff, Larry Bradley. That announcement caused something of a stir and a few laughs, which LaVoi Antler attributed to the sheriff's appearance on the reservation earlier in the week when he was trying to find the Jefferson Medal.

"A group of tribal members have asked that we take the occasion of this Buffalo Dance to circulate a petition denying the request of the Midwestern Archaeological Foundation Museum to keep the Jefferson Peace Medal," John Edward announced, and the room broke into enthusiastic applause. "I hope you will all find it in your hearts to sign it," he added when the room quieted again.

John Edward had started the petition on the side of the room opposite where Antler, Liz, and Buddy's family were seated. Almost immediately there was a stir around the petition, but neither Antler nor Liz could detect the cause. To Antler's surprise, the singers had already gathered in the center of the gymnasium floor and were setting up their drum.

"What's going on over there?" asked Liz, craning her neck to follow the petition.

"They're up to something but I can't imagine what it is," he whispered to Elizabeth. "The petition doesn't make any sense. They can't deny the museum anything."

Antler could not believe that his people were actually getting something as complicated as a Buffalo Dance together so smoothly and quickly. He'd been at such events dozens of times before when nothing was ready to go by ten in the evening. This night, everyone was cheerfully hustling around, passing the petition, clearing the floor of the gymnasium for the dance.

Also with unaccustomed energy, men and some women were rising from their seats, gathering bags and boxes, and making their way to the rooms around the gymnasium and out to automobiles to get dressed for the dance. Buddy Foster got up to leave, probably to go to the restroom, and Antler joked, "Are you going to dance tonight, Grandpa?" and Buddy laughed, "Maybe so, Grandson, maybe so."

One of the mysteries of the Buffalo Dance is who the dancers are. What with all the commotion of helpers dressing the dancers, cooks preparing the feast, mothers tending to children, latecomers arriving, people leaving to go to the toilets, it is impossible once the dance begins to know who the heavily costumed and masked dancers are.

Nor does anyone guess. The Nehawka understand that the dancers are now buffalo. The dancers are no longer their relatives, friends, and neighbors once they put on their Buffalo Dance regalia and begin to dance. In the matrix of the costumes, prayers, music, and ritual, those who were human beings earlier in the evening when they arrived at the tribal building are now buffalo.

As a boy Antler had been a Buffalo Dance helper and he understood the magic of the transformation that accompanied the dance. At one point in the tribe's history, when the Sky Bundle had become very powerful, the Buffalo Dance had almost completely died out; the dance had regained its importance when its adherents joined with the Sky Bundle followers. Then, only a generation or so ago, it fell into disfavor again, but there were always a few old men who kept the tradition alive. Antler was glad. He was proud that he had been a part of the dance since he was a child. The dance had always fascinated him, seemed to him to be something worth saving, even in the age of space and computers.

He had seen men too old and arthritic to walk, dance acrobatically for hours, only to be confined to wheelchairs again when the dance was over and they were once again old men rather than virile buffalo bulls. He had seen men lamed in war and women broken by poverty and childbirth transformed into young and powerful beasts for the duration of the dance. He had tried to explain the mystic metamorphosis to a few white people, even his anthropology professor from his college days, but the only one he had ever encountered who seemed to understand was Elizabeth. He reached for her hand. "What's that for?" she asked, taking his hand in both of hers.

"For being a good woman, a good *white* woman," he said. He watched the drummers set the drum on its stand, check their sticks, make a few tentative thumps, and test their voices, a ritual he had seen a hundred times before, one that never grew tiresome for him. He genuinely loved the music of his people, though most of his white friends thought of it as nothing but howling and pounding. Liz insisted that she liked it too, but he wondered if she endured it only to please him.

John Edward called Buddy Foster, tribal holy man and as much as anyone responsible for bringing the Buffalo Dance to its new prominence in life at Turtle Creek, to the head table to bless the gathering. Mr. Foster built a small altar of ordinary bricks in the middle of the gym, built a little fire of white ash sticks, and put a cast-iron pan over it. It took him nearly a quarter hour to get the fire going because, as befits a Nehawka holy man, he took great care in doing the ritual precisely right. He then prayed a long prayer and dropped white-cedar needles on the coals, sending a gray cloud of pungent white cedar smoke into the air above the basketball court's center circle.

He "gathered" the smoke with an eagle feather fan and walked slowly around the room waving the smoke toward the audience and patting the eagle feather fan on the dignitaries in attendance. At precisely the point when Buddy Foster reached Antler, Liz, and Buddy's family with his blessing of sanctified smoke, Alvin Kills Enemy handed the Jefferson Peace Medal petition to Liz. Antler concentrated as intently as he could on Buddy Foster's blessing. He always made a point of "catching" the smoke at blessing ceremonies and carefully "pulling" it down over his head and shoulders and patting it on his body, as was the custom among his people, especially when the blessing was that of his honorary grandfather, Buddy Foster.

"I don't know if taking the smoke really does any good," he once told Liz, "but it makes me feel good. And it's one of the few Nehawka things I still get to do."

Antler waved Liz impatiently aside, therefore, when she tried to speak to him and interrupt his thoughts just as Mr. Foster waved the smoke toward him. "LaVoi, LaVoi, for God's sake, look. Look at this. Look." She tugged at his sleeve insistently and held the clipboard with the petition toward him, high, almost in his face, as if to force it into his field of vision.

He turned to scold her for interrupting his blessing, but she stopped him short by pushing the petition before his eyes. And its adjunct—the Jefferson Peace Medal. There it was in Liz's hand, the Jefferson Peace Medal with a red ribbon passed through its hole, tied to the clipboard holding the petition.

Antler stared in astonishment. He reached out and took the clipboard and the Medal from Liz. He held it in his hand, the Jefferson Medal. He was suddenly so cold and faint that he sat down. He tried to read the petition, but all he could think about was that he, an officer of the court, had suddenly become a party to a felony.

He held the Medal for what seemed like hours as Buddy Foster finished his blessings and John Edward was about to signal the drummers to begin the music of the Buffalo Dance. Antler rose. "Mr. Chairman," Antler shouted. "My friends and relatives." His voice echoed in the gymnasium.

The ensuing silence suggested that those present had anticipated a reaction from Antler but were surprised by its abruptness. "I apologize to my grandfather, Buddy Foster, and to all of you who are my family and tribe, but I am also your tribal attorney and I must speak to what is happening here tonight."

"You may speak, Mr. Antler," said John Edward.

Antler held the Medal above his head and shouted around the dead-still gymnasium, "I am not only a Nehawka and a Turtle Creeker, I am also an attorney, an officer of the court. I cannot be a part of this tonight because it is a crime. I must report all this to the authorities."

"You are also *our* attorney, Mr. Antler," said John Edward, "and what we share with you is to remain between us."

"But I cannot allow myself to become a part of this crime, Cousin, and no matter what you think, no matter how justified the theft may be, no matter how angry you are, that's what we are dealing with here—theft. *Grand* theft."

"Will you wait until the Buffalo Dance is over to report to the police that we have the Medal at Turtle Creek?" John Edward shouted across the gymnasium floor to Antler.

"Yes, but then you are all . . . we are all going to be in trouble."

"What are they going to do, Cousin?" asked John Edward with a gentle smile. "Arrest the whole tribe? Do they have enough fry bread and corn soup in the county jail to feed all the Turtle Creek band? Cousin, when you talk with the sheriff, tell him that he will have no luck finding the Medal on the reservation. You know that, and Larry Bradley is good enough a man that he knows that. But tell him that all of this will be cleared up and taken care of at the powwow next month. Tell him he will have his Medal."

Without giving Antler an opportunity to respond, John Edward signaled the drummers to begin, and instantly the thunder of the drum and the high-pitched singing of the men at the drum filled the gymnasium and prevented any further debate. Antler passed the petition and the Medal to Naomi Foster, standing beside him. She signed the petition and passed it on and the petition and the Medal disappeared again among the Turtle Creek Nehawka tribesmen.

Antler was suddenly exhausted. He sagged in his place on the backless bleachers. Liz put her hand behind his head and softly rubbed the back of his neck. John Edward had made it clear that neither he nor the tribe would ask Antler to betray his profession. He had permission to report the location of the Medal. But what was to happen to his people? Didn't they understand the fury that would descend on them when Clarence Edgley found out that they had stolen the Medal and that it was on the reservation?

After a few preliminary songs the Buffalo Dancers filed in, covered with feathers, fur, bells, and ribbons, their heads encased in large masks shaped roughly like a buffalo's heavy head. The sound of the bells added to the chaotic sounds of drumming and singing. The lights of the gymnasium dimmed and the dancers swirled and eddied around the floor. Dancers left the room and new ones took their place. At one point there were only six dancers, at another nearly twenty. LaVoi Antler thought he knew just about every Buffalo Dancer on the reservation, since he had scarcely missed a dance except the few years he had been away to school, but now even the costumes changed and blended. Sometimes a familiar mask would appear on a costume unfamiliar to Antler, and then a familiar costume was crowned with a mask he had not seen before. He had no idea who the dancers were.

After nearly two hours of dancing, Antler recognized the songs that signal the closing ceremony, and dancers began one by one to dance off the floor and out of the gymnasium. Even now that the dancers were leaving and changing back into street clothing, back into human beings, no one could identify who had been in the costumes, because other people were stepping out to help the dancers, to get dishes for the feast, to go home if they had to work the next morning.

Finally only one dancer remained. He—or she, there was no way to know—danced wildly, whirling and flying. Where does he get the energy, Antler wondered, after dancing for two hours—if indeed he had been dancing two hours?

Suddenly the lone Buffalo Dancer stopped. Slowly, he raised his arms above his head and with a flourish showed that he held the Jefferson Peace Medal. For a full minute he stood staring at the Medal held above his head, the drummers and singers growing even wilder in their excitement. Then the dancer began to move again, stabbing with the horns on his mask just as Antler had seen bison do on the fields in the Black Hills bison range. The dancer pawed at the ground as if he were throwing dust over his shoulder. He charged the drummers and ran as much as danced around the floor. Antler wondered if the dance was one of anger or exultation.

The lights came up as the drummers and singers finished the last song. Elizabeth pulled a paper bag from beneath her bleacher seat and handed Antler his dishes, the customary plate, cup, spoon, and napkin. "Are you feeling okay, LaVoi? You look terrible," Elizabeth asked. "Should we skip the food and go home?"

"No, I'll be all right," he told her.

The food for the feast, contributed by the Turtle Creek American Legion and the Buffalo Dance Society, was piled on flattened cardboard boxes on the gymnasium floor: steaming wash boilers of soup, bushel baskets of fry bread, dozens of pies, buckets of baked beans from the commodity bank. Buddy Foster said a long and impassioned grace over the food, asking not only that the food be blessed but also that the tribe be victorious in its struggles. There was no doubt in anyone's mind which struggles Buddy Foster meant.

The corn soup and fry bread went a long way toward settling Antler's troubled mind. The tastes swept him with memories of the meals he had eaten in his grandma Smoke's kitchen, of the thousands of festivities like this he had attended in the past—powwows, prayer meetings, hand games, tribal reunions, funerals. His life among his people was concentrated in the tastes and smells of these foods. Even the commodity beans. These simple foods—corn soup and fry bread—were his people's soul food.

After the feast Antler and Elizabeth left the hall, loaded their dishes in the trunk of the car, and started on the drive back to Rising City. "Well, we got an earlier start than usual," Elizabeth said, clearly trying to give Antler something pleasant to think about.

"Sure. Not only did everything start early and move along on schedule for a change, but no one said a word to us after the dance."

"They're worried about what you think of the theft of the Peace Medal."

"God, Liz, so am I. What *do* I think? I haven't the fuzziest notion. Edgley is going to be fit to be tied. I don't know what the sheriff is going to expect of me. What a mess."

"What do you think they are going to do now? Where are they keeping the Medal? The sheriff can't possibly find it on the reservation, can he?"

"Liz, Grandpa Smoke once told me about bees. You know, worker and drone bees can never turn their backs on the queen. As she moves through the hive, they turn as she passes them so they do not show her their backsides."

"Oh, come on! Now you're just ribbing me."

"No, it's the truth, Liz. Later on when I was in high school I kept bees myself and I saw it. And no one can sting a queen either. She really is the queen. She is the mother of every bee in that hive. Every single one.

"So sometimes a queen gets very old and worn out and the hive clearly needs a new queen. Sometimes the workers make a new queen off in some other part of the hive—they can do that, make a queen—and keep the old one alive, tucked off apart from the vital young queen, as if to protect her. Sometimes they just leave with the new queen and start a new colony.

"But sometimes it comes down to killing a queen, and the question is, how does a bee kill a queen? Can't sting her. Can't even turn your back on her.

"So what they do is to begin to crowd in around her, as if by signal. The crowd gets bigger and bigger and tighter and tighter. Finally the bees in the center of the crush suffocate—a lot of innocent workers and drones, along with the old queen. No one kills the queen, exactly. No one is really guilty. They're all just sort of standing around and before anyone realizes it, there is a crowd, and before you know it, the queen is dead. You can just hear them saying, 'Gosh, I didn't know the queen was in there. I'm not responsible. I was just in the neighborhood.' "

"Collective guilt."

"No, collective innocence."

"And you think that's what they're doing with the Medal?"

"That's what that petition was all about. We all handled the Medal. We're all guilty. We were all equally innocent in our guilt. 'Gosh, I didn't know the Medal was there. I'm not responsible. I was just in the neighborhood. I didn't see where it came from; I didn't see where it went.' "

"So in fact, no one has the Medal."

"No human being. The last time I saw the Medal, it was in the hands of a Buffalo Dancer and a Buffalo Dancer is a spirit, not a human being." Antler paused. "God, Liz, won't that sound great in court? 'Your honor, my clients are clearly innocent of the theft because a buffalo spirit stole the Medal.' "

"I hope that's what's going on, LaVoi. I felt good holding that medal. Maybe it *is* a peace medal. You know what I mean? Not that it just symbolizes peace, but that it *is* peace. I hope the Turtle Creekers and the buffalo spirits hide it away forever."

"The Nehawka believe the Medal is peace, that hunk of silver. It was once part of the Sacred Sky Bundle. That makes it like a piece of the original cross for a Christian. I don't think the Nehawka people will ever have peace if they just hide the Jefferson Medal away though, Liz. Edgley and the law are never going to rest—or let them rest—until the Medal is back in the museum, and until it is back in the museum there will be no peace."

Antler was right. After he notified the sheriff that the Medal was indeed on the reservation, that he had seen it (he decided not to mention for the moment at least that he had held the Medal in his own hands), Edgley began a publicity bombardment that surprised even Antler. Edgley petitioned the federal and state governments to stop all payments of funds and all support of programs on the reservation until the people of the Turtle Creek Reservation returned the stolen medal.

"Do you mean," asked one incredulous reporter, "that you want the government to stop food programs on the Turtle Creek reservation until 10.3 ounces of silver is returned to you?"

"If that's what it takes," said Edgley firmly.

"But the children . . ."

"That medal is like a child to me," Edgley said. "My *only* child."

Antler was confident, especially with that sort of talk, that Edgley would eventually be his own worst enemy. Antler had figured out that Edgley operated on a forty- to sixty-day cycle, saying something outrageous in public with predictable regularity. Antler had every hope that Edgley would not disappoint him in the matter of the Jefferson Peace Medal.

Edgley's next tactic, however, left Antler uneasy. Edgley offered a $5,000 reward for information leading to the return of the Medal and the successful prosecution of those responsible for its theft. Most Turtle Creek Nehawkas would no more have sold out the Peace Medal for $5,000 than they would sell their mothers for the same price. The unsettling factor in that metaphor, Antler reminded Liz, is that there is always someone, even on the reservation, in every community and every family, at least one person, who *would* sell out his mother for $5,000.

Antler told Edgley, the sheriff, and the press that he had no idea where the Medal might be and had no notion who had stolen it, but that if it was safe anywhere, it was safe with the Nehawka tribe, to whom the Medal had been given nearly two centuries earlier and who considered it to be a powerful and holy talisman. The Turtle Creek people had assured him, he told anyone who would listen, that the matter would be settled at the powwow, now only a few weeks away. They had told him the Medal would be returned and he had no doubt that it would.

It was a week and a half before the powwow that the sheriff dropped in at Antler's home early in the evening. Antler was on the redwood deck overlooking the lake, about to throw some steaks on the grill, when Sheriff Bradley startled him by ambling around the corner of the house. "Scared me half to death, Larry," sputtered Antler.

"Guilty conscience?" laughed the sheriff. "Are you old enough to drink that beer?"

"Maybe *too* old to drink that beer. Would you like one?"

"No, but I would have a cold root beer, if you have one handy."

"Sure. Hey, Liz, would you send one of the kids out with a root beer."

"Can you take a few extra minutes for a steak, Larry?"

"I don't know. I've got a lot of paperwork to . . ."

"Liz, send out another steak, too."

Neither suggested a reason for Larry's visit—Antler knew he was there to see if he could find out anything about the Medal—until the meal was over and Larry and Antler were sitting alone on the patio, drinking one last beer. "I really hate to bring this up, LaVoi . . ."

"I'm not crazy about talking about it, Larry."

"You understand my position."

"You're the sheriff and you have a felony theft on your hands. Now, you have a pretty good idea who stole it and where it is, and you are not the least bit eager to jail the thieves. On the other hand, your constituents will drum you out of office if you don't."

"There's not a lot of time left."

"All I know, Larry, is that the people up at Turtle Creek tell me this matter will be settled to everyone's satisfaction at the powwow. Have you had any nibbles on Edgley's reward?"

"Not a word, and I hope I don't. If anyone from Turtle Creek spills the beans, I think I'll have a civil war on the reservation. At least a murder."

"You got that right, Larry."

The sheriff left with nothing settled and nothing learned, but both he and Antler felt better, knowing that the other understood his situation. Only Elizabeth knew how ardently Antler prayed that John Edward Rouliere had known what he was talking about when he told Antler the Medal would be returned, that Rouliere had enough control over the tribe and the Medal that he could carry whatever plan he had to completion.

Edgley continued to issue threats through the press and asked the governor to direct the state police, even the National Guard, to sweep the reservation in a search for the Medal. When the tribe denied any permission to trespass on tribal lands, Edgley demanded that a team of law officers be stationed at Elk's grave site to ensure that the Turtle Creekers did not try to rebury the Medal. "Let me see if I understand," mused John Edward to Edgley when he came to the reservation with the sheriff. "You want to be sure that the Medal is returned to the museum and not to where it was before the museum stole it. Do I have that right?"

"I don't banter with criminals," Edgley huffed. Sheriff Bradley convinced Edgley that he should wait for any further legal action and certainly stay away from the reservation until the powwow. Perhaps there would be a resolution to the problem then.

By the time of the powwow, Antler was as close to being an emotional wreck as Elizabeth had ever seen him. "LaVoi, there's nothing you can do, so why don't you do what you always say you do when you're stranded at O'Hare when the fog is rolling in. Shift into your Indian mode. Don't fuss about situations you can't control. Make the most of life. Look at all the goofy people around you."

"I know you're right, Liz, but this time it's not so easy. At O'Hare I'm dealing with white folks, but here it's these Indians. I think I've spent too much time away from the reservation. At this point I have no idea what sort of tricks they have tucked away in their wigwams."

Antler no longer camped on the powwow grounds for three or four days as he did when he was young. It was just too complicated with two kids and his work schedule. But he never missed being there for the Saturday festivities, the biggest day at the annual event. There was still enough Indian in Antler that he enjoyed seeing family, friends, and old schoolmates who came to powwow from all over the country. He loved the food, and music, hearing the language again, watching the dancers.

White visitors to powwow are always disappointed to find anachronisms like merry-go-rounds, cotton candy stands, and portable toilets at ancient tribal gatherings, but when Antler took white guests, he tried to steer them past such distractions. "Listen to the speeches, watch the dance, listen to the songs. That's the old stuff. The Nehawka are not a museum tribe, trying artificially to maintain some primitive lifestyle. We are simply a people living the way we live, and we like cotton candy and merry-go-rounds as surely as we like fry bread and the Buffalo Dancers."

Antler was pleased when he heard Liz or one of the children echoing his words. Especially Liz. The kids had Nehawka blood in them, so they had reason to stand up for Indian ways, but Liz had never been to a powwow until he took her to one the year before they were married. She was twenty-two at the time, as frightened by the strangeness of it all as she was excited. Now, she had as many friends on the reservation as he did.

"If you two ever break up," Buddy Foster once said to LaVoi, "us Indians are going to get custody of Liz and let you go to the Norwegians. She's the real Indian in your family, LaVoi."

The powwow committee had outdone itself with its guest list this year. They had managed to convince the governor to come—but then of course it was an election year and she needed every vote she could get, including those of the Turtle Creek Nehawkas. There were two state senators in the stands, and the congresswoman from Turtle Creek's district. The tribal council chairmen of the Osage, Pawnee, and Winnebago tribes were in attendance, the powwow chairman announced. The Episcopal bishop from Omaha was there and Sheriff Larry Bradley and a couple of deputies. The place was, of course, swarming with reporters, looking for a big story on the stolen Peace Medal.

Clarence Edgley was there too. He was clearly under the impression that he had taken a chance in showing up on the reservation. He kept close company with the sheriff and the two state patrolmen accompanying the governor. Now and then a young Indian war dancer with painted face, draped in wildly colored cloth, feathers, and bells, would dance straight toward where Edgley and the sheriff sat, menacing with a dance ax or lance, to see Edgley look uneasy and strike up a lively conversation with the sheriff, but the dancers' gestures were obviously meant only to draw laughter from other Nehawka. Even the sheriff laughed.

Antler was not certain if the sheriff or Edgley knew that the Medal was under the control of the Buffalo Dance Society. He wondered if they sensed the tension that filled the dance arena when John Edward announced the Buffalo Dancers from the speakers' stand. "Excuse me, Liz. I think I should be down closer to the dance arena for this, just in case someone suddenly needs a lawyer, if you know what I mean."

"I understand," she said. "I hope everything goes well."

He made his way through the crowd down to the dance floor and watched tribal members leaving the arena to get into costume or help others, the same unself-conscious shuffle that so successfully blurred the identity of the dancers every other time he had seen it. Finally the drum started, and the singers, and the dancers—perhaps thirty of them on this occasion—danced into the arena. Antler wondered how they could even stand in the July sun in the heavy costumes, yet dance.

The Buffalo Dancers were even more unrestrained than usual, and Antler wondered if the enthusiasm of the dance was in anticipation of yet another chapter in the history of the Jefferson Peace Medal. The dancers themselves answered his question only moments later. Not ten minutes into the dance the chief dancer charged across the arena, the other dancers following him just as tribal memory said the great herds followed their bull leader. As the dance leader approached the governor's seat of honor, he reached into an ancient buffalo-hide pouch at his side and brought out the Medal, which he held high above his head. This time the dull gray of the silver caught the sun and flashed like lightning around the tree-shaded arena.

Edgley leaped to his feet, but the sheriff pulled him back. Again and again the chief Buffalo Dancer charged at the audience, the bishop, tribal council members, the chairman of visiting tribes, holding the Medal before him and before their eyes.

The dancer even charged at Antler, stopping with the Medal held only a few feet from Antler's face. Antler wondered if the dancer was taunting him. He tried to look past the mask into the dancer's eyes but it was as if there were no dancer, only the mask. Antler took two or three fast war-dance steps, an abbreviated dance of triumph, to which the buffalo snorted approvingly and dashed off back to his waiting herd.

The chief Buffalo Dancer danced on another quarter hour holding the Medal above him and before him. Antler wondered if human strength was capable of that sort of endurance and he promised himself to try it sometime, just to see if he could. Antler watched the dancer, knowing that it was a man or woman he knew, knowing that he or she had been transformed. He wondered if the tingle in his arms was from the blood within or the emotion without.

Then suddenly the dancer charged the governor again, this time much closer than before, bringing his arms and the Medal over the governor's head. The two state troopers with her were so startled by this unexpected threat to their charge that they didn't have a chance to rise from their seats before the dancer lowered the silver Medal's red ribbon necklace over her head and dropped the Medal to her breast. A gasp went through the crowd of white visitors. Photographers dashed to the governor's seat in the dance circle and

flashes lit her smile as the reporters recorded the unexpected return of the Medal. Edgley rushed to her side, anxious to take
advantage of this moment of his victory over the Nehawka.

The music continued. The excitement among the white visitors
at the powwow did not surprise Antler but he was confused that
the Turtle Creekers were showing no distress at all at the surrender of their precious Peace Medal. The dancers were still crowding
around the chief and charging around the arena, oblivious to the
commotion at the governor's chair. Finally the governor motioned
for the reporters to clear the arena so she could watch the dance,
but the calm was only momentary because now the chief Buffalo
Dancer charged the Osage tribal chairman and lifted above his
head . . . a silver Jefferson Peace Medal on a red ribbon. The
dancer lowered it over his head. A few confused photographers ran
across the dance ring to capture this moment, too.

They were almost run down by yet another charge of the Buffalo
Dancers, this time bestowing Jefferson Medals on the Winnebago
and Pawnee chairmen. Medals dropped around the necks of the
congresswoman, the state senators, the entire Turtle Creek tribal
council, a very confused Clarence Edgley, the Episcopal bishop,
the Catholic bishop, the principal of the reservation high school, an
anthropologist from the state university, and Antler. A representative of the National Endowment for the Arts, at the Turtle Creek
powwow to deliver some ancient archival materials, and the reservation's medical-technical volunteer also got medals.

Antler wondered how it had been decided who got medals, but
the logic escaped him. Medals were everywhere. Why the Osage?
Why Edgley? Why him? By the time the Buffalo Dance had ended,
at least thirty-five—some guessed forty—medals had been distrib-
uted, all identical, all on red ribbons.

Antler could see Edgley, red-faced and sweating, arguing with the sheriff, the sheriff finally pushing him backward with one short, powerful sweep of his long arm. Antler walked behind the bleachers with the hope of hearing some of the discussion. "I want you to arrest these people and take back the medals until we determine which one is the real one, Bradley, and I mean now. What the hell kind of law officer are you?"

"Edgley, I am not about to arrest the governor and take a peace medal away from her. And people are already scattering with their medals to all parts of the country. How am I supposed to run them all down? You have your damned Medal: 10.3 ounces of silver is 10.3 ounces of silver. How do you know that even one of the thirty we saw today is real? Cool down and go home before I arrest you."

"Arrest *me*? You ass, I'm the one who was robbed. The criminals are out there in the feathers and beads, dancing around like idiots. I'll have your badge, Bradley, you jerk."

"That's it, Edgley. You're under arrest for disturbing the peace." Sheriff Bradley turned to Antler. "LaVoi, would you mind helping me subdue this agitator until I get cuffs on him? I thought not."

Antler talked with a few friends on his way back to Liz. Crossing the dance arena was difficult. Dancers were still trying to complete the closing ceremony but Turtle Creekers had crowded the dance arena under the huge oaks, congratulating themselves on their coup. They pounded each other on the back, danced spontaneous war dances. It was the first time in decades, certainly in his memory, that Antler had seen his people in a state of jubilation.

"Can I speak with you a moment, Cousin?" John Edward shouted in LaVoi's ear, over the noise of the crowd. John Edward pulled him over to a quiet spot outside the dance arena and talked intently with him for nearly a quarter of an hour, Liz wondering all the while what problems the two were trying to resolve. She was relieved when she saw LaVoi laugh and pat his cousin on the back.

They shook hands and LaVoi again made his way toward Liz through the jubilant crowd.

When he reached Liz, she was standing arm in arm with Naomi, tears of joy running down their cheeks. "We did it, we did it!" she shouted to him, throwing her arms around his neck.

"What do . . ." He was about to say again his old favorite line, "What do you mean 'we,' white woman?" but somehow it was no longer appropriate.

On the ride home the children fell asleep in the back seat—"part of the powwow tradition," Liz said quietly—and Antler and she talked. "What do you suppose they did, LaVoi? Where did they get all the medals? How did they do it?"

"I can answer some of your questions, Liz," he said. "John Edward explained a little of it to me. Do you remember a few years ago when an Indian named Bernalli, a silver worker, a Seminole I think, was arrested for counterfeiting Olympic medals? And they found out that he had been duplicating antique jewelry and coins for years?"

"Oh, sure. He was using some sort of homemade hydraulic ram to make the coins. I remember everyone was amazed at how good his fakes were."

"Right. They finally had to use some sort of electron microscope or something to sort the mess out. Now Bernalli's copies sell for almost as much as the originals. He's that good. I think Ed Carter defended him on the counterfeiting charges and got him off with a couple years' worth of probation."

"If Ed defended him, he must have been guilty," Liz laughed.

"No doubt. You know they're in trouble when they go to Mad Dog Carter. Well, Bernalli is down in Mexico now, where he can work his routine with a little less threat from the law, and when he heard about the mess with the Jefferson Medal, he called up the tribal council and said he thought he had a solution to the whole problem.

"The Buffalo Dancers sent Dennis Flint Hand and Luke Mapateet down to Bernalli with all the silver they could round up and Bernalli worked night and day for a couple weeks making dies and striking medals. He guaranteed the Turtle Creekers that when he got done, it would take the best labs in the world to tell the difference between the original and his reproductions. Didn't ask for anything in return but a ride back up here so he could be on hand when the . . . well, when the medal hit the governor. Ed Carter says he was sitting in the stands during the Buffalo Dance, even though he's wanted in God knows how many states."

"But where did the Turtle Creekers come up with all the silver? They certainly didn't have money to buy it. I . . ." Liz paused and sighed deeply. "Oh no, LaVoi. I wondered why Naomi wasn't wearing her squash blossom necklace today. Do you suppose . . ."

"Liz, I think there's every chance in the world that I have it here in my hand." He held out the medal the Buffalo Dancer had given him.

"Can't they do some sort of tests on the medals to find out which one is the original?"

"I suppose they could but I can't imagine the county, or the state, or even the museum at this point wanting to go through the trouble and expense of rounding up all those medals and trying to sort the mess out. Maybe even Edgley will realize now that silver is silver, and the symbolic importance of the Medal has nothing to do with the age of the metal in it."

"What about the original medal? Do you suppose they reburied it? Was it one of those they gave away today? Did they melt it down to make the new ones?"

"Liz, Grandpa Smoke used to tell a story . . ." They both

laughed: that introductory phrase—"Grandpa Smoke used to tell a story"—had become a standard formulaic story opening in their family. "Do you remember reading Ian Frazier's book *The Great Plains*? The part about where Crazy Horse was buried?"

"Sure."

"Well, Frazier, like every other white man who ever tried to solve the mystery, wasn't even close. Frazier, like all the rest, thinks like a white man. He's sure that the Indians don't know where Crazy Horse is buried either, since he talked with fifty of them and they all gave him a different answer. White men think it's funny that every Indian claims to know where Crazy Horse is buried and every single one of them has a different notion of where the place is. So, the white guys figure, 99 percent of the Indians have to be wrong. Maybe 100 percent."

"And . . ."

"And, as is so often the case with Indians, they are *all* right. See, a white man thinks that every problem has a solution and every problem has *one* solution, but that's not the way the world works. Some problems have no solution. Some problems have hundreds of solutions.

"When I was a boy my Grandpa Smoke told me that Crazy Horse's parents took his body into the badlands north of Fort Robinson and they hid it in a cave far from where any white man ever passed. But Crazy Horse's family and tribe worried more and more as white men became increasingly common in Indian territory and poked their noses into every square inch of land, looking for gold or treasure or God knows what. So the Indians moved Crazy Horse's body from hill to hill, cave to cave."

"When Indians point to ten different hills and say 'Crazy Horse was buried there,' they are all right!" Liz said slowly in wonder.

"It's even better than that, Liz. The Indians knew that white men would give a fortune for Crazy Horse's skeleton, to exhibit in medicine shows, or to destroy before it became a tribal symbol, or to 'study' at some museum or university. And they knew that it would be an enormous temptation for some drunk Indian to sell Crazy Horse's body to a white man for a fortune sooner or later. You don't like to think that someone would betray his own people like that, but you never know. Human beings are human beings, after all. Imagine how Edgley would like to have Crazy Horse's skull on his desk for a paperweight. Look how fast we lost the Sky Bundle.

"By then—that was maybe twenty years after he had died— there wasn't much left of Crazy Horse but some dry bones and a little hair maybe, so the holy men of all the Lakota tribes got together at a big Sun Dance and off in the hills somewhere they divided Crazy Horse's bones into little medicine bundles, wrapped with sage and deer hide, with eagle feathers and bear claws and his little brown stone. At the end of the Sun Dance, they all carried the bundles with them and hid them again in caves and trees and cabins and churches."

"So now it isn't even a matter of that hill and that hill and that hill being a place where Crazy Horse *was* buried because he may be—in part at least—still there!"

"That's right, Liz. No white man will ever exhibit Crazy Horse's body because white men will never find it. It is nowhere and it is everywhere."

"My God, LaVoi. I read Frazier and I wondered but I never guessed."

"No one *could* guess. The miracle is that there are whites like you who wonder."

"It's beautiful. The Medal is not a thing, it's an idea. But what about the Medal giving peace to the tribe? If the tribe no longer has the real Medal, if it's been destroyed, will the Turtle Creekers have peace?"

"I think they have the real Medal because they sure looked at peace when we left tonight. The Medal never brought Edgley peace when he had it. Maybe the one he has now will work. Any other questions, Mrs. Antler?"

"As a matter of fact there are. I saw you eyeing those girls in the round dance this afternoon. I was wondering if you were planning to run off with one of them or if you still have enough Indian in you to lust after us white women."

"I guess so. Would you like to come into my tipi tomorrow while the kids are at the bowling alley?"

"You men are all alike, Indian or not."

She squeezed his hand so hard the edges of the medal cut into his skin. "Take it easy, Liz. Here." He handed her the medal. "Will you wear this for me? That way you can share the guilt."

"Are you sure I should . . . ?"

"Yes, I am sure you should. You, of all people."

Liz took the medal's ribbon and pulled it over her head.

"You know, we have to talk with the tribal council about getting an Indian name for the kids. And for you."

"I thought you'd never ask," she said. "But you know, I'm very happy with the Indian name I have, Mr. Antler."

Buddy Foster was right, Antler thought. Twenty years earlier Antler had married a white woman, but now he knew in all confidence that she had become a Nehawka.

At this point in Nehawka tribal history, winter counts were no longer kept. Buddy Foster, John Edward Rouliere, and LaVoi Antler joked that if the tradition were still in effect, the year 1992 would almost certainly have been named after the events surrounding the Jefferson Peace Medal. Three weeks and two days after the annual Turtle Creek powwow, Clarence Edgley began a lawsuit that required Sheriff Bradley to determine the authenticity of the medal returned to Dr. Edgley and the museum.

In accordance with a court order, Sheriff Bradley seized medals held by Turtle Creek Chairwoman Virginia Ree Killer (elected to follow John Edward Rouliere and therefore heir to the chairperson's medal), six medals held by council members (two others could not be located), the Winnebago medal (the Osage and Pawnee medals were out of state and therefore not available for evidence), and one held by LaVoi Antler. The Episcopal and Catholic bishops, the governor, one state senator, and the congresswoman voluntarily surrendered their medals for study. The med-tech volunteer and school principal challenged the sheriff to take them to court for their medals. Clarence Edgley voluntarily submitted his museum's medal for analysis. No other medals could be located; none were volunteered.

The fifteen medals immediately available to the court were submitted to the American Numismatic Association's certification service in Colorado Springs, Colorado, for analysis. All fifteen were found to be authentic.

▼ ▲ ▼

The Story of Luke and
the Roadrunners

Luke Bigelow compared his work running down bail jumpers to bird-watching: "You spend two weeks reading everything you can about the purple-breasted cuckoo, then another
week talking to locals, a couple days looking for nests and signs,
and then all at once, when you least expect it, along come a couple
of goofy birds, do a dance where feathers fly all over the place, they
mate in three seconds, and that's it. You pack up your stuff and go
home."

That's not the way it went on this occasion, however. Luke had
watched the isolated Texas farmhouse only one full day before the
action started, and then the situation got complicated, and then life
was never quite the same again.

Luke had stashed his pickup truck in a shed at an abandoned
farm a mile or so from the house and made his way quietly, carefully through some scrub oak to a stand of mesquite and brush on
a low hill about three hundred yards from the farmhouse. It was a
comfortable stakeout, as Luke's stakeouts went. The September
day was warm and windless, no flying bugs to worry about, the
grass was soft under the shrubs and free of prickly pear, he had a
clear view of the front and yard side of the farmhouse, and he felt
confident because the two rabbits he was after weren't much more
than kids. No priors, no violence, no weapons in their records.
They didn't even have enough sense to tie a dog outside the house
to warn them of intruders. Not the way for junior drug smugglers
to become senior veterans, in Bigelow's opinion. He put down a
ground cloth, emptied a can of Sevin around it to discourage fire
ants, and sat down.

Through his Adlerblick binoculars he watched them—a thin girl
maybe nineteen or twenty years old and a boy not much more than

a year or two older and not much more substantial, both Indians — puttering around, closing sheds, putting stuff in a battered Chevy van: a cooler, a couple of suitcases, some heavy boxes, probably more of the stuff they had been popped for in the first place. The dumb punks had learned nothing from their first encounter with the law.

Luke figured that the two were about to head out on the road, which meant he would have to make some decisions. He didn't intend to try to follow them around the countryside until they settled down again. They might be planning to pick up a few friends on the road, which would only complicate his job. He could lose them in traffic. They might figure out he was following them. He was going to have to make his move quick and without the usual careful preparation he put into his captures.

Luke survived more on his care than his wits, more on timing than muscle. Usually, by the time he kicked in a front door, he knew so much about the people inside, what sort of weapons they had, how well they could use them, their strengths, their weaknesses, that his pulse didn't pick up more than a couple of beats when glass started breaking. Luke planned well, and if the script went his way, he was paid and the bondsman, the judge, the prosecutor had work; on the other hand, lose control and deliver corpses, and attitudes changed fast and the players changed sides. The point is, Luke made sure he always knew what was going on and how events were likely to go and that his targets had no idea at all.

Okay, so he hadn't had a chance to put a lot of time into this operation; the two rabbits had come in from Mexico only a few days before and they would be moving north soon. He had watched the house all day and had a pretty good idea that the young man and woman were alone. He saw no signs of weapons. The Indian kids didn't appear to be nervous, which meant that they probably hadn't done what nervous people do—like take precautions. He might have worried that the two would take off before he had a chance to get to his pickup, a mile away over a hill and through brush, but he had heard the unpleasant sounds the Chevy van made when the Indian kid started it up. Probably just a bad spark plug wire or distributor trouble, but the hood was up and the kid was digging around in the engine with screwdrivers and pliers, so it wasn't likely that they would be getting started until tomorrow. He would have a few more hours to watch them, time to get back to his pickup, pick up weapons, dump the binoculars and sleeping bag, and figure out a plan.

On a couple of stakeouts like this one—way out in the country, where his quarry could be pretty certain they wouldn't have visitors—he had seen couples engage in some interesting sex, and for a moment he thought maybe these two healthy youngsters might offer one of those chances for him to relax and smile a bit. Naked people having fun aren't much of a threat, bail jumpers or not. But while these two were friendly enough, they were pretty much all business. He worked at the van, she took some shirts and jeans off the clothesline, they talked now and then, laughed, but nothing that suggested they shared a bed.

The girl had long, black hair. Luke couldn't see a lot at this distance but she appeared to be pleasant-looking and had an attractive figure, if not a generous one. It would have been fun to watch her romp bare-assed on the porch or, like the couple he had tracked down the previous spring in Kansas, on an old mattress tossed right out in the middle of a farm's front yard, but Luke guessed that it wasn't in the cards this time around.

Shortly before sunset Luke caught the smell of something cooking—menudo, he guessed. The girl called something out from the back door of the house and the boy yelled something back. He

fiddled around a few minutes more under the hood, slammed it
shut, wiped his hands on a rag, and got into the van. He started it
and it ran fine. They would be leaving the next morning, probably
early, Luke figured. He'd make his move before they were up and
alive. He'd catch them sleepy-eyed. The way they were acting, they
had no intention of standing watch during the night.

He slid into his sleeping bag and ate some crackers and cheese
from his knapsack. He watched as the lights went out at the farmhouse below him. Finally, there were only two lights left, one in
what was probably the front room and a second upstairs, probably
a bedroom. The lights went out almost simultaneously. Suspicions
confirmed: one of the pair was sleeping upstairs—probably the
girl—and the other was downstairs, maybe on a couch or on the
floor—the boy. He might have been there as a sentinel, but chances
were, Luke suspected after watching them through the day, he was
simply being chivalrous and giving the lady of the operation the
safer, more comfortable accommodations in the upstairs bedroom.

Luke closed his eyes. He wanted as much sleep as possible before
the bust broke loose in the morning. He knew from experience that
he would fly awake at the slightest noise from the house; for him,
the sound of a car starting was like a fire alarm for anyone else. He
also knew from experience that he would sleep five or six hours and
then wake up, at which time he could make his way back to his
truck and set up the bust.

And that's the way it went. All routine, no problem. When Luke
woke, he looked at the position of the Big Dipper. He had noted its
position when he shut down at 11 P.M. and he knew that as the
earth rotated through its twenty-four-hour day, the Dipper would
appear to sweep counterclockwise all the way around Polaris, the
North Star. Halfway around in twelve hours. A fourth of the way
in six hours. When he went to sleep, the Dipper was straight up;

now it was a little more than a third of the way down the left hand side of the circle. He guessed he had slept five hours. Just right. The soundless, pulsating alarm on his wristwatch went off—precisely five hours.

He took his time getting back to his pickup through the dark night. He shed his stakeout equipment and checked his .308 one last time, choosing instead the 870 Remington riot gun—a short, twelve-gauge, pump action shotgun, the shells loaded with no. 4, alternating with double-ought loads. Anything the riot gun lacked in firepower it made up in intimidation. The quick-load magazine made the weapon look for all the world as if it had three gigantic barrels. In the back of his belt he tucked a .44 magnum revolver.

Guns like that aren't worth much in a long-range gunfight, but then Luke didn't want long-range gunfights. "Dead or alive" is Old West stuff. He wanted his opponents to see those black tunnels pointing at them, and if he did have to fire one of them, he sure didn't want to blow away his reward. He wanted the maximum noise and immediate destruction of property to impress the folks across from him. Impress the hell out of them.

He tucked several self-locking nylon pipe hangers into his belt and put a long, heavy eight-cell flashlight on the seat beside him, as much a weapon as a light source.

Luke drove out of the abandoned farmstead slowly, not turning on his headlights. It took him almost ten minutes to cover the half mile from the farmstead to the gravel road. He hated this part of his job. On the farm lane he knew there was no chance of encountering traffic, but out here on the gravel, who knew what drunk might be coming home, even at this hour, doing eighty miles an hour, and here he was, dinking along at ten miles an hour without any lights. Couldn't be helped.

He felt relief when he turned off the gravel county road into the lane of the farm where the two Indians were, he hoped, still sound asleep. He drove just far enough into the lane so no one would see his truck from the gravel—maybe two hundred yards—and opened the driver's side door so he would not have to make noise opening it when he was closer to the house. One of the first alterations he made when he bought a vehicle was to install a toggle switch that shut off all interior and brake lights, including the one under the hood, so he didn't have to worry about lights betraying his presence.

He killed the engine and let the pickup roll slowly to a stop, to avoid making noise on the dirt and rock. For a moment he sat quietly in the cab, waiting to see if his arrival had aroused anyone at the farmhouse. No lights. No sound. So far so good.

Luke slipped from the truck, adjusting the Kevlar vest that had saved his life at least twice. He took the shotgun and flashlight, left the door open, and slowly, one step at a time, he edged along the side of the lane toward the house, keeping to the dark of the trees. When he reached the edge of the yard, he paused and listened. Nothing. He stepped out of the dark of the trees and into the yard—dark but not obscured—making sure that the Chevy was between him and the house.

At the van he stopped again and for a quarter hour crouched there, listening, looking. He stepped out from the back of the vehicle and slowly approached the front porch of the house. There was a time when he would have crawled, but he hated the helpless feeling of having his hands on the ground instead of a gun. He would just as soon not have anything touching the ground, but two feet are sure as hell better than two feet, two knees, and two hands.

The porch was old and wood. It would squeak. He knew it would. He had watched the Indians walk across the porch three dozen times over the previous day, so he was pretty sure that the porch was solid enough, no loose or missing boards. Nonetheless, if he should stumble or if someone inside the house woke up, now there could be no faking, no retreat. He would have to react as quickly as he could and rip into the house spitting fire, doing whatever he could to maintain control of the situation and give the kids the impression that an airborne division had just landed on their front porch.

Luke could do that. There was a time when he earned his drinks by betting that he could kick tiles out of bar ceilings. He broke his collarbone twice, and his wrist, and his nose, but he drank free and local hard-asses always gave him more room after witnessing one of his berserk performances. If the porch collapsed under him, even on him, Luke would still be inside the house in two seconds.

He moved to the side of the porch. He knew better than to use the steps. That was precisely where anyone with any brains would put a motion detector, trip wire, or booby trap, and Luke, he liked to say, was no booby. Of course these two Indian kids weren't the sort to use high tech, but why take a chance. He pulled himself up to the edge of the porch and swung his left leg over the railing. So far, so good. A few pounds at a time he transferred his weight to the foot on the porch inside the railing. A few cracks and pops but nothing major. Luke sensed a slight breeze arising. Good. Even the sounds of a light wind could cover anything but a total disaster. He pulled his right leg over the railing and transferred all his weight to the porch. A few little sounds, about what he had expected. What he really liked was when his quarry were in the same room, in the same bed, like newlyweds, hearing nothing but themselves. But no, this time it was separate rooms, separate beds, separate floors.

He took a third step and then something in a damned board

popped and then squeaked so loud he might as well have stepped on a bobcat. He now had to balance his desire to get into the house unnoticed and the very real chance that someone inside had already detected him and unless he acted immediately could do him some real damage. He took two smooth, quick steps toward the door, trying to keep noise down just in case the two inside the house still hadn't heard him. He opened the screen and tested the door knob. It turned. He pushed it in firmly and quickly, but didn't let it hit the inside stop. He stepped into the house.

He heard heavy breathing to his left—probably the boy, still sleeping. Boy, these kids are real professionals, Luke thought. He slid his feet on the bare wood floor slowly in the direction of the breathing so he wouldn't step on anything or bump furniture. The sleeping sounds were now very close. He aimed the pistol-grip riot gun with his right hand, insofar as a riot gun needs aiming, and then the light in his left. He braced himself and flicked the button on the flashlight.

His aim was predictably perfect: the brilliant white beam exploded onto the boy's face. He tried to throw his arm up in front of his face to protect his eyes but hopelessly tangled himself in his bedding. Luke knew the feeling: the boy wanted to turn away from the light and yet he was so startled that he needed to see what this attack was coming from.

The boy made the first sounds of asking what was going on but didn't get past the first whistle of a "w" when Luke popped him squarely on top of the head with the flashlight and then pushed him back onto the couch, the shotgun pressing hard enough into his mouth to bring blood.

"Not a sound," Luke growled with as much threat as he could generate in a whisper. The kid sat on the couch, staring directly into the light. Luke knew that all he could see was that blinding white light and the cannon sticking out of it, right into his mouth. Luke could see he wasn't going to have any trouble here. He pulled the gun barrel back a few inches from the boy's face, and with a skill that comes only from practice pulled a nylon strap from his belt and pulled it tightly around both the boy's wrists, and said softly, "Call the girl down."

The boy hesitated. "She's . . ." the boy started, but Luke pushed the gun into the boy's face again. "Just don't hurt her," the boy said despite the threat.

"I'm not going to hurt anyone as long as you don't make it necessary. Call her down. Now."

"Silver!" the boy called. "Silver, come down."

"Silver," Luke thought. "Tonto and Silver. What goes through parents' minds when they name their children?"

"Is it time to go already?" a soft voice asked from up the stairs behind Luke, directly ahead of the door he had just come in. Luke waved the gun up and down in front of the boy's nose, to let him know that he should continue the conversation. Luke moved back toward the door so he could keep his eye on the boy but be ready for the girl when she came down the stairway. He made note of the light switch just inside the front door. He kept the light in the boy's face and held the gun's muzzle ahead of the light beam so there couldn't be any question in the boy's mind where Luke was aiming the gun.

"Yeah, come on down, Silver. It's time to go, all right," the boy said. A light came on upstairs. Luke heard sounds of the girl dressing. Then her footsteps across the floor. She turned on the stairway light. Luke moved back into the shadows of the front room. He kept the light and the gun on the boy but turned his body to his right so he could see her the moment she stepped into his view.

"Why don't you have a light on down here?" the girl asked as she reached the bottom of the stairway.

Luke reached out with the barrel of the shotgun and flicked up both light switches, turning on a ceiling light in the front room and another just inside the door. The bulbs were small and probably dingy, but the flash of light that early in the morning startled the girl.

Luke grabbed the girl and hurled her across the room toward the boy. She hit the couch so hard it almost went over backward. She struggled to regain her balance. Luke kept the flashlight directly in the boy's eyes; even with the ceiling light on, its brilliance would keep him blind. Moreover, this way he had the heavy flashlight out in front of him where it would do the job if he needed it.

"Don't even think of moving," Luke roared. He took a step toward them, swung the shotgun back behind him toward the wall between the front room and the stairway, and pulled the trigger. He was prepared for the thunder but the riot gun's noise in the confined room was still deafening; he knew that the shock of the explosion would petrify the two on the couch. The girl screamed, as Luke knew she would. Probably peed her pants, too.

"You, the girl, come here. Right now. Don't even think. Just move it." He screamed the words through the plaster dust and gun smoke the instant the reverberations of the gunshot died down. The girl started to rise from the couch, disoriented from the confusion of the past few seconds; Luke grabbed her and pulled her hard toward him. He twisted her hand forward on her wrist and forced her to her knees. With one hand he pulled a nylon strap from his belt and jerked it tight enough on her left wrist that she cried out.

At her cry the boy started up off the couch. Luke raised the shotgun to the ceiling and fired again. He knew that if the noise didn't end the incipient rebellion, the cloud of plaster dust raining down from the shattered ceiling would. Luke dragged the girl to the stairway. He threw her to the stairs and passed another strap through the hole he had blown in the wall.

"You, Geronimo. Get over here right now and I won't hurt the girl. Move it, move it, move it!"

The boy stepped forward, coughing from the plaster dust. Luke grabbed his arm and, as he had done with the girl, twisted him to the floor, on the other side of the hole in the stairway wall. Luke fastened a third nylon strap through the boy's wrist restraints, through the new hole in the wall, and then through the girl's wrist ties. Now everything was under control. Luke stepped back to admire his work.

The girl was now kneeling on the stairs, her back to Luke; the boy sat on the floor in the front room, facing him. Luke knew from experience that they would be more cooperative if they each knew the other was all right and close, but they couldn't see each other. He didn't know why. It just worked that way. They certainly weren't going to go anywhere, tied up through that wall.

Luke quickly ran his hands over each of them, checking for weapons, money, or any papers with information, but there was nothing. He would have a look around the house before he moved them down the road toward justice. He edged into the room to the right of the front door. Dining room. Chairs, a table, not much else. He could see through a door in the back of the dining room a small kitchen. "Don't do anything stupid," he told the couple, and stepped into the kitchen. He hit the light switch. It didn't work, but the room was small enough that the light from the dining room showed him nothing more than a refrigerator, a small electric stove, a sink, some cupboards.

He opened the refrigerator. Cottage cheese, a couple cans of

Coke, some lunch meat. Not even a beer. Damn druggies. He walked back through the dining room to the front door. He pointed the shotgun up the stairs. "Who else is up there, sweetheart?" he asked the girl. She shook her head without looking at him.

He walked slowly past her and up the stairs, his boots making crunching sounds as he stepped on the shattered plaster. He didn't exactly have to worry about trying to hide his presence in the house. The girl had left the light on in the bedroom. Nothing but a rumpled bed and a battered dresser. He stepped across the hall to an open doorway and flicked the light switch. Nothing. Not even a cot. A stack of *National Geographics* in one corner. He tore open the drawers in the dresser, threw the mattress off the bed, kicked over the *National Geographics*. No money, no papers, no maps.

Luke stepped back downstairs. The girl was crying softly. Still she did not look at him. "Mister, I don't know what you want, but you picked the wrong folks, I can tell you for sure," the boy shouted from the other side of the hole in the wall. "We got nothing, but you can take whatever you want if you'll leave us alone. Don't hurt the girl."

Luke stepped around the wall into the front room. "That's downright generous of you, Cochise. I could take just about anything I want and there wouldn't be a lot you could do about it, now, would there?" The boy said nothing.

"Here's a little riddle for you, kids: how can it be that you don't have shit, and yet you're worth a bundle of bucks. Hey! Get that? 'Bucks?' You know, like Indians. Not bad for a white boy, huh? So what's the answer? Can you figure out my riddle? How can someone worth nothing still be worth a lot?"

The boy glared at him but said nothing.

"I don't suppose you remember an insignificant $25,000 bond that Otis Bentsen put up for each of you two in a little matter of a drug arrest, do you? 'Possession of controlled substances for distribution,' I think the lawyers said. Doesn't ring a bell? How about you, Pocahontas?" The girl sobbed, her face in her arms.

"Leave her alone. She's had enough trouble from white men," the boy said.

"You talk pretty tough for sitting there in your underwear with your arm stuck through a hole in the wall. You know, when you missed that court date, my client had to come up with a lot of money because you were two bad little Indians. And that wasn't very smart. My client doesn't like to lose that kind of money. Here he tries to do you a favor and you give a bad name to the Noble Red Man by trying to pull an old-fashioned massacre on him. That's not very nice. And now he's angry. Very angry."

"I am sorry about that," the boy said. "I hoped that I could come back after this run and turn myself in so the court would give Mr. Bentsen his money back."

Luke looked at the boy. That was the first time he had ever heard that slime-ball Bentsen called Mister. "Let me guess: you're also innocent, right? You were just going to catch the real crooks and clear your good name."

"No, we were guilty. What we're doing may be against the law but it isn't wrong."

Bigelow pulled a chair from the dining room into the front doorway so he could look down the wall and see both of his prisoners. He wasn't in a hurry; he didn't want to drag them out of the house until it was light enough for him to have a good shot if he should lose control or one of them made a break for it. He wouldn't kill them but he sure would slow them down if he had to. He reloaded with a couple no. 9 target loads.

"You know," Luke said, putting on his nice-guy voice, "there is a way out of this. I'm getting five grand and expenses for taking you in. If you want to enter a silent bid on that offer, I would be glad to entertain it."

They looked at him, obviously confused. They didn't understand what he was saying. "No sense in being subtle with you two, is there? What I am trying to say is, you must have a lot of money stashed around here somewhere. It takes money to run a van of stuff north. You simply pay me, say, *eight* thousand dollars, maybe *six* thousand dollars, and I forget that I've seen you. Just like that."

"I have about fifty dollars in gas money, and that's it," the boy said.

"You know how I got into the bounty hunting business?" Luke asked. Neither of his rabbits answered. "Well, I'm going to tell you. I know everything about people on the run because I spent most of my life on the run." The girl looked at him for the first time, confirming his early suspicions: she was pretty in a childlike way—not Luke's type. She looked like an injured deer at the moment, but Luke had the impression that maybe she looked like that all the time. She immediately looked away.

"Yep. I was a drug runner just like you dummies, so I know all the tricks."

"We are *not* drug runners and we don't have any money!" the girl snapped.

"Oh, you can talk, huh? Well, that's great, sweetie, but you don't make much sense. What were those boxes you put in the back of your van yesterday? Designer clothes? Feathers and beads? No, that was peyote cactus, darlin'. Mescaline heaven. Hippie candy. And from what I saw you loading up yesterday, enough for every hophead between here and Minneapolis. That stuff is illegal everywhere I know, and taking it across state lines is a particular no-no."

"The word is 'peyot' ' and it is our people's sacred herb and . . ." the girl started.

"Don't even try to explain it to him, Silver," the boy interrupted. "Look at him. He's not going to understand. White men understand nothing."

"You might be surprised, kid," Luke laughed. "I know all about the 'religious experiences' dopers have from time to time. I'm not going to buy it and neither is the judge. And the word is pay-o-tee, take it from someone who is mostly English and we're the ones who invented the language."

"It's pay-oat, take it from someone who is mostly Indian and we're the ones who discovered the cactus," the girl snapped without looking at him.

"Look, smart-ass, just because you are an Indian and *look* like an Indian doesn't mean there aren't other people who have some Indian in them but don't happen to have black eyes and big noses."

Ouch. That hurt. Luke couldn't remember having ever told anyone that he had some Indian blood in him from way back—some great-grandmother who had married an Indian guy in southern Missouri a hundred or so years ago. His mother insisted that he keep the information to himself. She thought it was all right to have a Cherokee grandmother, but considered it something of a disgrace to have an Indian grandfather. Unless he was a chief or something.

"Okay, let's get organized for our little trip back to Austin. Is everything out there in the van? Do you have your money and papers out there or am I going to have to dismantle this place?"

"Everything's in the van, and don't mess up my grandma's place any worse than you already have," the girl snapped.

Despite his general dismissal of women as anything more than a receptacle for his sexual expressions, Luke didn't like people who kicked puppies or picked on children, and this girl had that kind of fragility, even in her momentary defiance. Besides, these kids weren't dangerous and he had spent a few hours himself on the wrong side of a bounty hunter's shotgun, so he saw no reason to do his usual tough-guy routine. "Where's Grandma now?" he asked.

"She's at a ceremonial in Gallup and is just letting us use the place. This is all she has, and look at the mess you've made."

"It could get worse, princess. A lot worse. Where's the money?"

"Everything we have is in my billfold, in the jeans on that chair over there"—the boy gestured back into the front room with his free hand—"and in her purse, in there on the table."

"Boy, you're talking to an old-timer here, not some college graduate cop, so don't be cute. You'll only make me mad. You don't run drugs and carry your money in a billfold or purse. You got a couple hundred thousand dollars worth of dope out there in that car, and that means you got a box of money someplace. Like I said, if you want me to take this place apart, fine. I'll do it. But why don't you save us all a lot of trouble—especially Granny—and just tell me where the cash stash is."

"Mister, we ain't drug pushers, and we don't have any money. Those boxes in the car are on their way up to churches in Kansas, Nebraska, Iowa, South Dakota. We'll be on the road most of the next couple months and we'll be lucky if we get enough to cover expenses."

" 'Churches?' 'Churches?!' Am I supposed to believe you're bootlegging sacramental wine or something?! Your 'churches' must be some kind of operation to use up a few hundred pounds of dope a winter! They pay you when you deliver the goods?"

"Yes, they pay us. If they can."

"Sounds to me, kid, like you not only need a good lawyer, you need a business manager too! Maybe even a guardian. Take this one word of advice, son: if you are going to survive in this business, you've got to learn—God, I shouldn't even start trying to tell you what you need to learn!—you should learn to at least see your money up front. Buyers are not nice folks. They're not even civilized. Have you heard the saying that a stiff dick doesn't have a conscience? Well, dope-folks *never* have a conscience, erect or not."

"Members of the Holy Indian Church are not dopers, and they pay whatever they can, if they can, when they can." The boy tried to stand up but the nylon restraints held him back. The girl moved closer to her side of the wall so he could rise to his feet.

Luke waved the shotgun at him. "Easy, son. Just relax. Sit down. Stay cool. Let's talk about something a little less troublesome than religion. How about them Cowboys?"

The boy did not sit down. "Look. It's real important that we deliver those boxes in the van. A lot of people are counting on us."

"They'll get over it. Even drugsters understand that now and then a load doesn't make it."

"Look, mister, you want the money. Why don't you let us deliver the herb we have out there in the van? At least to a stop in Kansas or Nebraska where we can leave it all. The people need the herb for their services this winter. They don't have much but they have the church and the sacred herb and their prayers. Whatever money we collect, you can have."

The boy paused and pawed away the tear running down through the plaster dust on his cheek. Luke looked at him, astonished. What kind of man cries? The boy continued: "I'll make you a deal . . . yeah, I know, I'm in no position for a deal, but just hear me out. You come with us, let us deliver the sacred herb to the Omahas or Winnebagos or the Turtle Creekers, and we'll agree to go back with you peacefully to the law officers in Austin. Whatever money we collect for the cactus, you can have. All of it."

Luke couldn't believe that he actually was considering the offer. He knew better. "Oh sure. So I drive all the way to Nebraska with you, burning my gas, for nothing that I don't already have except a couple dollars some Indians have left after the weekend sale at the local wine store. And on top of that, if I travel with you, I'm back in the business of smuggling. Real smart move for me, right? And then when we get to the Snake Creek . . ."

"Turtle Creek," the girl said.

Luke paused and looked at the girl. Somewhere in the back of his mind he remembered his aunt who had done the Bigelow family tree mentioning Turtle Creek. He shook off the memory and continued, "So when we get to Turtle Creek, your buddies push me around a little, take my guns, my pickup truck, maybe cut me up a little, and I wind up with nothing, including my bounty, except maybe my life, if I'm extra lucky. What kind of idiot do you think I am?"

"He's telling you the truth," the girl said. "He's telling the truth. I guarantee it."

Luke laughed. "You got some gall, sweetheart. You can't guarantee anything."

"I guarantee it," she said, looking down at her hands.

On the Texas Gulf shore Luke had once wavered at an offer not far from this one—bring the dope, come along, get your money at the buying end, take an extra bonus. On that occasion he wound up beaten half to death on a beach with nothing left to his name but his underwear and his breath.

A year later to the day he went through the same mess again, almost. A Mexican buyer showed up with no money and another proposition, centering, as Luke recalled, on a nine-inch blade. That was the only time Luke had ever simply aimed a .25 pistol and pulled the trigger out of cold anger and a desire to survive. The bullet popped the Mexican two inches above the bridge of his nose, precisely in the middle of his forehead. Luke was in a bar in Matamoros a few months later and there the son-of-a-bitch was, alive and well, sporting a long, narrow scar beginning right in the middle of his forehead and continuing up into his hairline.

Surprised the hell out of Luke, but the Mexican laughed it off, explaining that the bullet had gone under the skin, over his skull, and out the back of his scalp. The Mexican said he came to before Luke had reached his car—he heard it start.

The big Mexican tapped the scar with his forefinger and roared: "Roberto Duran, 'fists of stone!' Big Juan, 'skull of stone.' " Luke laughed at the macabre joke but he also hit the door before Juan got any drunker or his brothers in business showed up. Luke considered the experience part of his education; the next day he bought his first .44. And here he was, about to make the same sort of mistake.

"Well?" The boy's voice startled Luke back from his memories. Luke looked at his two prisoners. He saw nothing in their eyes even close to what he had seen in the eyes of his previous quarry—fear, hate, contempt, deceit, design. In the black, deep eyes of Silver and the boy, he saw nothing more than a confirmation of what they were saying. It was as if the truth was written in poster colors across their foreheads. They wanted nothing more than what they were asking, and were asking for nothing more than what was necessary.

There was also Luke's continuing contempt for the law. No, not really the law. The System. And he didn't care which side of the law he happened to be on at the time. He still didn't like the System. Like the kids in front of him, he had always been a small-timer, hauling five hundred pounds of pot now and then, or maybe a couple pounds of coke. Whatever he could afford without having to deal with backers. No mob shit or cartels. He had always enjoyed the outlawry of it. And he missed it. Like he missed cowboying.

He sure as hell wasn't about to say it aloud but he was like these kids in more ways than simply his past as a smuggler. He'd always thought there was more Indian in him than the family tree suggested, anyway. He'd taken a sweat once with a Nehawka friend, Cal White Shell, from Centralia, Nebraska. That was one of the few times in his life he had actually thought spiritually, considered life, weighed the possibility of there being gods and powers.

"Okay, boys and girls. I'll play your little 'sacred herb' game but I'm telling you right now, if you intend to pull something, you better make sure I'm dead when it's all over because if I'm not, you sure as hell are going to be.

"And remember: even if you get away from me, even if you drop me into the Missouri River, Otis Bentsen is going to send someone else after you. He doesn't really care how many bounty hunters you kill. Doesn't cost him a dime until one of them brings you in. And the next one might not be a sweetheart like me."

Luke reached forward and with a snap of his little Schrade skinning knife slashed the nylon tie binding the two together through the wall. "I know your name is Silver," Luke said. "And I know your boyfriend's name is Gaylord."

"We're cousins," the girl corrected.

"Whatever, smart-ass. I know your height, weight, birth dates, and Social Security numbers. I know more about you than your mothers do. Except maybe that cousin routine. That's why I am the bounty hunter and you are rabbits. You're Silver Mapateet, Turtle Creek Nehawka, with a little Kiowa on your grandmother's side. And this is her place I've just messed up. He's Gaylord Horse Capture, Nehawka and Lakota. I'm Luke, and that's all you need to know about me.

"Now, here's how we're going to do this little shuttle. You're going to get into the back of the van. I'll tie you together again through the back bumper. It'll be uncomfortable but it's only a short ride out to my vehicle and if you put up with a little discomfort, so will I. I don't want to keep pointing this cannon at you but it will always be where I can get at it if I need it. Understand? We're going to go down the road here to my pickup. Then Silver is going to come with me—"

"No," the boy interrupted. "She'll drive our van and I'll come with you."

"Just who the hell is in charge here, Geronimo?"

"It's Gaylord, and I'm not trying to make any trouble. Silver's had some bad times from a white man and she wouldn't feel good about riding alone with you. She's a good driver. She'll stick right with us. I'm not going to give you any trouble, and neither will she, if you'll stick with the bargain."

"Sorry, kids, but on this one you'll have to do it my way. A woman will always run out on a man but a man will stick around like a panting dog until the house burns down.

"Gaylord, you understand that if you get lost, your friend here is in deep trouble. In five minutes I'll phone a cop and have you picked up with a hundred pounds of controlled substance. They'll put you away forever. And the closest Pocahontas here will ever come to a wedding night is an ugly roommate or maybe a fat guard in the laundry room." The girl shivered and for a moment Luke regretted being quite so lurid in his threat. "It'll be just fine, princess," he added. "We're going to come out of this real good friends and if you are straight with me, I'll put in a good word for you with Bentsen."

Christ, Luke thought, a fat lot of good he could do them when Bentsen got his hands on them again, not to mention the state cops. If Silver had trouble with a white man before, well, Bentsen would almost certainly give her a lot more to have bad dreams about, for sure. Well, not his problem. He got them out to the van, secured them to the back bumper, and drove to his pickup truck. While they were still tied, he went through the van, ripping out a CB transmitter and radar detector. No money, no papers.

"Now, look, Gaylord. I don't want you drawing attention to us, understand? You have a lot more to lose in this operation than I do. I'll argue that I got missy here and I was trying to run you down. They won't like that story but they'll probably buy it. Don't speed; use your turn signals; drive carefully. How are you doing for gas?" He leaned in and looked at the gauge. "Full tank. Fine. We'll probably stop once or twice for gas. If you need to pee, hold up three fingers and we'll pull off on a side road. I'll pick the place. I'm not going to let you take off alone into a filling station. Do you need to go now? If you do, just step over there behind the van. You first, Silver. I hate to offend your sensibilities but the only other option is for you to pee your pants if you haven't already.

"Well, Gaylord, it looks like it's going to be a good day for a drive. Maybe a little rain. Good thing. I always liked running in bad weather. Keeps the cops in their cars." Luke was talking mostly to cover the sound of Silver urinating behind the van. He could tell when she stepped away that she was now more embarrassed than afraid.

"You know when I told you to take it easy with Silver?" Gaylord said with quiet urgency, glancing in the direction of Silver. "That she had trouble with a white man? Well, it was a deputy sheriff in Oklahoma."

"I told you I know more about you than you might think, boy. I know she spent some time in jail in Oklahoma. In Tulsa, as a matter of fact. I don't know the details."

"Luke, you were closer than you knew when you said something about guards. This deputy roughed her up, raped her, and then kept her in jail for a couple more days of fun. All she had there in jail was her faith in her people and the Indian church. That's why she's doing this roadrunning. She promised herself she'd do this if she got out of that jail and away from the bastard who was using her bad. His wife made a surprise visit to the jail one day just about the time he was dropping his pants, and Silver says she's sure that was an answer to her prayers."

Silver returned and Gaylord stepped behind the van. Luke ignored Silver and marked a map from his truck. When Gaylord returned, Luke said, "Boy, you go ahead of us. Stop at all lights, even if it's green and just turning yellow. We won't be far behind you. Follow this map. I usually drop a detonator into the rabbit's gas tank so if he makes a funny move, I just press a button on a garage door opener and he disappears in a puff of smoke. See? You've already learned something. I won't have to do that with you, will I, Gaylord? Good."

Luke paused and looked at the ground of the farm lane's shoulder at his feet. He bent and picked up a small, round, green object and rubbed it against the leg of his jeans, where it left a light green smear. He looked closely at it. "Look at-that," he laughed and passed the disc to Silver. It was an ancient Indian head penny.

"Good sign," Silver said, handing it back to him.

"Well, I guess so," Luke said, pushing it into his pocket.

Luke and Silver got into Luke's truck, and Gaylord got behind the wheel of the van. Luke turned his truck and pulled to the side of the lane to let Gaylord drive by. "Maybe you can drive a while later. But you're not much of a woman to drive a tank like this," Luke said to Silver without looking over at her.

"I do okay," she said. Those were the last words they spoke for almost four hours, except when Luke tuned the radio to a public radio station. "God, I hate them whining cowboys on country-western stations, forever complaining and moaning and groaning. I just want to tell them to get off their dead butts and do something for themselves, know what I mean?" Silver nodded but said nothing.

Everything was going along fine until they were about halfway across Kansas on Highway 183, not far from La Crosse, about nine hours into the drive. There aren't many hills on Highway 183 through Kansas, but as Gaylord topped a slight rise a half mile ahead of them, Luke saw the van's brake lights flash. "Something's up over the hill." Luke slowed down.

At the crest of the hill they came up behind Gaylord, who was now doing only twenty-five miles an hour. "Sweet Jesus, a roadblock," Luke blurted. At the bottom of the hill, less than a mile ahead, were six or seven patrol cars and ten or twelve cars and trucks lined up in both lanes. A large yellow sign at the side of the road read, "Kansas State Patrol Safety Inspection Station. Prepare to stop."

"If there was any chance of us getting by those cops, Gaylord's blowing it by driving twenty-five miles an hour," Luke exploded. "He might as well have a flashing sign on top of the van that says RUNNING DOPE!! RUNNING DOPE!!"

The van reached the end of the five cars lined up at the roadblock and stopped. In the van's rearview mirror, Luke saw Gaylord put his head down on the steering wheel. It didn't look good. Luke said, "Hang on," to Silver and eased up on the brake. By now they were going only ten miles an hour, but when the truck slammed into the back of the van the impact was enough to throw Silver hard against the truck's dashboard. "Oh God," she groaned.

"Shut up and stay right where you are," Luke growled. He kicked open the driver's side door and slid out of the truck.

Luke charged up to the van and tore open the door. He glanced into the back to see that the boxes of illicit cactus were still closed and covered. He grabbed Gaylord by his collar, leaned toward him, and hissed, "Don't say a word." Luke turned to the trooper who was walking back along the line of the cars to see what the trouble was.

He turned back to Gaylord. "Jesus, man, do you realize you don't have any brake lights on this heap? You can't just hit the brakes out here in the middle of nowhere and expect everyone behind you to stop. I hope to hell you have good insurance. Let me see your insurance card. And I want your license number, too."

"Everyone all right here?" the state trooper asked, looking back at the crumpled rear end of the van.

"Yeah, just a little bent sheet metal, but we have to sort out all the insurance stuff. It's not going to be easy. I busted up the rear end of his van enough that now you can't even tell if he had lights or not. And you know, I can't really blame the boy. Even if he had had taillights, we would have had trouble stopping. I know you guys are just doing your job, but, well, a roadblock at the bottom of a hill, and cars backing up near the top, and . . ."

Luke pointed back at the four additional cars that had now pulled up behind the "accident." "Hate to mess up your operation but my insurance company says not to move any vehicles in an accident until photographs have been taken and all information has been exchanged. We should be able to be out of your way here in an hour. Or so."

The patrolman took another look at the cars lining up, reaching ever closer to the crest of the hill, and said, "Look, buddy, why don't you just pull ahead up to that next intersection and sort everything out there? If you need an officer's name on your insurance forms, just put down 'Lyle Carson.' I'll tell 'em it was nobody's fault. We really don't have time to work this out now. Come on. Let's move along." He waved them through the roadblock.

Gaylord was obviously shaken by the close call. The two vehicles went only four or five miles before Gaylord pulled to the shoulder.

Luke stepped out of his truck and went to the van. "That's okay, pal. You did just fine. Take your time and when you think you're ready to start rolling again, drive on into La Crosse. Stop at the first service station on your side of the highway and we'll see what we have left by way of vehicles."

In La Crosse Luke looked over the van and the pickup. There was little damage to Luke's truck; a heavy pipe bumper and grill guard—useful in driving through brush, sheds, and houses—had protected the truck's sheet metal and radiator from harm. "About the only damage on the van is broken taillights and a bunged-up back door, which doesn't really make much difference on a piece of junk like this, but I don't like the growl in the transmission. We may have something broken there. Know what we call vehicles like this?"

Silver and Gaylord shook their heads.

" 'Indian cars.' We call them 'Indian cars.' Small wonder, huh? Anyway, I don't want to take the time to get the repairs. I don't intend to sleep with you along the road and I sure as hell am not going to buy you a motel room, so we're going to dump the van. I'll tell the guy in the station we'll pick it up in a few days on our way back. Start moving everything into the back of the pickup. Try not to be too obvious with the dope, okay?"

"It's not dope," Silver muttered.

"You weren't anxious to offer that explanation to the cops back there, were you?" he chuckled, patting her on the shoulder. "Just don't be obvious. Whatever you want to call it, we'll be rid of it by tomorrow at this time."

Luke went into the service station, where he explained the situation to the mechanic. "Nice guy," Luke told Gaylord and Silver. "He'll patch up the van at a decent price. I'll cover the costs. I'm the guy who banged it up."

They finished transferring everything from the van to the truck's camper shell and pushed the van behind the station. "I'll drive," said Luke. "If I'm going to smuggle drugs—okay, sacred herbs—I'll show you how to do it right. You kids are going to piss with the big dogs today. You've already learned two lessons."

Gaylord shook his head and laughed. "I think we've learned more than two lessons." Silver laughed, too. Luke stopped at a red light and looked at her, so small in the middle of the truck cab. "Nice laugh, Silver. Maybe that's where you got your name. Your laugh jingles like a handful of silver dollars." She smiled.

"Isn't that the way you people name your papooses? After the first thing you see the day the child is born? What's that joke? The kid says, 'Isn't it true, oh Father, that you named my sister 'Flying Bird' because the first thing you saw on the day she was born was a flying bird?' 'Yes, oh Son,' says the old chief. 'And you named my brother 'Black Horse' because you stepped out of the tipi the day he was born and saw a black horse?' 'Yes, that is true. But why do you ask, Brown Dog Shitting?' "

Luke could feel Silver's shoulder move as she laughed quietly. Gaylord laughed out loud. "You know," Gaylord said, "that's one of those jokes that is funnier when a bunch of Indians tell it."

"Yeah, I know what you mean. Drives me crazy when Mexicans call me 'Gringo,' but a buddy and I once ran a construction company in Laredo, and we called it 'Gringo Construction.' "

"What's your last name, Luke?" Gaylord asked.

Luke didn't like to give out that sort of information. "Luke" was enough. He especially didn't like to have felons he was hauling to jail know his name. He wasn't afraid of the scum he dealt with but it was just easier to avoid the problem. "Bigelow," he said nonetheless. "Luke Bigelow."

"Luke Big Blow. Not much better than 'Brown Dog Shitting,' " said Gaylord. Luke looked across the truck cab with a threatening frown, but he could see from the expression on Gaylord's face that he was joking, so he laughed. "You're not in much of a position to talk, Gay-lord."

"How about them Cowboys?" asked Gaylord.

The rest of the drive was uneventful. Not much was said but somehow Luke felt easier than he had before the crisis at the roadblock. Before, no one was talking because they were uncomfortable; now they weren't talking because they were comfortable. As long as *he* didn't get too comfortable, Luke thought.

He should have been thinking about what he was going to do once they reached the peyote buyers on the reservation but instead he was mulling over a brief exchange he had had with Silver not long after they left La Crosse. Gaylord was leaning heavily against the door, sound asleep, when without preamble Silver said, "You know what you said about what kind of church uses dope? Well, you know you were wrong. It isn't dope."

"Yeah, yeah, yeah. You've made that point. Still, what kind of church uses 'sacred herbs?' "

"What are you?"

"What am I?"

"Yes, what religion?"

"Ten thousand years ago I was a Catholic."

"I grew up Catholic."

"But now you're a sacred herb worshipper?"

"No," she laughed her silver laugh. "We don't worship the herb. It is part of our prayer service. It helps us share the mysteries, it helps us understand that we'll never understand. I'm still a Catholic. Most of us respect more than one religion. The Holy Indian Church, the peyot' church, is Christian. It takes the best parts of the old religions and the new ones and puts them together, you know."

"No, I don't know."

"Now you do." He nodded. She continued, "You celebrated the Holy Mass when you were a Catholic 'ten thousand years ago,' and you saw the priest take the host and the wine? And he told you that it was the body and blood of Christ, and he wasn't just talking dreams, was he? He meant it. Body and blood. They call that cannibalism. Well, the sacred herb is the same for us. You know drugs. You know peyot' is no fun."

"No one in his right mind eats that crap," Luke sputtered, recalling a horrible night in Los Lunas, New Mexico, when he was sure he was going to die and would have welcomed death.

"My people take peyot' prayerfully. They call it 'the bitter herb.' They take it only during prayer meetings and only because Jesus gave it to us for that purpose. You'll see when we get to Turtle Creek. Indian church people try to avoid any drugs, including alcohol. That's not easy for an Indian."

There was a long, painful pause as Luke remembered the Indians he had seen puking in alleys and gutters, fighting and killing, ravaged by the poisons that had come to them along with "civilization." He remembered looking in the little refrigerator at the farmhouse where he had taken Silver and Gaylord prisoner. Not even a can of beer.

"Do members of the Holy Indian Church eat burgers and fries?" he had asked. And for the first time since that morning when she was tied through the wall of her grandmother's stairway, Silver had turned and looked at him. He pointed at a Golden Arches sign down the road and turned into the McDonald's.

It was dark when Gaylord directed Luke into the driveway of a little house—scarcely more than a cabin—in the reservation town of Turtle Creek. "My uncle Ralph Pete's place," explained Gaylord. "We can stay here until we talk with the church elders tomorrow. There's not much room in the house for luggage so just bring in whatever clothes you need. Everything else will be okay out here. No white folks around to steal stuff." Luke pushed his guns under the seat of the truck, except a small 9 mm that he stuffed into his toiletry kit. He took a shirt from the hanger behind the seat and a pair of socks from a canvas bag in the camper shell.

"Do you have dishes?" Silver asked.

"Dishes?"

"Yes, Indians always carry dishes. Where there's Indians, there's food. You wait and see. Gaylord's Aunt Lillian will have food."

"She's expecting you?"

"No, but she'll have food." And she did. Lillian answered the door at their knock and greeted Gaylord and Silver with generous hugs and laughter. She smiled a toothless smile at Luke and shook his hand, barely touching him in the process. Then there were greetings from Uncle Ralph Pete and some other people whose relationship to the hosts Luke couldn't figure out. And there were three or four children running around who seemed to belong to everyone and no one.

The house was jammed with people, and yet wasn't crowded— perhaps because no one touched. People moved around in the cramped quarters gently and slowly. The conversation was quiet and polite. Women put their hands in front of their mouths when they laughed. The joking was good-natured, almost naive. There was no cursing—not even a "damn" or a "hell." Luke couldn't help but think how . . . how *civilized* it all seemed.

This was nothing like the company Luke Bigelow was accustomed to, and yet he felt perfectly at home. In this most unlikely of contexts, with the family of his prisoners, he almost forgot his fears.

Lillian handed him a plate of fried chicken, sweet fruit salad, a fist-sized piece of dark brown, fragrant bread, and a cup of black, sweet coffee. He was the first guest served, though he was furthest away from the kitchen—closest to the door. (He was comfortable in the Pete home but he was still careful; he was careful even when he was in his own home.) He could see that he was first served because he was a guest. Did they understand, he wondered, that he was taking their kids to prison? Probably not. Gaylord and Silver laughed and talked and paid no attention at all to their captor. That was fine with him.

It was eleven or twelve o'clock before the conversation turned to bed. Luke couldn't tell how late it was, because so far as he could see there wasn't a clock in the entire house, but he was totally worn out.

"Mr. Bigelow, we are poor people and don't have much to offer by way of hospitality, but you would honor us by taking the room at the top of the stairs, over on the east side," Ralph Pete said to Luke.

The uneasy, unwelcome feeling of fear swept over Luke again. He didn't like those arrangements at all. He would be at a dead end on the second floor, as far from the door as they could put him. He looked at Gaylord and then Silver. "We'll see you in the morning," Silver said. Gaylord nodded in agreement, and Luke could tell they meant it.

"You can wash up in the kitchen," Ralph Pete said.

"Thank you, Mr. Pete," Luke said. He splashed water in his face, stepped out the back door to pee one last time, and looked up at the black sky, jeweled with more stars than he could imagine. A complicated day, he thought. Twenty hours ago he was one hell of a lot surer about where he was. He thought about Silver's summary of the peyote—uh, peyot'—people "understanding that we cannot understand." Well, here he was, on peyot' ground, and he sure as hell didn't understand. He walked around his truck and checked the doors. Dogs barked around the little town. He heard someone laugh at another house. He also thought he heard the sound of drums and singing somewhere not very far away. He remembered something. He put his hand in his pocket and felt the rough Indian head penny.

Some of the guests were leaving the Petes' house, walking across the big open square in the center of the town. Luke went in the front door—a small precaution, going out one door and coming in another—and found people making beds throughout the house, laughing and joking. Not very threatening. Gaylord was spreading blankets on the kitchen floor. Silver was laying out cushions and pads on the front room floor with three children who were mobbing her, dogging her every step, hugging her even though she was not all that much larger than them. Silver caught Luke watching her. "My cousins," she laughed, as the children once again swarmed over her.

He went up the stairs and went to the room to the east. He realized at once from the furnishings that he was in Ralph and Lillian's room. The hair on his neck bristled. They gave him a room to himself, *their* room, either out of altruistic generosity—oh, sure!—or because they wanted to isolate him, to know exactly where he was. He checked the door: it didn't have a lock. He looked out the window: it opened on a porch roof, an easy exit. Or access. Nah, he hadn't seen anyone all evening who could climb the stairs easily, yet the porch roof. Mostly old folks and kids.

He couldn't believe he had been dumb enough to get himself into this mess, and yet the evening had been so calm, so pleasant, so much like a home he hadn't seen in a long time. Still, he would avoid risks. He looked around the room. He noticed a heat register in the floor, the kind that is nothing but a hole to the downstairs;

he opened it slowly and carefully. He looked down into the front room and could see Silver tucking the children into bed. She laughed with every movement she made. She was obviously comfortable here, too. Perhaps she would be getting ready for bed herself soon, right below him. Perhaps he could watch her through the floor grate.

This momentary sexual attraction to Silver surprised him: this plain child had less of a figure than the boy she was traveling with, and he was usually drawn to the buxom type. "Not me," he said to himself, quietly closing the heat vent. "She may have had trouble with white men, but not from this white man. This is a business trip, Bigelow."

He decided that he could sleep on the floor on the window side of the bed so the bed would be between him and the door. Anyone opening the window would expect to find him in bed but pass directly over him instead. He pulled the covers from the bed and bunched them on the floor. He was about to throw a pillow on the floor, too, but when he saw that it was handsomely embroidered with pink roses, he made sure he put it on a blanket rather than on the bare boards. He removed the 9 mm pistol from his toilet kit, took the safety off, and laid it beside his makeshift bed.

He was about to turn off the bare bulb hanging from the center of the ceiling when there was a soft knock at the door. For a moment he wished he had brought back his shotgun from the truck. He stood up and measured the distance to the window. He tucked the pistol into the back of his pants. "Come in." A pause, and then again a knock. "Come in," he repeated.

He watched the door knob turn. Aunt Lillian stuck in just enough of her head that her eyes showed. "Excuse me, Mr. Bigelow. I . . ." She stopped when she saw the dismantled bed. "I just wanted to see if you need anything."

Oh shit. Here this sweet old lady had offered him her bed and he took it apart and threw it on the floor. "Mrs. Pete, I apologize for making a mess of your bed but I'm just not used to sleeping on a bed and I hoped you wouldn't mind me sleeping here on the floor."

Dumb excuse but she bought it. Lillian Pete put her hand in front of her mouth and laughed softly. "You sleep wherever you want, Mr. Bigelow." She closed the door. He imagined her going down the stairs, shaking her head and wondering at the strange ways of white men. Well, she was pretty much right, Luke guessed. He considered moving his bed, now that she had seen where he would be sleeping, but said to himself, "To hell with it," and for the first time in a long time Luke Bigelow slept until the sun came in the window and the smell of coffee, eggs, and bacon—and the laughter of children—woke him.

As he dressed, he looked out the window over the small reservation town of Turtle Creek. Children were walking across the open square toward the school. Luke watched as Silver led three of the children he had seen in the front room the night before as far as the dirt street in front of Ralph Pete's house. She waved to them and they took off toward school on the dead run. Silver turned and walked back to the house. She looked up at his window, but Luke couldn't tell if she saw him standing there, watching her. He hoped not. He didn't want her to have the wrong idea about him, him being a white man and all.

Downstairs he found that Aunt Lillian—she told him to call her that—had set a place for him at the table, where she was clearing dishes from the previous shifts of breakfast eaters. "From our own chickens," Aunt Lillian said, pointing to the orange-yolked eggs on his plate. "And I made the fry bread"—the dark lumps of bread he had wolfed down the night before.

"Fry bread, huh?" Luke laughed. "Sure is good stuff."

"Eat too much of it and you'll turn into an Indian," Gaylord laughed as he came in the back door and through the kitchen. "There's an old story among my people about a Nehawka boy named Black Deer, who went off on a raid to a Pawnee village and came back a Pawnee even though that was the last thing he had on his mind. Maybe that's going to happen to you, Luke Bigelow. You come here on a raid and you're going to eat so much fry bread, you're going to go back to Texas a Nehawka. You just might be turning into an Indian."

"Well, I could do worse. Once I turned into a dark alley," Luke laughed back. Aunt Lillian put her hand over her mouth and giggled.

"We're supposed to meet at Buddy Foster's house in a half hour. Take your time eating. It's just across the town over there." Gaylord pointed out the window and across the dusty square toward another small house in a grove of cottonwood trees.

"Why are we going over there?" Luke asked, suspicions rising.

"I figured you'd want to be around when we ask them to take the boxes and the money changes hands. We're going over to Buddy's house because he keeps a fireplace and we go to him out of respect. We can't ask him to come to us."

And then before Luke could ask, Gaylord added, "He keeps a fireplace. That means he's like . . . like . . ."

"Having a fireplace is like being ordained in a white man's church," Silver interrupted from the front room. "Mr. Foster is like a minister, except more like a holy man. He conducts prayer meetings and does blessings. Buddy is the great-great-great-whatever grandson of my ancestor Seeks Wood Mapateet, the last Keeper of the Sacred Sky Bundle. So it's like I told you: he combines the good parts of the old ways and the new ways, the peyot' church and the Buffalo Dance, the white man's world and the Sky

Bundle. He is working right now to get the Sky Bundle back for us, from some museum that's had it forever. Buddy has remembered the old ways and kept them for us—the Sky Bundle and its songs. I can't have anything to do with that because I'm a woman and the Sky Bundle is man stuff, but Buddy is also working at keeping the Buffalo Dance going and women can dance the Buffalo Dance. Maybe sometime you'll get a chance to see a Buffalo Dance. You'd make a good Buffalo Dancer, Luke."

Luke was startled. It was the first time she had called him Luke. It was the first time he had seen her talk as if she couldn't stop.

She continued to talk, almost bubbling: "Mr. Foster is entitled to our respect because he has earned it. We go to him. He doesn't come to us." She stepped in from the kitchen and poured more coffee in Luke's cup.

"Thank you, Silver. For both the coffee and the information. That was some speech."

After he had eaten and thanked Ralph Pete and Aunt Lillian, Luke went out to his truck and tossed his dirty shirt and socks into the camper shell. He leaned against the hood, looking across the open plaza of the village toward Mr. Foster's house. Everything was quiet. Two or three "Indian cars" parked in the yard, but nothing threatening; if you're going to cause trouble, you make a point of having good wheels under you, and it didn't appear to Luke that there was a car in the whole village that would have made it to the state capital, yet the state line.

"Aw, everything's probably all right anyway," he said to himself. And then, "You must be going soft, Bigelow." Nonetheless, the cold barrel of the 9 mm pistol down the crack of his ass felt good.

Silver and Gaylord joined him at the truck and they drove the short distance around the square to Buddy Foster's house. "Drive right up to the front door, Luke," Gaylord directed. "No sense in carrying the boxes any further than we have to."

"Maybe we should see the color of Mr. Foster's money before we start making deliveries," Luke said without looking at Gaylord or Silver.

"I can tell you right now, he's not going to have much money. He was expecting just enough for his fireplace for this winter, and he probably doesn't have much more than fifty or sixty dollars even for that. Unless you want to drive around the northern Plains with us a good part of the winter delivering the boxes and collecting expenses, we're just going to have to leave what we have here and ask Mr. Foster to send us whatever the other tribes give him as time goes along."

Luke hadn't thought much about this whole mess but he didn't have much of an alternative but to accept it. "It's good you're a roadrunner delivering sacred herbs because you sure as hell don't amount to much of a dope dealer," Luke said, shaking his head. "Fifty or sixty dollars. Is that what you expect to make on this transaction?" Luke was surprised at the embarrassment he suddenly felt that he was thinking of profit in what was clearly a religious transaction; it was a feeling he had rarely experienced, embarrassment at being white. Echoes of his Catholic upbringing, he guessed.

Neither Silver nor Gaylord offered an answer to his questions. They knocked at the screen door and respectfully shook the hand of the tall, distinguished man—Luke was surprised that this revered holy man was actually not more than fifty years old—who answered the knock. They introduced Luke as a friend to Mr. Foster, who waved them into the house and to the kitchen table. An attractive woman, also in her forties, poured each of them a cup of coffee. "Not me, thanks," said Luke. "I'm coffeed out."

Everyone stared at Luke as if he had announced that he had just soiled his pants. "What kind of Indian are you, turning down a cup of coffee?" Mr. Foster laughed, pushing the full cup right back in front of Luke. "We Nehawkas don't take no for an answer, certainly not in the Turtle Creek, do we, Silver? And you'll need the coffee to wash down lunch, and pie, when Naomi gets it to the table."

Luke thanked Mr. Foster and accepted the coffee. Lunch? Luke wondered. How long was this transaction going to take? A young, hard-muscled man with long braided hair stepped into the kitchen from another room. Uh-oh, Luke thought. This could be trouble. "My son Clark," Buddy Foster said. Luke shook the young man's hand. Luke felt the odds shifting toward the Indians' advantage.

The situation took another unpleasant turn: Gaylord, Silver, and Buddy Foster began to talk about the boxes of peyote they had just delivered, or at least that's what Luke assumed they were discussing, but the conversation was in Indian. "God, I must be crazy," Luke thought when he choked back the urge to demand that they speak English so he knew what the hell was going on. Instead he drank his coffee and fidgeted. He looked across the table at Silver. She did not return his glance but she smiled, as if to let him know that she knew he was looking at her—and that she realized and was enjoying his discomfort.

Luke turned in his chair so he could look out the front door, his back to Silver. She made a noise, as if suppressing a laugh, but he refused to give her the satisfaction of turning back to see. He spoke and understood some Spanish and had been in many situations like this where he faked ignorance so he could eavesdrop on business conversations between dealers. Once that skill had saved his life and many times his fortunes. This time he would have to try another feint and pretend that either he understood what they were saying or didn't care.

Even in format the conversation was not the sort Luke had come to expect in drug sales. Most dealers want to make a deal as fast as they can in order to shorten exposure. Luke's own motto, widely known at one time in the circles of southern smugglers, was "Count, weigh, and drive."

In deals, everyone knows what the merchandise is worth and so not much discussion should be necessary. But Gaylord talked maybe fifteen minutes, and then Mr. Foster thought his words over for ten or fifteen minutes. Then Mr. Foster talked fifteen minutes, and Gaylord listened and thought. Then Silver spoke, and everyone listened and thought, and on and on it went. Now and then they would all three look at Luke. After a while Naomi—at least that's who Luke assumed the woman was—brought cherry pie and more coffee to the table.

"Luke, go get that cooler out of the pickup," Gaylord said, his first words in English in nearly an hour. Christ, first I have to sit and listen to gibberish for most of the morning and now I'm taking orders from my prisoner, Luke thought. What next? But he did as he was told, and Silver and Naomi took meat, fruit, bread, potato salad, and a gallon can of fruit cocktail from the cooler and brought it to the table.

"What are the chances of us getting out of here before sundown?" Luke whispered to Silver when everyone was resting after the lunch.

"Such things take time," she said.

After the noon lunch, everyone left the house to lounge and nap in the shade of the cottonwood trees. "Beautiful fall afternoon, isn't it?" Gaylord asked Luke.

"Yeah, it is. It really is, but you know, Gaylord, I would like to get out of here before nightfall. I don't want to impose on these people again tonight."

"Well, it's just a matter of sorting out how we're going to do this. Mr. Foster hasn't had much in the way of donations for the church this summer. Things have not gone all that well on the reservation. And he feels uneasy about taking all the sacred herb we have without paying us for it right away. I'm trying to tell him that he will be doing us a favor and we will be grateful if he will help us out."

"You're not arguing about price?"

"No," Gaylord laughed. "Except that he wants to pay more and we want to take less."

"You Indians are crazy, know that? No wonder you lost."

"Who says the war is over?"

Luke felt uneasy again. He regretted eating so much. "Are you saying something about us, you and me? Are we still at war, boy?"

"It's Gaylord, and no, you can relax. But you'll have to admit that it's getting harder and harder to tell who's the rabbit in this operation."

Gaylord was more right than Luke wanted to admit. Moreover, there was nothing Luke could do to change matters. Screw it, he thought, and closed his eyes. He woke up an hour later when Gaylord kicked the bottoms of his boots. "Time to go. Mr. Foster accepted my terms. He'll see that the other tribes get their herb and he'll collect whatever he can for us. He needs to know where to send the money."

Though he was still groggy from his nap, Luke knew better than to give a prisoner his address. And he knew better than to have such a piddly amount sent to Otis Bentsen; Bentsen was going to be mad anyway that there wasn't going to be any easy, unaccountable drug money to split up, but he would be fit to commit murder if he learned that Luke had jeopardized this capture for a couple of fifty-dollar transactions.

"Tell him to keep the money until I get back this way. I know where to find him," said Luke, rising from the ground and dusting off his shirt and pants.

"You're going to trust an Indian drug buyer to hold the money for you? It's good you're a bounty hunter because you sure don't amount to much of a dope dealer," Silver laughed. Luke didn't have much of a choice except to agree.

Everyone said their farewells, including Luke, and Silver told Luke to put the cooler back into the truck. "Yes, dear," Luke said with false politeness. He was surprised to find that the cooler weighed more now than it did when he had brought it into the house a few hours before. "Naomi packed us some lunch," Silver explained when she saw Luke struggle with the cooler.

"And some breakfast, another lunch, and maybe a supper from the feel of it," groaned Luke. He should have checked it for weapons. He would have two days ago. Today he didn't.

By three o'clock that afternoon Gaylord, Silver, and Luke were back on the road, this time headed south, Gaylord driving. Luke was relieved to be rid of the contraband, happy to be off the reservation and back to where the standard language was English, and delighted to be headed back toward Texas justice with two fugitives who showed no potential for making trouble. He looked across the cab at Silver, then past Silver to Gaylord. Well, maybe he wasn't all that delighted.

The drive south was uneventful. Gaylord drove well into the night, and then Luke drove until dawn. Finally Silver made a fuss about being left out of the driving schedule just because she was a woman, and so Luke turned everything over to her, and just as she said, she did fine.

They stopped now and then to dig some food out of the cooler, or to make a pit stop—Luke said it with a hiss so you couldn't be sure he said "pit stop" or "piss stop." Silver shook her head and made pretensions of being embarrassed every time, but Luke could tell she was just giving him a bad time for being so crude. Once she even said, "Luke Bigelow, you are crude and disgusting, know that?"

"Yeah," he laughed, "and that's why you women are crazy about me."

"Not this woman," she smiled.

"Woman?! You're not much more than half a girl, if you ask me."

"You'll never know."

"I'm talking about your figure."

He could tell at once that he had touched a sensitive point. "Maybe we can go skinny-dipping sometime and you can show me I'm wrong."

"Dream," she snorted.

There was disappointment when they reached La Crosse. The repairman at the service station was still working when the travelers arrived. He wiped off his hands and shook his head slowly. "Looks to me like when you got rear-ended you broke something loose in the transmission, and cracked some seals," he told Luke. "I'd like to help you folks out, but no kidding, the repairs would cost more than the van is worth."

"Well, that's okay. These folks aren't going to need a vehicle for a while anyway," Luke said, pointing to Gaylord and Silver in his truck. "Why don't you just keep the heap for your trouble? Maybe you can get some parts off it."

"I can't do that. The vehicle's worth something, at least. How about if I give you fifty bucks for it?"

"You bargain like an Indian," Luke said.

The mechanic laughed. "My grandmother always said she was part Cherokee, but then everyone is part Cherokee if you believe grandparents!"

"I wouldn't take the money from you, buddy, but the van belongs to those kids over there in the truck, and they are going to need every dime they can get. How about twenty-five?" Luke took the money the mechanic pulled from his cash register and Luke put it into his billfold. When he got to the truck he explained the situation, took out his billfold, and handed a fistful of bills to Silver. "He says the best he can do is give you two hundred for it."

"That's about what we paid for it when it was running," Silver laughed, poking Gaylord with her elbow.

As they drove through the night, Silver and Gaylord slept. Luke was pleased that Silver leaned against him as she slept. She could have leaned on Gaylord.

No, Luke protested to himself when he found himself enjoying her warm breath on his right arm. No, it's not anything like sex. Not this time. It just feels good to know she trusts me enough to lean on me when only a couple days ago I was blasting away with a shotgun in her general direction. He worked so hard at not disturbing her as he drove that he wound up with a stiff arm and shoulder he'd be nursing long after he was rid of them.

Hmm. Rid of them. A thought that hadn't crossed his mind in a while. For the first time in six years of bounty hunting Luke Bigelow wasn't going to feel comfortable turning a fugitive over to Otis Bentsen. But he would turn them over. He wasn't about to blow the generous bounty Otis had promised. Luke reviewed all the usual rationalizations: someone would get these kids sooner or later anyway, and sooner or later they'd have to pay the penalties they owed Bentsen and the law. That someone might as well be Luke Bigelow. Maybe he could give them a little of the bounty money so they could get themselves a decent lawyer. Yeah, he would give them some money and maybe they could get a better attorney than a public defender. If they did serve time, maybe they would be smarter when they got out.

Silver moved against his arm. *If* they got out. Silver didn't strike Luke as a likely candidate for bully of the cell block. They'd eat her up—the dykes, and guards, and tough cases.

And Bentsen, *that* son-of-a-bitch . . ."

It was a little after noon when Luke drove his truck up onto the front lawn in front of a house, right across neatly mowed grass and up to the sign reading, "Otis Bentsen, Bail Bondsman, Let Otis Be Your Friend in Need." The bastard had no shame, Luke thought. He spun the truck's wheels twice to snug the truck's stout bumper against the signpost, shaking it, bending it, throwing grass and red dirt up onto the sidewalk behind him.

Silver and Gaylord looked across the cab at Luke. "It's just something I do," he explained. "You'll understand it better after we've had our little negotiations with *Mister* Bentsen." He said "mister" as if it were a dirty word. "I hate to do this, guys, but I am going to have to put straps on you. Believe me, it's better that I do it than Otis, okay?" Luke said apologetically as they got out of the truck.

Silver and Gaylord held out their arms. "Will you take care of our clothes and the cooler?" Silver asked.

"Yeah, do you want me to return them to the farmhouse? I'm going back there and settle up for the damage with your grandmother in a couple days anyway."

"Thanks," said Gaylord. "Tell her what's going on with us, too, okay?"

"Sure. This way. Be careful on those stairs. If you fall with those restraints on you can get hurt." Man, what a change from the way he usually treated the slime he had slammed up and down those stairs over the past three years. The pillar on the right was nearly worn out from the times Luke had thrown prisoners against it on the way into Bentsen's office, just to calm them down a little.

Bentsen met them at the door. "I told you fifty times, you ass-hole. Don't drive up on the lawn like that."

"When I bring you merchandise I want to make sure it arrives here safely, Oats. I have no intention of parking halfway across town and strolling here with dangerous felons. Get used to it."

"I'm telling you for the last time, cut it out or you'll get no more easy money from me. But look what we have here." He put his hands under Gaylord's and Silver's chins, turned their faces up so he could look into them, and smiled a smile that would spoil milk. Gaylord jerked his head away; Bentsen ran his hand down Silver's neck and down the middle of her chest, between her breasts, or where her breasts would have been if she had had breasts.

"You can stop that shit right now," snarled Luke. "Just get in there and start rooting around in your desk for cash. They're not yours until I have my bounty and expenses, and this wasn't cheap. I had to chase them all the way up to Nebraska."

"Bullshit. Carl Schantz told me that he saw them in North Austin not a month ago. I pay you enough that you don't need to screw me by padding the expenses. Take it out of the cash you stole from them."

Luke dug into his shirt pocket and took out a wad of crumpled papers. "They didn't have a dime. Take a look at those gas re-ceipts—Nebraska, Kansas, Oklahoma, and all within the past seventy-two hours. I'm not going to stand out here and argue with you, Oats. Get in there where you bury the money." Luke opened the door and Gaylord and Silver filed in. Bentsen quickly stepped in line immediately behind Silver. Bigelow grabbed his right shoul-der before he had completed his first step and whirled him around. He jammed a stiff forefinger hard against Bentsen's nose. "Leave the girl alone, you dirtbag." Bentsen wanted to smile away the confrontation but he could see that Bigelow was in no mood for joking.

In his office Bentsen sat down behind a large desk, mounded with papers and files. Luke pointed Silver and Gaylord to two chairs on the side of the room away from the door. Luke sat directly in front of the desk, across from Bentsen. "Money," Luke said.

Bentsen unlocked a drawer at his left hand and pulled out a large, black tin box, which he also unlocked. He counted and handed Luke a wad of bills. "There's your percentage. How much on expenses?" Without hesitation Luke answered, "Seventeen hundred twelve dollars and sixty-seven cents."

"You got receipts, you crooked bastard?"

"You want your prisoners?"

Bentsen counted out more bills. "We'll round it off at seventeen twelve."

"We'll round it off at seventeen thirteen," Luke said.

Bentsen pulled another dollar bill from the wad and added it to the pile in front of him. He shoved it across the mountain of papers on the desk toward Luke. "Wanna count it?"

"Oh, I'll count it, Oats. And you can bet your fat ass that if there isn't seventeen hundred and thirteen dollars in that pile, you are going to get a visit from me that you're not going to like. Smithie Preen, the bail bonder over in San An-tone, shorted me once. Remember Smithie?"

Without taking his eyes off of Bigelow's face, Bentsen pulled another hundred-dollar bill from the tin box and tossed it across the desk toward Luke. Luke picked up the pile and stuffed it into a battered Rock County High School gym bag. It had been a long time since gym shorts and sneakers or a bullrope and spurs have been in this old bag, Luke thought to himself.

"Okay, you two," Luke said to Gaylord and Silver. "Let's go. I'll take you over to the courthouse and we'll check you in."

"They're my property now," frowned Bentsen. "I'll get 'em over there after I've scolded them for being a bad little boy and girl." He smiled his chilling smile again toward Gaylord and Silver.

"I'm taking them over," said Luke, leaning back again into the chair. "I don't want to leave you alone with these thugs, Oats."

"You've been paid. Get out of here," sneered Bentsen. "On second thought, if you want to be helpful, why don't you take the boy over. I think I'll be safe enough with Silver. Maybe we can be friends."

"No dice. I'm taking them, and I'm taking them now."

"You'll never work for me again, Bigelow, you smart-ass. It won't be two months before I'll have one of my boys out looking for you. Now, get out of here. The girl's staying."

Bentsen leaned forward and to the right. Luke leaped to his feet, grabbed the front edge of the desk, and threw it upward. The heavy desk rolled from the floor directly onto Bentsen's lap. His chair went over backward, the desk still atop him, and he hit the floor on his back, the back lip of the desk smashing into his chest.

Luke took one step forward, directly onto Bentsen's unprotected crotch, and grabbed into the desk's kneehole for the gun Bentsen was trying to reach—a small, cheap .22 caliber revolver. Luke leaned over the desk front, now its top. With the gun he swept aside the tangle of papers and peered down into Bentsen's face, which was all he could see because the rest of him was under the desk. "Jesus Christ, get off! You're killing me," Bentsen mumbled in agony.

"Listen, you scum-bag, don't ever pull a gun on me again, or you are automatically dead. Say you understand that." Bentsen groaned. Bigelow pitched his weight on and off the desk, rocking it onto Bentsen's face. Bones broke. "My God, I understand, I understand," Bentsen screamed through the papers, wood, and blood.

Bigelow pocketed the little pistol. "Don't bother to tell me I won't work for you again. The reason you hire me is because I know how to deal with the worst scum on earth—of which you are a prime example. And if you send any of your other boys around, they'll scamper away from me to some peaceful place like Da Nang. I'm going to check your prisoners in for you now. You can sleep soundly tonight knowing your bail money is safely in your pocket, you slimy jerk."

Bigelow grabbed the straps joining Gaylord and Silver, who by now were standing in the corner of the room, trying to stay out of the way of whatever was going to happen next between Luke and Bentsen. "Let's get out of here." He pulled them past Bentsen's secretary, who was standing behind her desk, her face a mask of terror. "Hi, cutie," said Luke, with a grin. "Better call the veterinarian for your boss."

Luke pushed Gaylord and Silver into the truck and drove off Bentsen's lawn, throwing sod onto the porch, directly over the sign that said, "Let Otis Be Your Friend in Need."

At the courthouse Luke pulled his prisoners across the reception area and toward the escalator without a word. At the top of the escalator he turned left down another small hallway and opened a large, heavy door with translucent white glass and a number, but no sign or name.

"Looks like you've done this before," Gaylord said. Luke did not answer. He stepped up to a receptionist's desk and said, "I want to talk with Jim Coons. Now."

The secretary looked at Bigelow coldly, and then at Silver and

Gaylord with contempt. "Mr. Coons is in conference, Mr. Bigelow. Did you have an appointment?"

Bigelow walked around the end of the desk, pulling Silver and Gaylord behind him. "Hey," the secretary shouted sternly. "You can't just walk in there!"

"You're hurting me," cried Silver.

"Sorry, honey," said Bigelow, looking back at her and shaking his head. They burst through the closed door behind the secretary.

The room was the exact opposite of Otis Bentsen's—large and stark. A clean desk sat directly in the middle of the room, a large, dirty window immediately behind it. One wall was filled with shelves of dark red books. A wooden bench was the only furniture along the other wall. A man sitting in a wood chair in front of the desk stared at Luke and his prisoners with amazement. The man behind the desk was obviously annoyed, but collected. "What do you want, Bigelow? Why can't you come in here like normal people for a change? It's okay, Shirley," he said to the furious receptionist standing at the door of his office. "I'll take care of Mr. Bigelow and his friends. We don't want them cluttering up the office any longer than necessary. Morton, would you mind coming back in a quarter of an hour or so?"

The little bald man who was staring at Luke and whose mouth was still agape nodded, stood slowly, and left the office. Luke took his seat.

"You working as a bail bondsman now, too?" the man behind the desk asked.

"No, I just didn't want to leave them with Bentsen."

The man looked at Gaylord and Silver, who looked all the more helpless in front of the wall of leather-bound books. "Yeah, I can understand why. When I get prisoners from you and Bentsen, they wind up spending more time in the hospital than in jail. Good to have you back, Silver, Gaylord. You disappointed me when you missed your court date. I really hoped we could make life a little easier for you, but you haven't made life easy for me."

"I have a proposition for you," Luke interrupted.

Coons looked down at the papers on his desk, paused, and said, "So, now you're a bail bondsman *and* a lawyer, huh? Your versatility never ceases to surprise me, Bigelow. Now you've been everything in our legal system except a judge."

"Wrong again, Coons. I'm ready to be judge, too. I want to make you a trade. You know as well as I do that these two are small potatoes. They're not dealing hard stuff. In fact, a good lawyer could probably get them off with the argument that there is still some right to freedom of religion in this country."

"Ooh, now he's a Constitutional lawyer. Bigelow, they don't have a good lawyer. Dope is dope. Laws are laws. Dead meat is dead meat. Why don't you spend some of that bounty money on a lawyer for them?"

"That's exactly what I intend to do if you insist on being stupid," Luke said to Coons. Coons looked into Luke's eyes. "I don't want to play games, Coons. I just busted up Bentsen pretty good and I am out of patience."

"Are you threatening me, Bigelow?"

"No, Coons, I am not. I'd threaten you if I wanted to. But this time I am just being honest, and I'm asking you a favor. And I'm going to do a favor for you. If you insist on prosecuting this case, I'm going to call in the Native American Rights Fund. They'd love a case like this. They'd tear you a new asshole, you know." Bigelow turned in his chair. "Excuse the language, Silver." He turned back to Coons. "NARF will explode this silly case into racial discrimination against Indians, rich against the poor, religious oppression. Even if you win, Coons, you know you're going to lose. Especially if you win."

Coons looked at Luke without moving, saying nothing, not even blinking.

"On the other hand, if you, one, dismiss this case, and, two, make sure Bentsen gets his bail money back so he'll leave these kids alone, one, I'll owe you—"

"Big deal," said Coons.

"And, two, I'll give you the full story on the Sanchez murder in San Antone." He paused. Coons said nothing but he looked interested.

"You and I both know you want to nail down that case, and I'll name names."

Coons blinked but still said nothing.

"I'll give you a witness to the murder."

Coons sucked air. "A witness I can count on? In drug-murder cases folks have a way of changing their minds at trial time, you know."

"This witness will show up. It's me."

"You must want to spring these kids pretty bad."

"Is it a deal?"

"I want one more little thing in this bargain, Bigelow. You're doing all the talking here. I want to hear something from defendants Mapateet and Horse Capture." Coons looked across the expanse of his desk at Silver and Gaylord. "You two are guilty as hell. You and I both know that. There's not a doubt in my mind that I could put you both away for a long time. Bigelow's right: I want to take care of this Sanchez matter and, frankly, no one around here gives a damn about you. I'm going to turn you loose, dismiss the charges, but I want a promise from you that there'll be no more of you two hauling hallucinogenic cactus for distribution, religion or not."

"They promise," Luke said.

"Wait a minute . . ." Silver said.

"They promise, Coons." He turned to Gaylord and Silver. He winked. "It'll be all right. Just promise the man that there'll be no more of you two hauling those whacky cactee. Do it. Believe me, it'll be for the best. Just think about that automobile accident you had in Kansas. As it turned out, that accident wasn't as bad as it seemed, was it?"

Silver and Gaylord looked at each other. "Okay, we promise."

"They promise," Luke said victoriously.

"No more hauling drugs for you two, ever?" Coons insisted.

"Right," Luke said.

Coons looked at Luke and then Silver and Gaylord. "Right," Silver and Gaylord affirmed.

Outside the federal courthouse, Silver and Gaylord rubbed their wrists, red and bruised by the nylon straps.

"Well, thanks, Luke. That was pretty darn decent of you," Gaylord said.

"What are you going to do now? The two hundred dollars you got for the car isn't going to take you far."

Silver laughed. "We have a lot of Indian friends here in Austin, Luke. They'll take care of us. We'll get everything put back together before too long."

"Tell you what," Luke said. "Since I'm going up to your grandmother's anyway, I could just take you along. And I'll split the bond money with you since you stuck to your side of the bargain."

"You're a real credit to your race," Gaylord laughed. "But I'm still not comfortable with that promise you made us give Mr. Coons."

"We may eventually have to come back and take our medicine, Luke," Silver said. "I just can't promise not to work with the church and carry the sacred herb north any more. I don't want to break my word, but I can't promise honestly that I won't do it again. I've made some other promises."

"I know, Silver, but white man speak with forked tongue. Gaylord told me some of what you owe to the Holy Indian Church. But now listen to this: what exactly did you promise Coons?"

"Not to run peyot' any more."

"That's not what you promised. Coons is a lawyer. He dots every i and crosses every t. One word's wrong and the law is no good, the case is dismissed, the contract's null and void. Like that wreck we engineered in Kansas, your promise is not exactly what it seems. What did Coons make you promise, *exactly*."

Silver thought a moment. " 'I want a promise from you that there'll be no more of you two hauling hallucinogenic cactus for distribution, religion or not.' "

"There you are," crowed Luke triumphantly. "You two aren't going to haul hallucinogenic cactus for distribution, religion or not. There's no way in hell you hopeless babes are going to go out on the road again next fall without ol' Luke there to save your butts—sorry, Silver—every time you do something stupid. See? There will be *three* of us next time. Coons didn't say a word about three of us hauling hallucinogenic cactus for distribution, religion or not."

"You'd do that for our people?" asked Silver. "Why do you care if Buddy Foster has sacred herb for his services?"

"No, I wouldn't do that for your people, or Buddy Foster, Tinkerbell. I'm doing it for me. That sneaky kid of his, Clark, is probably skimming on cactus sales right now, and I don't intend to let him steal us blind. And I sure would admire another breakfast like Aunt Lillian cooks up. Especially that fry bread. Good stuff."

"Yeah, you look worried about your money. You're just not used to dealing with honest people. Next fall when we get to Turtle

Creek, we're going to get you an Indian name," Silver laughed. "How does 'Fry Bread Big Blow' strike you?"

"Terrific, Skinny Squaw with Smart Mouth. Get in the truck. Does your Kiowa grandmother make fry bread? They tell me that if you eat enough, you turn into an Indian." Luke jammed his hand into his pocket and felt an expected shape, texture, and weight. He pulled it out. It was the Indian-head penny again.

Buddy Foster was busy that year trying to re-organize and revive what remained of the Buffalo Dance Society and seeking infor-mation about the Nehawka's long-lost Sa-cred Sky Bundle. He asked four of his sons, under the leadership of his eldest son, Clark, to take on the task of delivering the supply of the sacred herb brought by Silver and Gaylord and their friend to other Plains tribes that winter, a task they carried out with devotion and caution. The young men made new friends in their visits across the northern Plains. When Buddy Foster held a Thanksgiving feast to celebrate the safe return of the four, he laughed to Silver, Gaylord, and Luke Bigelow, "If we kept winter counts the way the old-timers did, this would probably be 'The Winter of the Nighthawks.' "

None of the young people understood the curious allusion, but the old people who did understand laughed at the incongruous thought of the erratic, scattered flight of summer birds like the nighthawks in a winter sky, like the young Nehawka men rico-cheting from reservation to reservation, urban Indian community to solitary fireplace, delivering the sacred sacramental herb of their faith.

The Story of Grandma Pipe

Pirch Beck was outside feeding his dogs when Thomas Jefferson White Shell drove into the yard, which surprised Pirch, because Tom didn't usually drive into the yard. As a rule, Pirch saw him and his boy Calvin heading down under the bridge about this time of the morning to do a little fishing. Pirch banged the pot of scraps into the dogs' bowls as Tom got out of his car and straightened to greet him. "Ho, Injun," said Pirch.

"Ho, white man." It was their greeting ritual. It never varied. Hadn't for years.

Tom was wearing new blue work dungarees and a slightly faded, plaid western shirt. He was definitely not dressed for fishing. "What's up, Tom?"

"My grandma Pipe died up at the Turtle Creek Reservation."

"Oh, I'm sorry to hear that. I only met her once, at a powwow you took me to, but I could tell she was quite a woman. Was she your father's mother or your mother's mother?"

"Neither one. I don't think we were even related in the white man's way. She was everyone's grandma in the tribe. A lot of white folks's too."

"I could tell that, all right. So, what can I help you with, Tom? Anything I can do to ease your loss?" That was fancy talk for Pirch, but he figured a death in the family is time for fancy talk.

"I'm heading up to the reservation for the funeral and I could use some company. Wanna come along?"

"Well . . . yeah. Let me tell Calla and grab some clothes. Is there anything else I should bring?"

"Bring your dishes, and maybe you'd better grab a bedroll. Accommodations are likely to be a little crowded."

Whenever Pirch had gone to the reservation with Tom before,

about all he needed was dishes. He guessed from Tom's suggestion that he would need a bedroll that they might be staying a while. Pirch told his wife Calla, "Don't expect me back for a couple days. I'll be okay with Tom and his friends. That Nash of his isn't much up to snuff so the trip there and back might eat up a little time, too. Why don't you throw together a couple of egg salad sandwiches for us." He grabbed the sandwiches, kissed Calla, waved good-bye, tossed his few things into the car, and they left the farmyard with a backfire and the squawk of chickens.

A turn down the farm lane and onto the gravel road and the two travelers were underway for the three-hour drive to the reservation. The Nash cooperated more than Pirch had expected and they only had to stop to blow out the gas line to correct a vapor lock once, so they drove up to the little farmhouse of Tom's Aunt Chastity and Uncle Jack about noontime.

They were greeted by a mixture of kids and dogs at the farm. Some relatives—a few of whom Pirch recognized from earlier visits to the Turtle Creek Reservation—waved from the porch. Women were cooking in copper wash boilers over open fires in the yard. "Looks like it's about lunchtime, Pirch. Better grab your dishes," Tom said.

Food was a good way to start the day, a good way for Pirch to slip easily into Indian life. The meal was the usual corn soup with a hunk of beef of unidentifiable cut, fry bread with chokecherry jelly, presweetened black coffee, and fresh apple pie. Pirch got into the end of the meal line but everyone ahead of him gently pushed him up toward the front; even though everyone at the farm was a guest, the white man was a special guest. After all, he traveled with Tom, and he let Tom and his boy Cal fish under his bridge. And unlike a lot of white folks, he wasn't afraid to get out his dishes and eat Indian food.

An hour or so later—part of being on the reservation, to Pirch's mind, was forgetting about time—when everyone had finished eating, Tom asked one of the relatives, jerking his thumb over his shoulder toward the house, "Grandma in there?"

"Yeah, back room."

"Want to come see Grandma?" Tom asked.

"I guess so," Pirch said. He wasn't anxious to look at another dead person. He never quite understood it, but his experience in the Battle of the Bulge had not hardened him toward death, just made him all the more sensitive. Even so, he had come to support Tom, and part of that support, he supposed, was being with him when he visited with his dead grandmother.

Pirch still found it peculiar that Indians spoke of the dead as if they were still alive—"Grandma in there?"—but Tom had once expressed his own confusion about the way white people say, "The body of Bernice Collins was pulled from the river . . ." as if only the body were there, but something else wasn't. Why not say "Bernice Collins was pulled from the river?" Tom had asked Pirch, but Pirch didn't have an answer for that one.

White Shell and Pirch went through the front room of the small house, crowded with women, some crying, some talking, a few even laughing. They greeted friends and relatives to all sides, moved through the crowd, and stepped into the dark back room, lit only by a couple of candles on a dresser and reflecting from the mirror. Heavy woolen dance shawls darkened the room's one small window.

On a kitchen table in the middle of the room was the body of Grandma Pipe, not much bigger than a child's. Her black hair, speckled with gray, had been oiled and braided. She was dressed in the full, dark, old-fashioned dress favored by older Indian women. She was wearing her finest beadwork and silver. Her hands had been folded over her breast so that her star tattoos, evidence that she had once been a virgin chosen to cut sage for the rituals surrounding the Sacred Sky Bundle, were clearly visible. That must have been a long time ago, Pirch thought. The Sky Bundle had been gone from the reservation and the Nehawka people for generations. Only people like Grandma Pipe even remembered there had been a Sky Bundle.

Tom nodded by way of greeting to the sobbing women seated at the wall around the room, and stepped up to the table. "Ho, Grandma Pipe. It's your grandson Thomas Jefferson White Shell . . ."

As if in response, the women began to keen, a high-pitched wailing scream that sent shivers up and down the spine. "Your great-grandson Calvin couldn't come along because he's in school today. I know you understand that," Tom continued, and then, his large, muscled body poised over her empty, fragile shell, Tom told Grandma Pipe what had been going on in his life, as if he hadn't noticed that she was dead. Like a Greek chorus, the keening women punctuated his recitation.

When Tom and Pirch stepped back into the daylight, Tom began to cry. It was not simply a matter of tears running down his face, but of great, body-wracking sobs, as if a contained prairie storm had suddenly broken loose. Pirch didn't know what to do. He didn't know if it was more appropriate to console his Indian friend or to leave him alone with his sorrow. Pirch stood clumsily at his side, as men do on such occasions, not knowing where to look or what to say. Long ago, at hand games and powwows Tom White Shell had taken him to, Pirch Beck had learned that the movie-show image of the stolid, unemotional Indian was strictly Hollywood stuff. If anything, what he had seen told him that Indians tended to be more thoughtful, more emotional, more demonstrative than most white people he knew.

After a few minutes Tom regained his composure, patted Pirch on the shoulder as if he were the one who needed comforting, and said, "Thanks. I'm really glad you're here with me, Pirch, and I know Grandma Pipe appreciates it too. There aren't many white people would do that. Come over here and meet some more of my relatives."

Pirch knew that Tom meant his words as a compliment, as thanks, but instead they made Pirch ashamed that his people were so much less than these, whom they despised. Sometimes he wished Tom would just say something nice without reminding him that in acting with common courtesy he was almost betraying the long, sorry legacy of his people.

Despite the fact that his people were poor, uneducated, and shattered as a culture, Thomas Jefferson White Shell was tenaciously proud of his people and their past. Pirch knew Tom was one of the few young men of the Nehawka who still listened to the stories of the old men and learned the ways of things like the Buffalo Dance. Pirch had always secretly wished that Tom would bring him to a Buffalo Dance but he knew better than to ask for an invitation.

One of the times Pirch had seen Tom White Shell filled with fury was the occasion when Tom spoke of his return from the war in Europe. He had stopped for a week's furlough in Boston with his lifelong friend Buddy Foster. Through clenched teeth Tom had told Pirch of the visit of the two young Indian veterans to the Densmore Museum and the display of the Sacred Sky Bundle of the Nehawka people. Tom told Pirch that the Bundle was lying open in a glass case, where women, children, or uninitiated white men could look freely at its powerful, secret, and sacred contents. Tom had immediately closed his eyes, and run from the room, ashamed and terrified that he had seen the forbidden contents without having gone through the necessary training and rituals. Tom and Buddy had almost been arrested when they went to the museum director's office and insisted that the Sky Bundle be moved from public view at once. An Indian woman in the Director's office— Tom thought he recalled that she was Ojibwa—finally convinced the two Nehawkas to leave the office peacefully.

Tom and Buddy came back to the Turtle Creek Reservation from that experience intent on learning all they could about the Sky Bundle. They made a pact to return to Boston and the Sacred Sky Bundle someday with the appropriate status, to beg its forgiveness and offer it thanks. Perhaps they would ask the museum to give it back to the Nehawka people, or if necessary take it back by force.

Pirch wondered if one of the connections Tom White Shell felt for Grandma Pipe might not be the fact that she had been one of the last virgins of the Sacred Sky Bundle. Pirch Beck made a mental note that someday down the line a ways, maybe when they were fishing under the bridge, he would ask Tom about that.

Through the day Pirch sat around the yard, greeting other relatives and friends of Grandma Pipe as they arrived, smoking hand-rolled cigarettes, eating, drinking cheap wine and homebrew beer, and telling stories—a lot of them about Grandma Pipe.

"I remember the time I knocked a baseball through some curtains she had hanging outside her house when she lived over there by the Mormon church. She had the curtains stretched on some kind of frame and the ball went right through them as if they were paper or something. Left a hole exactly the size of the baseball."

"Yeah, I remember that. She was really mad."

"And when Grandma Pipe got mad, she could really be a fury."

"I never understood how someone that small could be that mean."

It was peculiar to Pirch, this gossipy remembering. At first he found it vaguely irreverent, maybe even sacrilegious, and yet it was so thoroughly honest, so thoroughly filled with love that before long even Pirch could sense that the conversation was a narrative tribute to the little woman lying dead in the house. These men appreciated that she had been tough on them when they were kids. And in some cases, when they were adults.

"If it hadn't been for Grandma, I'd have never stuck with the tribal sobriety program and the Holy Indian Church."

"Jeez, Reuben, don't start witnessing right here and now!"

"If it hadn't been for Grandma Pipe, I would have never sat those winters with Alvin Fire and learned what I know about the Buffalo Dance and the Sky Bundle songs."

"If Grandma Pipe hadn't taken me in when my folks died, by now I'd be a white man."

Everyone laughed, and then everyone cried.

By evening there were a couple hundred people crowded into the farmyard, passing in and out of the house. About sundown some men set up a drum and began singing strong-heart songs; from inside the house there came the faster, higher-pitched sounds of a peyote drum and singers. Pirch was leaning up against Tom's car in the yard, chewing on a piece of fry bread, when a big late-model Dodge drove into the yard. Definitely a white man. Pirch recognized the driver as Dr. Evans from the reservation agency hospital.

Pirch had always appreciated Doc Evans because he worked for next to nothing instead of using his education to amass wealth, and he seemed to have a real appreciation for the people he served. Through the hard years of the Depression—even harder for people on the reservation than the non-Indian people around them—he had worked for years for almost nothing, taking corn, calves, eggs, fry bread, beadwork, and promises instead of money. There was no money. He never expressed anything but respect for his dirt-poor patients. He acted as if he were actually there to *serve*.

"Another credit to our race," Pirch thought. Pirch watched Doc Evans go through the rituals of greeting and expressing sympathy. The good doctor clearly knew his way around in Indian company. He stepped into the house to pay his respects to Grandma Pipe and accepted a plate of food and a cup of coffee. Eventually, after an hour or so, he made his way over to Pirch's station at the Nash. "Hi, Pirch. How's it going? Haven't seen you for a while."

"No. It's good to see you, Doc, but I'm sorry it has to be because of Grandma Pipe."

"Well, she was an old woman. She had a good life, and she was ready for death."

"You sound more like an Indian every time I talk with you, Doc."

"Thanks. I'll accept that as a compliment."

"That's how I meant it."

"In some ways, Pirch, I envy Grandma Pipe her death."

"What's that supposed to mean? Are you getting suicidal or something?"

"No, not at all. If anything, these people have given me hope. I mean, I wish I could die when my time comes like she died. I watched my mother and father die a couple years ago, and I wish they could have died like Grandma Pipe. You know, she died right here, surrounded by her relatives. I came here a few days ago and checked her out, and there was no question but that she was dying. I could have had her hauled to the hospital and kept her going a few days or weeks, but, you know, she was *comfortable* here with her relatives and friends, in a familiar place, with familiar food. She knew that everything possible was being done for her. I brought her whatever I know from my people; her people were doing everything they could with plant medicines and prayers. And, Pirch, you know, I'm not at all sure what I offered was any more than what they did.

"And that music." He pointed toward the singers outside the window of the room where the women were now washing Grandma Pipe one more time in preparation for her funeral. "Those are peyot' songs. You know, Pirch, Grandma Pipe was one of the people responsible for bringing the Holy Indian Church to the Nehawka."

"I thought the Nehawka had always had the peyot' church. I thought that was an Indian religion."

"Well, it is, but it came to the Nehawka from the Kiowa not too many years ago, about 1910 or 1912, I think. Grandma Pipe and a lot of the old-timers like her liked the new church because it combined the best of the old ways and the new. She was one of the last virgins of the Sacred Sky Bundle and she was one of the first to pray all night at the peyot' meetings. That was a pretty daring and progressive thing for an old lady to do, and she was already old—Indian old—by that time. She was a kind of rebel.

"She stuck with the Buffalo Dancers and remembered as much as she could of the Sacred Bundle to pass along to youngsters like your pal White Shell, and she threw herself into the Christian ways of the Holy Indian Church, too. She was quite a woman, Pirch, and now she is surrounded by the sacred songs of all the sacred ways she followed in her long life—the peyot' singers, the Buffalo Dancers, what few remember the Sky Bundle.

"They've been singing for her day and night for the last four days of her life. At any time when she was awake, she could hear those songs—powerful, spiritual songs—and she knew that every single thing possible was being done to make her journey to the Hereafter easy. Her relatives helped her remember the days when the Nehawka were alive and strong. Pirch, I'm not sure that when I die, probably in my own hospital, I'll be that confident and comfortable. We don't know how to give our dying people that kind of comfort yet."

"Doc, if you're not sure, how do you think the rest of us feel?"

He shrugged, said goodbye without giving an answer to Pirch's question, walked to his car, and drove into the night.

As the evening grew late, there was more drinking, more laughing, some good-time songs, good-natured kidding of some young couples who had retreated to parked cars for privacy. Pirch could still hear keening from the house, and the singing from the drums. It seemed a strange combination to him, intense sorrow and good cheer, but it was a combination Grandma Pipe had lived with almost all her life, so perhaps it was all the more appropriate tonight as her people prepared to say good-bye to her.

Tom eventually left his relatives and walked over to where Pirch still leaned against the Nash. "What do you think?" he asked, sweeping his hand over the yard and house.

"I think it is wonderful stuff, Tom. See to it when I die that I get the same treatment."

"I'll do what I can, white man," Tom laughed. Then he stopped and leaned his ear toward the drummers in the yard. "Listen to that, Pirch. Sacred Sky Bundle songs. Anthropologists and most of the Nehawka thought the Sky Bundle Society was dead years ago, but here they are, still singing the songs. And they're not all old-timers either." White Shell quietly sang along, as if to show Pirch that he knew the songs, that they were still alive in him.

He continued, "They tried to outlaw the Sun Dance and Ghost Dance songs among the Lakota." He pointed northwest. "But it didn't work. Up there on the Rosebud and the Pine Ridge they still sing the songs and dance the dances. You can burn books and papers and even drums, Pirch, but you can't kill the songs that live in the people's heads. The Buffalo Dance was dead, and most of the Indians who did it, the white man thought, but we're still dancing. Some day, Pirch, when everyone is more comfortable with the situation, I'll bring you to a Buffalo Dance. It's something, Pirch. We turn into buffalo, you know."

Pirch looked at his old friend to see if he was smiling, perhaps making fun of him. But he obviously was not. "I'd like that, Tom."

"I've talked with some of the Nehawka elders already and they are considering it. Letting a white friend come to a Buffalo Dance."

Pirch was almost overwhelmed by the confidence Tom White Shell was showing him. And the immense gesture of friendship. "Thank you, Tom," he said.

Tom said only, "Let's go over to Turner's farm. He has a tight barn with clean straw in the loft and he says we can sleep there."

White Shell steered the clattering Nash over rough dirt roads for about a half hour before he turned into a dark farmyard. A dim kerosene lantern burned outside the barn's door. Without bothering their hosts, the two friends went into the hayloft of the barn and slept hard. Pirch Beck's last thoughts as he went to sleep were of his friend's remarkable words, that in his lifetime he might witness a Buffalo Dance, something most of the world thought persisted only in anthropology books in libraries.

The next morning Tom White Shell and Pirch Beck washed up at Turner's pump and drove to town to the tribal community building, an old gymnasium. Once again there were women cooking in the ever-present copper wash boilers over smoking fires, and groups of men and women standing around eating and talking. There was laughter, especially when someone recognized a long-missed face of a relative or friend in town for the occasion of the funeral, but it was considerably more subdued than the party the previous night at Charity and Jack's.

A little before noon Tom and Pirch took their dishes and got in line to eat—this time there was buffalo and blue corn pudding in honor of Grandma Pipe's antiquity. And then the funeral began in the open yard in front of the community building.

An Indian funeral is not an easy experience for a white man. Women keened and wailed; some threw themselves onto the coffin and were torn away by their family. Prayers in Nehawka, passionate, long, *long* dissertations, drew the ceremony on for hours. The white undertakers from Rising City stood around fidgeting, looking at their watches, wondering when and if this funeral would ever be over. The Catholic priest from Lakota Falls blessed the corpse and the mourners and said a few words in Latin, but as increasingly seemed to be the case with Catholic churchmen among Indians, he left almost immediately after his brief part of the ceremony, not so much to avoid embarrassing himself or the church as not to make anyone else uncomfortable. Almost all Nehawkas at Turtle Creek held membership in two or more churches, sometimes churches with widely disparate views. The Nehawkas did not see any contradictions in being, for example, members of the Mormon, Holy Indian, and Catholic churches all at once. It was simply a matter of covering as many spiritual bases as possible.

They knew that the churches frowned on such multiple allegiances, and didn't want to embarrass their priest or preacher friends by rubbing their noses in this very real reality, so they were uncomfortable when the reality became obvious. Considerate churchmen, like the Catholic priest from Lakota Falls, avoided complications by ignoring the obvious. Seeing the peyote blankets and drum at Grandma Pipe's funeral ceremonies, and smelling the cedar smoke, he realized it would be easier for everyone if he did his part and then went away without making a fuss. Everyone loved him all the more for his sensitivity.

In the shade of the oak and cottonwood trees everyone was fairly comfortable. As relative after relative, friend after friend made speeches, Pirch couldn't help thinking about Dr. Evans's words the night before: there could be no question that Grandma Pipe was loved, even now in death.

Perhaps the hardest part of an Indian funeral for most white folks is the gift-giving. Pirch had seen this process three or four times before he understood it. A Nehawka spouse, with the help of children and siblings and friends, gives away everything she or he has when a wife or husband dies. On flattened cardboard boxes laid on the dirt before the open coffin, they pile the household's blankets, kitchenware, furniture; the dead person's clothing, shoes, jewelry, coats, hats, everything. And bit by bit friends and relatives are called forward to receive the tokens so everyone goes home with something of the dead person's, something by which to remember the dead.

Pirch was a little embarrassed when he was called forward to receive a towel, washcloth, and blanket that had belonged to Grandma Pipe, and yet he was glad to have something that had been hers now that she was gone. More than that, Pirch had come to understand that by this cleansing, he was helping the family. The first time he understood the whole process was when Tom had brought him to Canby Mitchell's funeral. Canby was a fairly young man, maybe forty, and his widow, only thirty-five or thirty-six, gave away everything in the house. She was left with nothing but three children and the beds. She even gave away her dishes.

"Now, what the hell is she going to do?" Pirch had thought. Then he put aside his own cultural understandings and tried to forget his pain for the widow, and watched. He saw people come forward again and again with gifts—money, blankets, towels, food, dishes. He grew to understand that the gift-giving process would go on through the week. People would come to Canby Mitchell's widow's door with armloads of gifts.

Instead of returning to a house full of painful memories, instead of having to sort out her husband's clothing, instead of being haunted by seeing his favorite cup and favorite bowl and favorite chair for years, Charlotte Mitchell went into a house cleansed of those painful artifacts. She had new dishes and new bedsheets and new chairs, with no memories associated with them at all. Whatever else she needed, she could buy with the gifts of money. What Pirch had at first seen as cruel and senseless was in reality a marvelous social system to ease mourning. Pirch wondered at the genius of "primitive" societies.

Grandma Pipe's procession to the cemetery on the hill behind the village was long and sorrowful—no limousines or hearses, just mourners walking, and pallbearers, all nephews, with plenty of replacements, walking alongside, carrying the simple wooden coffin on their shoulders. When the first members of the procession reached the cemetery, the last mourners were still leaving the community hall. Nearly every member of the tribe was in the cortege, everybody on the reservation and all the visitors.

Pirch had been to the cemetery before so he was prepared for what might have shocked other non-Indian visitors. The Turtle Creek Nehawka cemetery would have been stark even if no one were buried there. It lay on the very crown of a parched and naked hill, windblown and weedy. There were very few stone markers; Indians can't afford them. Wooden markers were broken off, tipped, faded, eaten by grasshoppers, and sandblasted by the wind into battered sticks. Here and there were a few faded plastic flowers. Not for the convenience of the groundskeepers, as is so often and sadly the case in white man's cemeteries, but because there was money for nothing more.

Earlier in the morning some of Grandma Pipe's grandsons had dug a grave, near the grave of her husband, Alfred Pipe, who had died almost twenty years earlier. "How did they know where he was buried?" Pirch asked Tom. "There's no marker."

"You'll see," he replied, smiling because he knew that there were still some things he could teach Pirch Beck about death among the Indians.

More grandsons than could easily perform the task used hemp ropes to lower Grandma Pipe's coffin clumsily into the grave; some pulled back the keening women who still tried to throw themselves onto the coffin in their grief. When the coffin rested firmly on the solid earth at the bottom of the pit, an old wooden door was placed on top of it, perhaps to muffle the sound of the clods as they fell on the coffin, not for the mourners but for Grandma Pipe.

For the mourners, the wooden door was like a sounding board, amplifying every shovelful of dirt into an explosion as it hit. Again, it was relatives—nephews, grandsons, great-grandsons, now and then a niece or granddaughter—who came forward from the crowd massed around the grave, took one of the four or five shovels, and threw several shovelsful of dirt into the grave, saying a few words during the slow and final admission of death's reality:

"I remember when Willie Parker and I went camping and got lost down by the river when she and Alfred had the wood farm." Shovelful of dirt into the grave. Thud.

"We came to her early in the morning, after sleeping all night in the rain, and she took us in." Shovelful of dirt. Thud.

"She fed us cookies and hot chocolate and made us feel good." Shovelful of dirt. Thud.

"She told us the story of Black Deer's raid on the Pawnee, and not two weeks ago she told the same story, word for word, to my own grandson." Shovelful of dirt. Thud.

"When the rain cleared and the roads were good a couple days later, she went with us when Alfred took us home so our mothers wouldn't be too hard on us because we had been gone so long." Thud. Stick the shovel into the loose earth at the grave's edge, and another hand takes it.

When Grandma Pipe's grave had been filled, grandsons and granddaughters worked the top earth carefully, making certain that it was tidy and symmetrical, with no lumps marring its regularity. Pirch prepared to leave the gravesite, then noticed that rather than leaving the cemetery, most of the families with children were moving closer to the grave. Obviously, the ceremony had not yet ended. He turned to Tom. Tom put his finger to his lips and pointed back at the grave.

Despite his long history with the Nehawkas, Pirch was not at all prepared for what happened next. He had never been through this part of a large Indian funeral. If he had ever had any argument with the way Indians treat children, it was that they were far too indulgent with them. Indians let their children run wild, eating any kind of junk they wanted, doing whatever crossed their minds, having whatever the family could afford. Tom had explained to Pirch, "Indians have damned near nothing when they're adults anyway, so they might as well have whatever they want when they're children. Whatever they want is cheaper then."

One of Pirch's first impressions of Indian mothers was the time he had gone to a gourd dance with Tom and a woman showed up with her new child. The baby had been fathered by a black man who abandoned the mother, a notorious drunk and prostitute in the community, almost immediately upon learning that she was pregnant. Most white folks called such children "illegitimate."

"Being a human being automatically makes you legitimate," Tom said to Pirch on that occasion, bristling. The baby was passed around from woman to woman, cooed over, loved, dandled, welcomed, sung to, tickled, and kissed, recognized as innocent of all of its mother's and father's transgressions.

So at Grandma Pipe's funeral, Pirch was shocked to see some Nehawkas he had known as loving mothers and fathers take their children one by one and shake them—not hard but firmly—and say directly into their little faces, "*This* is where Grandma Pipe is buried. She is *dead*, Leon, and she is buried *here*," and then the bewildered, crying children were made to walk up and down the length of the grave, *on the grave*. Some were so terrified that they had to be dragged from one end of the new grave to the other, the toes of their shoes making little ditches in the pristine, groomed soil.

As soon as one child had finished the macabre desecration, another child was taken to the grave and force-marched from one end of it to the other. "Robert, Grandma Pipe is in the ground *here*. She died and *this* is where we buried her."

The air that had been filled not long ago with the keening of mourning women was now ripped by the screams and sobs of children. Pirch was shocked. He didn't know how much more of the mistreatment he could take. He turned to Tom.

"Come here," Tom said, taking Beck's arm before he could ask his question and leading him a few paces away to a naked slope of the cemetery hill. "Right here is where my father's mother is buried. Right here." He pointed directly down to the ground and outlined a rough rectangle in the otherwise unmarked soil. "Over here is my mother's brother. He died when I was only three." He traced the edges of a grave in the dirt with his toe, where there were no other marks. "Over there by that thistle is the grave of my father's brother. He died before my father was born, but his brothers and sisters showed him the grave's location, and he showed me.

See the little depression by that box elder tree? That is the grave of Seeks Wood Mapateet, last Keeper of the Sacred Sky Bundle. I pray there often when I come home to Turtle Creek. Get it, Pirch? Those children crying over there, Pirch? They'll never forget where Grandma Pipe is buried."

"Neither will I, Tom. Neither will I," Pirch said.

While they were on the reservation Tom wanted to visit with some of his relatives who were home for the occasion of Grandma Pipe's funeral, so he dropped Pirch Beck off down at Sacred Ring Park down by the Missouri, the Smokey River, with some fishing equipment he borrowed from Tom's Uncle Jack. "I'll check back tomorrow noon to see if you need anything," Tom said.

"Don't worry about me," Pirch said, putting his hand on Tom's shoulder. "I've got pioneer blood in me. By the time you get back I'll have enough fish to keep us fed for a week."

"Wasn't it you who told me that the Pilgrims would have starved if it hadn't been for the Indians?"

Pirch again patted his friend Tom White Shell on the shoulder, by way of thanking him, and then remembered that Indians are not eager to be touched by others. He was about to apologize when he thought, "Ah, what the hell. This guy understands more than I ever will anyway so he probably not only figures that I want to be friendly but that I don't know how to show it and that I want to apologize but don't know how to do that either."

White Shell laughed as if he could read Pirch's mind. Pirch waved good-bye and turned toward the river. Pirch enjoyed having the next day and a half to sit at the edge of a big river and think about what he had seen at Grandma Pipe's funeral. He missed Calla but he knew that she would do just fine taking care of the farm on her own. Pirch thought about Calla and about the Indian women he had come to know and was surprised that what he loved most about his wife was what he admired most about the Indians: they were strong and independent without trying to be men, and allowed the men to be men without demanding that they be women. He liked that he did not have to explain to Calla why he needed to go with Tom and why he needed this time by the river to think about what he had seen and heard and learned. She seemed content to lie at his side when he returned and hear his stories without being mad that she had not been able to be there herself.

"She has wanted to go visit her sisters in Torrington for a couple years now," he thought as he watched his bobber spin in a slow river whirlpool. "I think we can afford a train ticket for her. And Clara, too. It's about time I gave both of them some time. I can take care of those damned chickens myself. Yessir. Next month. Calla would like that, and Clara, too."

He caught a few catfish, cleaned them, and left them with Tom's Aunt Chastity. The day they got home, Pirch spent most of the evening telling Calla and their daughter about how civilized societies handle death. The next weekend he bought two round-trip tickets to Torrington on the Burlington Zephyr for Calla and Clara. While they were gone, he wrote a brief will outlining what he wanted done in the event of his death.

WINTER COUNT

Winter Counts were no longer kept among the Nehawka people at Turtle Creek at the time of Grandma Pipe's death, summer, 1948.

The Story of
Seeks Wood Mapateet

The struggle to reach the top of Holy Hill took Old Man Mapateet the entire day. When he was a boy and went to Holy Hill to seek a vision, it had taken him less than an hour to scramble to the top, but that was long ago. Long before he was Old Man Mapateet, when he was Seeks Wood Mapateet. He was proud of his name because it said so much about the history of his tribe, the Nehawka. He was given the Indian name of Seeks Wood from his uncle Ten Skull. It was a good Indian name, not at all like the pale, meaningless names parents were giving Nehawka children these days—John, Fred, Chauncey.

Mapateet was a name a French trader, one of the first white men the Nehawka had ever seen, had given his great-grandmother, a name he understood and came to love only when he visited Paris.

In the old days, when he was a vision seeker, Seeks Wood Mapateet had come to Holy Hill to explore the Mysteries and seek an understanding of life; now Old Man Mapateet was here to remember, and to die.

He spread his blanket and sat as he had when he was a boy— insofar as his legs would still bend properly—with his back to the Turtle Creek village far below, looking out over the wide valley of the Smokey River, as the Nehawka people called the Missouri. He wished he had taken the time and trouble to come up here more often in his long life, but then this was a good place to come to die and this was a good day to die. He sang his family's death song:

Hey! My friends, I, Seeks Wood Mapateet, know this: every bird comes at death to earth.

Hey! You Thunderers, I, Seeks Wood Mapateet, know this: every summer wind that blows north, again blows south in the winter.

Hey! You Powers, I, Seeks Wood Mapateet, know this: a man leaves
his lodge by its door and returns by the same path.
Hey! My enemies, I, Seeks Wood Mapateet, know this: it is good to
live, but it is fitting to die,
And this is a good day to die.

He had sung the death song once before, when the sickness
called smallpox had come to his village, killing so many people, but
he had lived. Old Man Mapateet had lived a long time.

So much had changed during Old Man Mapateet's life, but to his
surprise, not much had changed atop the prominence called Holy
Hill. It seemed to him that the same clumps of buffalo grass were
growing that had been there when he had come for his vision sixty
years before. The four oak trees were not only still there but
appeared to be no larger than they had been so long before, and so
many years had passed. The scar behind his left shoulder, the scar
of his vision, was still there. So much was the same.

So much had changed. The people of Turtle Creek were no
longer proud of being Nehawkas; now they were embarrassed to be
Indians and wanted to be like the white people. Old Man Mapateet
could not imagine why. He had seen both ways, the way of the
white man and the way of the Indian—the *old* way of the Indian—
and he could not imagine why anyone would want to be a white
man and not a Turtle Creek Nehawka.

Especially the way the Turtle Creek Nehawka used to be. The
Nehawka had never mounted a single battle against the white
man's incursions during Mapateet's life. Not one. A few warriors
and a couple of soldiers and soldiers' women had died in fights,
especially when the traders brought whiskey up the river, but there
was nothing that could be called a military engagement, even by the
whites who were always eager to call any trouble with the Indians

a battle or a massacre, depending on who won. There was a time when Seeks Wood Mapateet was proud of his people's civility in dealing with the whites, but now he was not so sure. Perhaps, if his people had fought the whites just once, had had just one moment of warrior pride they could remember, they would still be the Turtle Creek Nehawkas he had known as a boy.

In the old days he and his friends and relatives had gone on the annual winter and summer buffalo hunts and still made raids against the Pawnee now and then. As a young man he had been initiated into the Buffalo Dance Society and he had learned how to pray and sing the songs that would let him become a buffalo himself. He knew the feeling of being a bull buffalo and it made him feel good to remember it. Now only a few old men remembered the Buffalo Dance and risked dancing it; white men had outlawed the Buffalo Dance twenty years ago, just as they had outlawed the buffalo themselves.

Old Man Mapateet looked out across the hazy valley below him, its fields and pastures. Now, instead of the good, powerful buffalo, he saw only stupid and weak cows, pigs, and worst of all, sheep. How could anyone think that is better? he wondered. He couldn't understand.

Well, there was much he did not understand. In fact, that had been the way of his life, not understanding. Mapateet laughed to himself, at himself. He couldn't believe how innocent he had been as a young man, when he first encountered the Black Shirts, the curious people whites called missionaries. Seeks Wood remembered the year the Black Shirts first crossed the Smokey River to set up their missions and schools in Nehawka territory. They were so insignificant, so harmless then. The Nehawkas welcomed them as they had traditionally welcomed everyone, giving them food and shelter until they managed to build homes and gather food for themselves, little knowing the poison they were bringing to the Turtle Creek village.

Seeks Wood was a young man then but he had already entered his training to accept the responsibilities of the Sky Bundle, since that was his birthright and obligation as a member of the Antler family. It occurred to him then—Old Man Mapateet laughed aloud again at his hopeless innocence!—that this would be a natural alliance, he, a member of the Antler clan and the Keeper of the Sky Bundle, and these Black Shirts, the Keepers of the Cross.

He had dressed in his finest regalia and rode his most handsome horse into the mission yard the second winter the Black Shirts were there, planning to present his plan to the missionaries' chief who lived there. He liked the idea of the two holy men from such different traditions exchanging ideas and knowledge. He imagined that they would talk with each other for many years, exchanging songs and prayers, burning cedar together and smoking the powerful pipe. Perhaps between the two of them, they could understand Mysteries that neither of them could understand by themselves. Seeks Wood had no doubt that the Black Shirt would be as excited about the potential of spiritual cooperation as he was.

As he approached the mission, however, he saw the Black Shirt's woman drop the clothing she was hanging on a line in the yard and run into the house as if she were afraid. Surely by now she knew there was nothing to fear from the Turtle Creek Nehawka. By the time he rode into the yard, the Black Shirt chief was standing in front of the small wooden house with one of his young Indian charges—and a long rifle across his breast.

"Reverend Benwell says you should get out of here with your feathers and arrows and painted face because you're a pagan and a bad influence on us students," the boy said, staring impudently into Seeks Wood's eyes.

Seeks Wood was shocked. This was no way for a child to speak to a warrior and future Keeper of the Sacred Bundle. He said to the boy, "You look like Hollow Horn, the son of the good Turtle Creek Nehawkas Charging Bull and Grassfire. But you have the manners of a Pawnee."

The boy stood quietly, no longer grinning a white man's grin. He took his eyes from Seeks Wood's and looked at the ground between his black shiny shoes.

"Tell the Black Shirt that I have come here to exchange words about the great Mysteries. Tell him that I will teach him and learn from him and he will teach me and learn from me. We are both seekers and together we will be like a war party, five times stronger than each of us alone. Tell him."

The boy turned and spoke to the Black Shirt. The Black Shirt laughed, but not a happy laugh. It was the kind of laugh a warrior might make upon counting coup on a hated enemy. The Black Shirt spoke to the boy, and the boy spoke to Seeks Wood: "Reverend Benwell says you look like a messenger from the Bad Place and there's nothing you know that he wants to hear. He says that if you don't reject the animal ways of the Nehawka and put on white man's clothes and live in a box house and work in the fields like a woman and accept the teachings of his holy book and of the great chief Christ, you are going to go to the Bad Place. I mean no disrespect, Seeks Wood. I am just saying his words."

"I know, Hollow Horn. Though I do not understand his words, I can see that this is the way he speaks. He demands much and offers little. I want to know about the words in his book and of his Mysteries. Are you sure that he does not want to know about the Sky Bundle and the Buffalo Dance and the visions of our people? Ask him again. Perhaps you said the wrong words."

The boy did not refer to the Black Shirt before he responded to

Seeks Wood: "I may have spoken the wrong words, my uncle Seeks Wood, that is true, but I have heard enough of the white man's ways here at the mission and enough of Reverend Benwell's words that I am sure this is what he believes."

"You let me answer his questions, Benjamin," the Black Shirt said angrily, using the name he had given Hollow Horn, and thumping the boy on the head with his forefinger.

"Yessir," Hollow Horn said. Seeks Wood liked it better when the boy was impudent than now when he acted like a whipped dog under the finger of a man who didn't care to learn about Mysteries.

"He does not want a vision," Seeks Wood said.

"No, Seeks Wood, he does not want a vision."

The Black Shirt grabbed Hollow Horn by his shoulder and shook him, hard. "I told you to let me answer his questions," he hissed in the boy's face. The boy's lip quivered.

"What kind of man are you to fight a child?" Seeks Wood shouted.

Hollow Horn hesitated. He didn't want to translate Seeks Wood's words because he knew the Reverend Benwell would beat him for them, but he could not respond to Seeks Wood himself, for Benwell would have beaten him for that, too.

"He says he wants to know more about Jesus," the boy said to the missionary.

"Well, tell him I will be glad to instruct him in the ways of civilization when he comes back with the right spirit in his heart and decent clothing on his back."

"Reverend Benwell says that he is so busy with us children that he doesn't have time right now to learn all that you have to teach him," the boy said.

Later that year, when the students were released from the mission school to their parents for Christmas holidays, Hollow Horn told his parents that he had spoken false words to a Nehawka warrior, and why. His mother and father immediately went to the Elk family lodge and apologized to Seeks Wood for their son's disgraceful behavior, but Seeks Wood told them that he understood, that the Black Shirt apparently treated his students worse than the Pawnee treated their women. He could understand the boy's fear.

Seeks Wood did not in fact give up his quest to learn more about the holy ways of the Black Shirts. During the Christmas holidays that winter Seeks Wood sat with the children and asked them what they had learned at the Black Shirts' school, and they told him as well as they could. Seeks Wood was fascinated by the Mysteries the children spoke of and he especially admired the holy books they had. They showed him how they could make words from the scratchings on the thin papers in the book. Despite the unpleasant welcome he had received on his visit to the Black Shirt's house, Seeks Wood was ever more certain that the book and Jesus and the saints and all were ideas worth exploring.

What surprised him most, Old Man Mapateet recalled again with a smile, was how much the beliefs and ways of the Black Shirts, as the children told him in those early days, were precisely the ways of the Nehawka people. This Jesus spoke of the importance of a spiritual life and chided those who worshipped wealth — precisely the traditional way of the Nehawka. The book of the Black Shirts spoke of the importance of welcoming the traveler, and the Nehawka prided themselves and were justifiably famous for their hospitality. Jesus spoke of peace, and the Nehawka wanted nothing more than peace. How curious it was, Seeks Wood Mapateet had thought, that these two peoples, so different in so many ways, from such distant places, had so many holy ideas and practices in common.

How young he had been! How stupid!

By now night was falling on the Holy Hill. Old Man Mapateet pulled his blanket over his shoulders. He saw dim and distant lantern light in some of the farmhouses below him in the river valley.

And he remembered a time when he was older but still innocent. Still an Indian. He was traveling to the place where the tribes—all tribes—found the soft red stone of sacred pipes. He had still not had much contact with white people though the countryside was now spotted with their flimsy homes and towns; at that time there were not many of the whites on the Nehawka side of the Smokey River. Old Man Mapateet couldn't help smiling as he recalled a conversation he had listened to among the elders, a discussion that reached the conclusion that there was little reason to worry about the whites. The elders thought that the whites had enough land over in Meskwaki territory, across the Smokey River toward the sunrise. Though a few had the courage to cross the great river, surely not many would come. Surely, they concluded.

On the long trek to the pipestone grounds with six of his friends, all of them good travelers and carvers of the red stone, they came upon a settler's cabin along the river they called the Pipestone Road. The band saw faint smoke rising from the chimney and smelled a wonderful food smell. They had traveled long and hard with little to eat, so this was a welcome discovery.

Seeks Wood and his companions stopped their horses in a patch of chokecherry brush not far from the homestead and talked about how they should approach the house. By now they all understood that white people were uneasy about Indians, and knew how dangerous and nervous, frightened white people could be. Yet Seeks Wood recalled all the words the children had brought back from the mission school, Jesus' words, about welcoming the hungry, and about giving being better than receiving, and how food should be shared. The only surprise about these ideas to Seeks Wood was that children had to be taught such things. It was all fairly obvious to him, since open hospitality was the way it had always been among the Nehawka people.

Seeks Wood and his companions approached the frontier cabin of Tom Bishop, but with considerable caution, following all of the protocols of good behavior. Before entering a lodge or a tipi, especially the home of a young couple, particularly the home of a young couple recently together, visitors would lift the flap quietly and look in to be sure that they were not arriving at a private moment. If the couple were not being, as the Nehawka people put it, "young," the visitor would shake the flap—one doesn't knock at buffalo hide—by way of indicating that they would like an invitation to enter.

Seeks Wood decided to do what he could to follow the same courtesies with the somewhat clumsier house of the settlers. He peered in at a window for a moment until his eyes became accustomed to the dark interior. He saw a woman at her cooking. It was obviously a good time to visit.

The woman turned from her fire and saw her unexpected guest's face at the window. He smiled to acknowledge her and show he was a friend. He could see the woman's mouth open wide and even through the thick walls of the white man's lodge he could hear her scream. Well, she was a little skittish for a grown woman, Seeks Wood thought.

He moved quickly to prove his friendly intentions. He pulled open the door and shook it several times before stepping in. The woman screamed again. Seeks Wood and his band stepped into the house and explained to the woman that they were Nehawka people, always friends to her white relatives, that they were on the way to a hunt and smelled her food across the prairie, that they had learned about the ways of Jesus and the sacred book, and that they had come as friends to share her food.

The woman cowered in the corner, crying, trembling. Seeks Wood was confused. When he tried to approach her and comfort the poor woman, she grew even more frightened, tried to be even smaller in the cabin's corner. Seeks Wood said to his friends, "Perhaps if we show that we are willing to accept her food, that we appreciate her hospitality, she will calm down a little. Maybe one of us should go find her man and tell him that she is not behaving well."

Seeks Wood and his companions decided to eat first and then find the woman's man. The woman had been making small circles of bread in a pot of hot grease and a pile of the breads lay on her table. So Seeks Wood took some of the warm breads and ate them. They were very good, for white man's food, rich and tasty. He motioned to his friends to show the woman the courtesy of eating some of her food, and they did.

As is the way of the Nehawka, they ate all the food, and Seeks Wood thanked the woman with a long speech about how, given the right circumstances, his people and hers could be allies, though her people certainly had not made it easy. He pointed to the pot of hot lard and rubbed his stomach by way of telling her, since she probably did not understand the poetic language of his people, that her food was surprisingly good and he and his band appreciated her kindness and cooking skills.

The woman rose slowly from where she had been cowering in the corner, at last quiet and behaving like a proper woman. She edged her way to the table, took some white powders and water and tools and ingredients Seeks Wood did not understand, and began mixing them. She was still crying but her actions were so peculiar, so mysterious that Seeks Wood could not bring himself to leave.

She made a kind of mud and then dropped little circles of it into the hot liquid in the pot on the iron firebox. In only a few moments she dipped the brown circles out of the fat and dropped them on the table. Seeks Wood picked one up but quickly dropped it again because it was so hot. He turned and laughed and told his friends to take one, but they sensed his joke and said they would wait until the breads cooled, thanks, and they laughed too.

They were surprised that the woman insisted on feeding them when they were already quite content, but they were determined to be good guests, so they again ate all the food she put on the table for them. Despite their best efforts, the woman continued to cry uncontrollably. And to make doughnuts endlessly.

Seeks Wood tried to explain to her that her cooking was wonderful and they appreciated her kindness but they really couldn't eat any more, and that as soon as her man came home so they could offer him their thanks, they would be on their way. But still the pale woman mixed the white dust into mud, dropped the circles into the hot fat, and piled the breads on the table. And Seeks Wood and his kinsmen continued to eat, although there was some grumbling about this fine situation Seeks Wood had gotten them into.

Then there were hoofbeats in the yard. Seeks Wood looked out the hole in the cabin wall, into which he had peeked when this whole mess started, and he was much relieved to see that the woman's man had finally come home. He must have sensed the problem that his absence had caused because he ran into the house as fast as he could, pushed his way past Seeks Wood and the others without so much as a word of greeting, and clutched the woman in his arms, apparently to keep her from burdening the visitors with any more breads.

"Tell him, tell him," the others urged Seeks Wood, obviously anxious to get out of the house and walk off some of the weight in their bellies.

"My friends and I thank you very much for your hospitality but we really need to be on our way. If you are ever near the Turtle Creek village, know that you are welcome and we will offer you all the good food you can eat. But probably not *more* than you can eat," Seeks Wood said to the man, who didn't really listen, but continued to comfort his sickly wife.

Seeks Wood could see that the man didn't understand a word he was saying. Seeks Wood had experience with the sign language that many Nehawka warriors, especially those who traveled far for flint and pipestone and for trading, as he had done often himself, used to speak among other tribes and even some white people. He thought that sign was worth a try in this situation because he certainly didn't want the woman to start making the breads again.

Seeks Wood made the sign for "thank you," and the white man seemed to understand. He made the sign for "friend." Seeks Wood smiled and made the same sign; he made the signs for "food" and "good," and then "woman" and "sick." The white man smiled and said something to his woman. She buried her face in her man's arm.

The white man put his woman on the small bed in the corner and set about making a packet of some of the white powder the Nehawka called "sweet water," a twist of tobacco, a piece of the fat white people peel from their pigs, and, to Seeks Wood's dismay, more of the brown bread circles. The man smiled and handed the cloth bag to Seeks Wood.

It was a friendly gesture, and Seeks Wood told him so, as best he could in the clumsy sign language. Seeks Wood had not encountered many decent white people, but this was certainly one of the best. It was a shame, however, Seeks Wood first thought and then told his companions, that a good man like this should be burdened with a troubled woman. Seeks Wood and his friends talked the situation over briefly and came up with a plan for helping their new friend.

Seeks Wood turned back to his host and offered his solution, still in sign language. He explained that he was headed toward the sunrise to the pipestone quarries and the white people and Indians there, he had heard, were in an even worse condition than the settler was suffering in this sorry excuse for a lodge with this difficult woman. Seeks Wood had seen the dark women of that country, so ugly their men must surely be desperate for another woman, even one as pathetic as this one. There, among those people, Seeks Wood reasoned, there would be a place even for a woman this puny and skittish.

And then, Seeks Wood continued laboriously with his hands, perhaps he could arrange for a woman of one of the northern or eastern tribes, perhaps one that had been brought to the pipestone quarries and had turned unpleasant, to come back with them for the settler. Perhaps they could find him someone who could at least keep him in children and get the farming done until they could see if a Nehawka woman would consent to come from Turtle Creek and relieve his loneliness. A widow maybe.

Seeks Wood continued, "I will trade you two horses for your sick woman—more than she's worth, obviously—and on our return we will bring you a fine Indian woman. Even a Pawnee would be a blessing to you, believe me."

The white man turned and said words to his woman; again she began to cry, but the man laughed. Curious people, these whites. Seeks Wood assumed that they must both understand that his proposal was the best course of action for both of them. But to Seeks Wood's amazement, the white man then signed that, no, he wanted to keep this woman and would not trade her for even one hundred horses.

Seeks Wood and his men were astonished, but they knew that a man can be fond even of a difficult woman. They told the man again that they thanked him, that if he should ever change his mind, they would be glad to be his friend and bring him another woman, a good woman, a stronger and well woman, one who could help this one who seemed so helpless and sick. Yes, one can be fond of a woman like this but one must also think of survival and the strength of the people.

Seeks Wood and his friends left the little house, shaking their heads, still confused. Pipe, one of Seeks Wood's companions, suggested that maybe it was the breads. Perhaps this man had an insatiable hunger for the breads, and that is why he wanted her. Even that didn't make much sense but it made more than any other explanations they could think of. That night when they camped, they ate only a few pinches of the dried meat called *wasna* and they talked way too late about the strange experiences of the day. They fed the round breads to fish in the creek.

Seeks Wood had learned since that the breads were the white man's doughnuts, and he learned how to knock on doors, and he learned that white men have many strange ways. And he learned that the white man had rejected his proposal to take the sickly woman off his hands because, while white men when it was to their taste took Indian women, the thought that a white woman might willingly go with an Indian, even an honorable man like himself, was incomprehensible.

Seeks Wood remembered when he traveled, many years after the last buffalo hunt, far across the oceans to places like France and Germany and England, where he did his people's dances for Cherokee Bill's Wild West Show. There had been white women there who had no difficulties going to bed with an Indian. There were women who sought him out after the show and invited him to their homes. He thought especially of Ciel, the strong woman in Paris, France, who laughed so well with him. When he told her that upon his return to America's Plains and his home at Turtle Creek, he would become keeper of the Sky Bundle, Ciel told him that she was destined to be his lover. Her name, she told him, meant "Sky."

And it was Ciel who had laughed a good laugh and told him about his own name, Mapateet. The Frenchman, she said, must have loved his great-grandmother a good deal.

When Seeks Wood was with Ciel, he had thought about the man in the log cabin on the road to the red stone quarry, wondering what he would think if he knew that the Indian who knew no English and did not understand doughnuts and laughed at the idea of his wife with an Indian husband was now lying beside a beautiful white woman, laughing, touching her, enjoying her love.

He never really understood Ciel's feelings toward him. He did know that when the Cherokee Bill show left France, Ciel cried and said she would miss him. She sent her prayers to the Sky Bundle, to the Sacred Sky Bird and Holy Feather Stone in the Bundle, and again she cried. This, Seeks Wood had thought at the railroad station, remembering the woman in the log house who cried at the wrong time, was an appropriate time for a woman to cry.

And a man. Seeks Wood cried too.

It was not as if Seeks Wood did not have his own concerns about what would have happened if he and Ciel had somehow continued. Seeks Wood had serious responsibilities among his people, especially the caretaking of the Sky Bundle. There was no question that he would have to return to Turtle Creek. And there was no question that Ciel would never have been at home there.

When he thought of it, Seeks Wood laughed again as he had the first time he realized the truth: that there was every likelihood his people would consider it a terrible disgrace for the Keeper of the Sky Bundle to have a white wife, and white children who would in turn become eligible to be Keepers of the Bundle. And there was the truth: his own people could be just as stuffy about the worthiness of other people's women as the white man in the log house— for that matter, all white men—were about the worthiness of Indians.

So Seeks Wood did return to Turtle Creek, alone. He courted and won the finest woman in the village, Star Elk, a distant relative. She gave him eight good children, of whom six lived to be adults. He became an elder, a respected member of his people, and respected by many of the white families who moved in around Turtle Creek.

Once he became Keeper of the Sky Bundle, he was even less welcome at the mission and the mission school than he had been when he was a young warrior. The Black Shirts—priests, teachers, government officials—seemed afraid of his strength and his knowledge of the ways of the Sky Bundle. They behaved as if they were afraid of the Sky Bundle. They wanted to know nothing about it.

Seeks Wood couldn't understand their fear. The Sky Bundle was losing its powers. When he returned from Europe, prepared to take on the responsibilities of serving the Bundle, he found that there were only a few old men who still cared about it. He was becoming an old man himself and yet he was the youngest follower of the Bundle, and the only one interested in following its ways, saying its prayers, learning its songs.

When at last he became the Keeper of the Bundle, there was little left to keep. He usually sang and prayed alone. He was the only one who observed the ways of the Bundle. It seemed terribly out of place, hanging in the closet of his reservation home. Perhaps that is why no one ever came to seek his counsel or perform the rituals of the Bundle.

Soon it was not even a matter of no one wanting to follow the Bundle; there was no longer anyone *eligible* to see its contents or sing its songs. The missionaries and teachers had shamed even Seeks Wood's own children, so they had no respect for their father and his old-fashioned ways. There were times when Seeks Wood doubted himself and his ancestors. He wondered if perhaps he had not himself witnessed the events that spelled the Bundle's loss of strength.

Before he was born, white men with power came to Turtle Creek and met with leaders from the Nehawka village. They gave Seeks Wood's grandfather, Elk, a silver medal, a direct gift from the Great Father, Thomas Jefferson, that guaranteed peace to the village of Turtle Creek. Elk wore the Medal every day for a full year. That year's winter count called the time the Year of Plenty and Peace. Elk believed in the Medal. He believed that the Medal was responsible for the peace and plenty of that year. So he took the Medal and its red ribbon from his neck and added it to the other sacred objects of the Sky Bundle. For the next twenty winters the Medal was an integral part of the Sky Bundle.

When Elk died, the responsibility for the Sacred Sky Bundle passed to Seeks Wood's father, Elk Dog, and Elk Dog was faced with a very difficult decision the first day of his stewardship: should the Jefferson Medal, which had been given after all to Elk as a gift, be buried with him or remain in the Sky Bundle?

The problem was the only topic of the village for the two days before Elk was buried. Should holy objects be buried, the people wondered? Can caretakers take things out of the Sky Bundle once they are put there? Elk himself had once said that nothing sacred should ever be buried because only the dead are buried and sacred things are alive. Was this medal Elk's possession that died with him or a part of the Sky Bundle that lives forever?

Elk Dog had decided to take the Medal from the Bundle and bury it with his father. Everyone in the village respected Elk Dog and knew that he, like his father, had his ways, and that his ways were never guided by greed or pride but by visions no one else had. Elk Dog also understood his people's questions: "I put this medal in my father's grave because it is his. This was the Great Father Jefferson's gift to him. It belonged to the Sky Bundle while it was alive but now it belongs with Elk, its owner. The Medal is not lost. It remains with my father, our leader. It will always belong to our people and the Sky Bundle because it is forever in the breast of our Mother Earth with Elk." Seeks Wood had watched his father place the Medal around his grandfather's neck as he was buried.

It was not easy for Old Man Mapateet now that all such serious thought was lost to the Nehawka. Perhaps the loss of the Nehawka way had been because Elk Dog had made a mistake in burying the Medal. No, such problems should not be blamed on things, even if they are sacred. The responsibility for the decline of Turtle Creek belonged to the people of Turtle Creek, Old Man Mapateet decided.

Once, in a fit of rage, Old Man Mapateet went through the village the way the elders occasionally did when he was a child, lashing out with a rawhide whip, chastising those who had slipped from the Nehawka way, holding up for ridicule those who bedded other than their husbands and wives, insulting those who drank whiskey and soiled themselves, slapping those who used bad language with his whip.

"Sometimes I wish I were a Pawnee!" he shouted to the villagers. "They have an excuse for losing their ways because they have lost their land. You are Nehawkas, and you are still on Nehawka land. But you disgrace that land! Shame! Shame!"

A few of his people listened to him and were ashamed—mostly old people. Most of the villagers ignored him, or called him a crazy old man. A few of the younger people laughed at him. There was no doubt in Seeks Wood's mind: the Nehawkas were dying inside.

Eventually, Seeks Wood Mapateet became Old Man Mapateet, alone with the Bundle. Star, his wife, helped him as much as she could, but so much of what he needed to do had to be done by men, men who were warriors, men who had sought visions, men who were elders, men who knew the ways of the Nehawka, men who respected the Bundle, men who sought the Mysteries and the Powers and the Thunderers. And there were no more such men. Old Man Mapateet was alone. With the Bundle.

Then he began to feel the approach of death, and that is why he had come again to the top of the Holy Hill, to die. And here he was, at last, really alone. He no longer even had the Bundle. He had been the last Keeper of the Sky Bundle, but he hadn't kept it. The Sky Bundle was now gone from the Turtle Creek people where it had been at home from before time began. No one among his people cared, but Old Man Mapateet felt shame that he had failed as the Keeper. Of course it had not been his fault, but the fact remained.

Over the past year he had faced the hardest decisions of his long life, trials to which there were no good solutions, only bad ones. There were many things one needed to know about when dealing with the Bundle—how to open it, how to fold it, what to say, how to think, where it should be in the lodge, its relationships with fire and water, who could touch it and who could not, the directions in which it had the most power, the Mysteries from whence it came.

But there had never been any rules about how to dispose of the Bundle. The presumption had always been that it would live forever. When the Bundle was alive and powerful, no one ever thought it would die; now that it was dying, no one cared what happened to it.

Old Man Mapateet spent long hours praying and considering what to do. He wondered if it should be buried with him so he could continue even in death to be its Keeper, but all across the countryside there were stories about white men looting Indian graves, some even before the flesh had gone from the bones. It would be terrible for all mankind if the Bundle should fall into the wrong hands and be mistreated—especially terrible for those who mistreated it.

Perhaps it would be better, Old Man Mapateet thought, to burn the Bundle so no one ever could mistreat it. But that in itself would be mistreatment and might bring disaster to his family and perhaps all of the Turtle Creek village or Nehawka people.

He considered giving the Bundle for caretaking to another tribe, but that again would be delivering it into the wrong hands, and innocent hands at that. Those wishing to help might suffer terrible consequences, and besides, why should they take care of the Bundle? No one among the Turtle Creek Nehawka, the people with whom it belonged, wanted it.

Several white men had offered to buy it from him but Old Man Mapateet shuddered at the thought. Selling something as sacred and powerful as the Sky Bundle was out of the question.

The only option that was at all acceptable to Old Man Mapateet, the last Keeper of the Sacred Bundle, was an offer from a museum in the east, the Densmore Museum in Boston, to keep the Sky Bundle for the Turtle Creek Nehawka. Seeks Wood was uneasy about this option, too. He worried about the potential disaster the transfer might cause the people at the museum. He had met and talked with many of the museum's representatives over the past two years and they struck Old Man Mapateet as good people. All the more reason not to bring disaster down on them.

The curators of the Densmore assured Old Man Mapateet that

they would do everything they could to treat the Bundle with respect and keep it whole for his people. He wanted to tell them all the things they needed to know, all the prayers and songs, but these too were sacred things that shouldn't fall into the hands of the wrong people. Again, they assured him that they would treat the materials with respect. They also told him they would have to publish in their books pictures and words about the Bundle and its ways, but Seeks Wood decided that what was holy about the Bundle was the Bundle itself and the songs themselves and the words themselves; pictures and words on paper were not the same.

He gave the Bundle and all the things that went with it—his pipe and tobacco pouch; a brush for applying coyote fat, valuable because of its rarity; an ancient robe; a hand-sized splinter of wood that he himself had removed from the blue post in the last of his family's earth lodges—to the museum for good keeping. He sat at the table without a word as the white men opened the Sacred Bundle, which no white man had ever done, and inventoried what was inside.

They called the Sacred Sky Bird a "southern parakeet" and the Sky Stone "a nugget of native copper." They carefully wrapped the burnt fragments of wood—"cypress" they called it—and the two halves of the Atlantic surf clam, the "fire shell" in which the Nehawka had always kept them, and the fragments of blue corn. They examined the tooth of the Thunderer Big Elk had found many years before and added to the other sacred objects in the bundle, and they said to Seeks Wood, "It's a mastodon tooth," clearly sure of their judgment.

"It's a Thunderer's tooth," Seeks Wood said, equally certain.

"No," the two white men laughed. "These are not unusual fossils. We are quite certain that it is indeed a mastodon tooth, but a rather nice one."

"What's a mastodon?" Seeks Wood asked.

"Well, it was a huge, extinct beast weighing perhaps four or five tons—more than this house, Mr. Mapateet! These great animals tore up the earth with their shovel-like tusks to get at their food, which they also ate by the ton. They were huge beasts, all right, and had very few natural enemies because of their size and defense mechanisms. In battle, they could kill even the ferocious saber-toothed tiger, a cat as big as a brown bear."

"Sounds like a Thunderer to me," grumbled Old Man Mapateet.

"Is there anything else that is a part of the Bundle?" the white men asked. For a moment Old Man Mapateet considered telling them the story of the Medal and how it had once been a part of the Bundle, but the heart had gone out of him and he didn't want to tell them anything more. The white men wrapped all the sacred things from the Sky Bundle and put them in a wooden box, put the box in the back of their wagon, and drove off, taking the Sacred Sky Bundle away from the Nehawka and Turtle Creek forever.

And like his people, the Nehawkas, Old Man Mapateet began to die inside.

He watched his people fall further and further into the white man's ways, mocking the old ways, and his pain grew. The news came from Wounded Knee in South Dakota that hundreds of innocent, unarmed Lakota had been shot down by soldiers with machine guns throwing two-pound exploding shells—women, children, and sick old men, blown to pieces by a people cruel beyond anyone's worst dreams. A Nehawka deer hunter came crying into the village one day and reported that people from the big museum in the city were on the burial hill digging and they had dug up many graves and taken many things from the graves of Nehawka ancestors.

And Old Man Mapateet realized that this had become a world where he no longer cared to live. The white man's world.

Not only was Old Man Mapateet dying, he preferred to die. He had decided to die. That was why he had come to Holy Hill. The Sky Bundle had died, his people were dying, and now he was glad to be dying. He closed his eyes, sang his death song, and died. Just like that. Just as old people used to do when the people cared for sacred things like the Sky Bundle.

For the last time, Old Man Mapateet sang:

Hey! My friends, I, Seeks Wood Mapateet, know this: every bird comes at death to earth.
Hey! You Thunderers, I, Seeks Wood Mapateet, know this: every summer wind that blows north, again blows south in the winter.
Hey! You Powers, I, Seeks Wood Mapateet, know this: a man leaves his lodge by its door and returns again by the same path.
Hey! My enemies, I, Seeks Wood Mapateet, know this: it is good to live, but it is fitting to die,
And this is a good day to die.

The year Old Man Mapateet died was one of the last times Nehawka elders gathered to name the year. They called it "The Winter the Sky Died." That winter was long and difficult; some of the elders attributed the hard times to the loss of the Sky Bundle. The spiritual winter of the Nehawkas was even longer—several generations long—and only a few Peculiars at Turtle Creek continued to practice the old ways—the Buffalo Dance and the songs of the Sky Bundle—and to tell the old stories about Black Deer who became Elk and his medal.

But there were always a few.

The Story of Black Deer

T wo old women from the north side of the lodge, the side in charge of the morning meal, were already up, stirring the fire. A young mother talked quietly to her baby as she removed the soiled cattail floss from the seat of his soft leather breeches. She reached into a deerskin pillow for a fresh handful. The grandfathers snored heavily in their beds behind the fire.

Small wonder. They had droned long into the night telling stories about Rabbit and Coyote. Most evenings they stopped their storytelling when the others went to bed, but the night before they had continued talking and laughing among themselves long after the last member of their audience had crawled under the warm buffalo robes.

Perhaps the people were sleeping well this morning because the summer crops had done so well. There were years when grasshoppers destroyed the crops, or there was no rain, and the storage pits were not filled for the winter. And there were years when the buffalo did not come near the village and the hunting parties that ventured out onto the grasslands west of the Smokey River found few animals. There was nothing to be done in those years but to try to gather more wild turnips or trap rabbits and to hope for an easy winter and better fortune the next year.

This had been a good year. The storage pits were full of dried corn and beans, the smoking racks groaned under the weight of dried squash strips, and there were some sheets of fresh meat and ribs from a young buffalo cow that had stumbled right into the village only a few days before.

This late in the fall, the days were short and the sun low in the sky. The shaft of light that usually pierced the earth lodge through the smoke hole had not yet made its appearance. The family compartments around the edge of the lodge were still dark, but in the center, in the communal area of the large lodge, the fire threw a soft light, burning with little sound, for the people of the lodge had taken care this year to gather plenty of good cottonwood—important for lodge fires because it does not throw sparks into people's laps, or into the food, or onto the bed robes.

The smell of sweet smoke filled the house and soon mixed with the aroma of the cornmeal and meat cooking for the morning meal. Slowly the thirty residents of the earth lodge, one of twelve in the village, began the day. They stepped down from the compartments around the perimeter of the lodge, folded their beds, and greeted the rest of the household. Sleepy-eyed and shivering as they stepped into the cold Plains morning, they joined others walking to nearby Turtle Creek to wash before eating.

On the path they talked about the fine weather and commented on the long storytelling session that had gone on the night before. There was a lot of laughter, several neighbors commenting that if the women of the lodge weren't such good cooks, the rest of the people could get some sleep. Since nothing better could be said of a lodge than that it was generous to its guests, the joking was more compliment than insult. It was not the sort of thing one spoke about, for fear of discouraging good fortune by mentioning it, but everyone clearly hoped it would not be long before there was another such evening of stories about Coyote, the Thunderers, the origins of the Sacred Rain-Fire Bundle, of the people themselves, and tribal heroes of the hunt and war.

The morning was chilly and frost stayed on the grass of the lodge roofs until the sun was well into the sky—a good morning to sit around the fire inside, to talk and to eat. There were important matters to discuss. The old men talked with disapproval about the five young men who had attacked a Pawnee village against the advice of the elders of the war council.

Some argued that it was simply the hot blood of young Nehawka warriors—as it should be—but others shook their heads and noted that the small, undisciplined band was once again under the leadership of Black Deer, a boy who had shown contempt for the elders and the ways of the people three times before. Black Deer, some said, was teaching the young boys disrespect. No, others said; it was Black Deer who was showing them courage, and who was clearly becoming a leader of the young Nehawka warriors in Turtle Creek.

Three autumns in a row Black Deer had rallied a small band of followers who made the eight-day journey to the Pawnee Village on the Plenty Potatoes River. They had left their village well before dawn, and headed toward the Pawnee villages to the west to strike coups. It was about the time of the first frost, during the moon called "When the Deer Paw the Earth," after the old men had counseled that this was not the time to rouse old angers.

By the time the boys' absence was discovered, they were out of sight of the village, well on their way to the west. The first and second days out, they walked proud and tall because they were still in the territory of their own people. They camped with a fire and loudly sang strong-heart songs to build their strength for the raid.

The third and fourth days the young warriors walked with more caution, watching the horizon for signs of Pawnee hunters or the smoke of an enemy camp. And nights they built a small fire well down in a creek bed. They sang no songs and slept less soundly. There were no boundaries in this endless grassland, no marks or borders, but the boys even in their youth knew that they were safe when they were close to home, more in jeopardy as they approached the Pawnee lands.

The fifth and sixth days they walked well below the horizon and scouted their route from the tops of hills, lying flat on their bellies in the crisp, red grass. That night there was no fire and one of them was always awake, well away from the camp, watching, watching.

The seventh and eighth days they crept along the lowlands, through the tallest grass and willow brakes, crawling, probing, watching, listening. Little matter if their caution made the adventure a day or two longer. In fact, the young braves relished the anticipation of the raid almost more than the attack itself.

This was the fourth time they had gone against this same village of the hapless Pawnee. How foolish the wretched Pawnee had looked the three previous times the boys ran through the village, slashing at ugly, dull Pawnee faces with their bows, humiliating their enemy beyond redemption. The Pawnee were barely wiping the sleep from their eyes when the boys struck.

Last year, as the raiders fled from the Pawnee village, Black Deer had run upon an old Pawnee warrior in a draw outside the village. The old man hadn't expected coup to be counted on him as he squatted there behind a plum bush with his leggings down around his ankles. When Black Deer hit the aged warrior across the face with his bow, he fell backward into his own waste. As the boys ran from the village, they could hear the old man howling with rage, "Hai, hai, hai!" a sound the young boys still imitated whenever they told the story of their strike against the Pawnee. A sure way of generating laughter in the Turtle Creek village was for one of the boys to see a young man of their own village heading off to the grasslands or woods to relieve himself and yell mockingly, "Hai! Hai! Hai!" The sight of the old Pawnee standing there stinking of his own smell, howling with indignation, had become deeply embedded in Turtle Creek storytelling.

The boys had tipped over the meat-drying racks of the Pawnee women on each of the previous three adventures, killed several of their dogs two years before, burned tipi covers three summers earlier, and the last summer, besides humiliating the Pawnee elder, had surprised a band of young women at the riverbank, doing their early morning bathing. They were homely wretches, being Pawnee, the Nehawka laughed, especially as they screamed, fell, and splashed through the water when the boys lifted their breechcloths and exposed themselves, showing their contempt, the women disgraced and violated simply by seeing the proud and superior nakedness of the Nehawka warriors.

Yes, the boys had come home from their previous three raids into Pawnee land full of stories of courage and humor. To be sure, the Turtle Creek Nehawka had been at peace with the Pawnee for almost three generations now, but boys must become men, and the raids reminded both the Turtle Creekers and the Pawnee how superior a people the Nehawka were, many of the older warriors argued, and the Pawnee would have their chance to raid in the spring—sometimes with greater effect, after all. It was only last spring that a Pawnee raiding party had come to the Turtle Creek village to capture a young girl for their Morning Star ceremony.

They had taken Three Song, a girl of particular beauty and good humor. The Turtle Creek villagers offered little resistance. They knew that the Pawnee were not raiding out of anger or cruelty or pride but because the powers of the stars, powers the Pawnee alone understood and served, required that a young woman of another tribe be tied to their scaffolds and shot through with arrows from the bows of Pawnee warriors.

The loss was painful for Turtle Creek village, of course, but this was the way it had always been and would always be and one could scarcely ignore the demands of the great Sky Powers that govern life and death, the buffalo and the corn, the sky and the earth. The Turtle Creek people had their own rituals to perform to guarantee that the world and its creatures functioned in proper order and peace, most notably the Buffalo Dance and the rituals surrounding the powerful Rain-Fire Bundle.

At any rate, the boys had always returned from their raids against the Pawnee with honor and distinction; concern about whatever risks had been taken was swept away by the stories of valor.

Until now. This time the results were different. This time Black Deer came back with shame for himself and his people, and possibly for the Sacred Rain-Fire Bundle. This time Black Deer had taken the Rain-Fire Bundle from the blue pole where it always hung in his lodge and carried it with him on the expedition, hoping to draw success from its influence on the weather and the sky.

Black Deer's family had always been the caretakers of the Rain-Fire Bundle, so if anyone had a right to use its powers, approved by the elders or not, it was Black Deer. Had his carelessness jeopardized the welfare of the Rain-Fire Bundle, and therefore the people, and therefore the nature of life itself? It was not a small question for the village.

Rashness ran in Black Deer's family, one elder noted. His father, Big Elk, and his grandfather, Two Elk, had been just as unreasonable. And yet the old men laughed as they remembered the exploits of Big Elk, because some of them had been the young warriors who followed him on his adventures—raids, treks to gather flint in the west and pipestone to the north, stories in the south and women from the east. Others coughed and frowned at the laughter, not at all appropriate where the welfare and power of the Sacred Bundle was in question.

Nothing had happened to the Bundle, the laughers argued. Black Deer had not carried it into the Pawnee village but left it with Early Cry and Birch Bark, who were too small yet to run through the village insulting the Pawnee but who had insisted on going along on the raid anyway. The very fact that the Bundle was hanging where it belonged, on the blue pole behind the fire in Black Deer's earth lodge, was an indication that it had never really been in danger. Besides, the Pawnee had behaved like men. Though Black Deer had been humiliated, that might be just what he needed to become a responsible member of the Turtle Creek village and the Nehawka tribe.

As the villagers learned later, the boys had camped a short run from the Pawnee village, just as the band under Black Deer had done the three years before. They dozed through the night and just as the very first blush of the sunrise began to show behind them, back toward their homes on Turtle Creek, they initiated their attack. Just as planned, the two youngest, Early Cry and Birch Bark, were left with the Rain-Fire Bundle and the few supplies the boys had brought with them, while the other three advanced on the village.

The three raiders crept quickly but carefully toward the village, knowing the path very well by this time as a result of their earlier adventures. They said nothing. There was nothing to say. They knew exactly what they would do and how. They could talk about their victory when they returned home.

The raid did not go quite as smoothly as the boys' plans. The Pawnee had discussed this matter of the annual raid of the Nehawka boys and the annoyance they had caused the village the past three years. Some of the Pawnee elders, including Four-Finger—the old man who had been surprised at his morning relief the year before—had called together the young men of the Pawnee village earlier in the fall and again told them the stories of how their mothers and sisters had been disgraced by having the private parts of Nehawka—by far the least attractive feature of a people known among the Pawnee for their general ugliness, the old men reminded them—waved at the helpless, noble women as they ran screaming from the river.

Coup had been counted among children and women and old men, the village elders growled to their young men. Young girls had been insulted and embarrassed, sacred girls of the blessed Pawnee people violated by insults from the basest of their neighbors, the Nehawka. The sanctity of the Pawnee village had been desecrated by the profane ways and words of Nehawka boys—Nehawka! Among whom not even the best warriors were worthy of much by way of respect from the Pawnee people, the real people, the *only* people.

The Pawnee boys heard the stories of the elders and understood that this must not happen again. They prayed and built a sweat lodge, where for four days they renewed their spiritual strength and sought guidance. For almost a full moon they rose early in the morning, painted themselves for battle, and waited. They scanned the grass to the east between the creek and the village and listened for the warning sounds of birds. Each evening they asked the elders to remind them again of the base ways of the Nehawka, so they would not grow tired and fall asleep the next morning. And they remained alert.

While Black Deer and his companions Digger and Ribs approached the village that morning through light ground fogs, the Pawnee boys hidden just over the tops of the earth lodges watched the trio coming from nearly a mile away. They held their voices, glad that they had gone through the trouble again that dawn to muzzle the dogs and tie them inside the lodge entrances. They watched Black Deer and his companions and smiled. They poked at each other with their bows and lances, anticipating what was certain to follow.

They saw Black Deer creep up within arrow-shot of the village and pause. They watched him sniff the air and listen. Passionately but silently they prayed that nothing would disturb the trap. Black

Deer signaled Digger and Ribs to follow him and he advanced into the village. The Pawnee boys knew from their own experience that the Nehawkas would go through the village almost to the other, western side, then make their dash of destruction and challenge back through to the east, toward their home and safety. The Pawnee boys watched.

Black Deer reached the last outlying lodges on the far western edge of the village and stopped. He crept to the meat-drying rack, obviously gauging the force and direction he would need to throw it onto the smoldering fire, a flying start to his fourth and most glorious raid on the pathetic Pawnee mice. He waved Digger and Ribs over to the fronts of other lodges where they could begin their run. He raised his hand, looked around once more, and then screamed at the top of his lungs, "Once again the noble and proud Nehawka spit on the Pawnee boys and girls of the shabby village along the river Plenty Potatoes."

It was, Black Deer considered later, too much to yell, for by the time he had finished and pushed the meat rack into the fire, the Pawnee boys were already charging down the steep sides of the lodges around him. He saw Ribs go down almost immediately under the blows of Pawnee sticks and bows; he couldn't see Digger, a lodge was between them, but he heard shouts and blows and assumed the same had befallen him.

Black Deer made a good effort at escape by dashing up the slope of the lodge behind him. The Pawnee boys were running down so fast they couldn't turn in their headlong path to pursue him, but one dark-faced boy twice Black Deer's size threw himself directly into the Nehawka raider. They both rolled back into the village. Black Deer jumped to his feet and tried to take advantage of the confusion by running back along the route he had originally planned, but by now women had come from the lodges and were coming directly at him. And dogs. He stumbled over a dog and tumbled head over heels, rolling to a stop at the feet of six or seven young women who began beating him with sticks. The blows disoriented him, and he was seized by many strong hands.

In a moment it was over. Pawnee victory cries filled the air as Ribs, Digger, and Black Deer were bound and brought together, surrounded by a crowd made up of every soul in the village. Children and women counted coup against them, dogs snapped at their shins and heels, women sang their victory trills, and warriors and old men laughed and insulted them. An old man approached them through the crowd; Black Deer recognized him as the man he had struck coup against the year before, the man who had fallen back into his own excrement, the man who had cried after them, "Hai! Hai! Hai!" The old man had a flint knife in his hand.

Black Deer began to sing his family's death song.

> Hey! My friends, I, Black Deer, know this: every bird comes at
> death to earth.
> Hey! You Thunderers, I, Black Deer, know this: every summer
> wind that blows north, again blows south in the winter.
> Hey! You Powers, I, Black Deer, know this: a man leaves his lodge
> by its door and returns by the same path.
> Hey! My enemies, I Black Deer know this: it is good to live, but it
> is fitting to die,
> And this is a good day to die.

This was the song of defiance that every warrior in his family threw at his enemies as he was about to meet death, and it had been that way as long as anyone could remember. He stood as tall as he could and sang directly into the face of the old man. When he finished his song, he cried, "Hai! Hai! Hai!" and looked at Ribs and Digger, also in the hands of strong captors. They didn't laugh this time, but they admired Black Deer's courage, singing in the face of death. They knew this good story would be told by many camp and lodge fire, among the Pawnee as well as the Nehawka.

The old man stepped up and spoke some words in the language of the Pawnee, a crude clatter of noise, not at all the musical language of his own people, Black Deer thought. The people of the village laughed a little and looked at the boys. The old man made more sounds of the rough language and the people laughed aloud this time, pointing at the boys, looking at them. The girls who had shrunk from them with fear when they were captured were laughing now too. Everyone was laughing. The dogs of the village smiled and laughed. Fire filled Black Deer's face. Fear and death he could understand and endure, but laughter . . .

Some women left the assembly, still laughing, and rushed into the lodges. They came out with packets and bundles, robes and feathers. Giggling, the girls opened the pouches and bags and approached Ribs, the youngest of the three. Two strong older warriors took him by his arms and untied the thongs from his wrists. An old woman brought a bowl of water and washed the dirt and blood from Ribs's face, body, arms and legs, laughing all the while like a coyote who has just killed a rabbit. Black Deer and Digger, still bound and helpless, looked on, trying to maintain their courage in the face of the tortures the Pawnee had planned for them.

When Ribs had been washed clean, two young women smoothed his hair with coarse-grass brushes and groomed it with sunflower oil. A young warrior came directly in front of the unflinching Ribs and renewed his face paint. A woman came forward and motioned for Ribs to lift his feet. When he resisted, two men forcibly lifted first his left and then his right foot while the woman put on his feet beautiful new moccasins, brightly decorated with porcupine quills.

Ribs looked uncertainly at Black Deer but Black Deer had nothing to counsel.

Someone pulled a fine new robe around Ribs's shoulders and replaced the tattered turkey feather in his hair with an eagle wing feather. A braid of sweet-smelling grass was pulled around Ribs's waist. A pouch of ground dried meat and dried berries was fastened over his shoulder with a strap. A strand of dried turnips was tied around his waist.

Four young girls pulled Ribs to the angle where the long lodge entrance met the round body of the building and held him there. He might have tried to escape the humiliation of being held captive by girls but he knew that alone, surrounded by the villagers, laden with all the fancy goods the Pawnee had draped on him, he wouldn't take more than a couple of steps before he would be brought down again. He would wait for Black Deer's move.

Digger was next, and his treatment proceeded in precisely the same manner—washing, painting, dressing, provisions, feathers. Desperately Black Deer searched his mind for any memory of stories he had heard about this Pawnee behavior. Was this another rite of the Morning Star in which the Pawnee would murder them on a scaffold to appease the Sky Powers? Strong arms thrust Digger into the corner of the lodge opposite Ribs. Digger too was surrounded by brazen Pawnee girls who stared directly into his face the way no Nehawka woman would ever do.

Then the Pawnee pulled Black Deer into the center of the crowd. He too was bathed and clothed, decorated and gifted as if he were being honored.

Honored!

"WAAAUGH!" Black Deer screamed as he realized what was happening to him and his friends. Again, "WAAAUGH!"—the only curse his people knew, the sound of an angry grizzly bear, the worst sound any man could ever hear.

Several warriors sprang forward in case Black Deer tried to escape or harm one of the people, but it was not necessary. Now Black Deer knew his fate and the humiliation of it was enough to make his knees weak and his stomach sick. He felt his bowels and bladder seethe but he choked his body back into control, not willing to add that humiliation to the rest.

The Pawnee were not going to kill him, or Ribs, or Digger. They were not going to torture them, or scalp them—as they would an honored enemy. A feared and respected enemy. The Pawnee were playing with them, mocking them, treating them as welcome, harmless guests.

Guests! It was as if the Nehawka had come to court Pawnee girls, as if they had come to exchange stories or trade robes, as if they had come to sit around the fire to eat and talk and smoke. "Kill me, you Pawnee dogs, but do not disgrace me like this," Black Deer snarled—or wanted to snarl. His voice came out a squeak and the Pawnee girls laughed again, even louder.

The old man who had fallen in his excrement waved to the crowd and said some words and the young girls brought Digger and Ribs to where Black Deer stood, his knees now trembling. The old man stood before them and talked with dramatic gestures, waves, and bows. He talked and talked until Black Deer felt sweat running down his naked legs into his new Pawnee moccasins. Now he had to fight even harder to avoid soiling himself in front of the Pawnee village. Tears of disgrace neared the surface of his eyes and he bit his lip to fight them back.

Another man came to the side of the old man and began in halting Nehawka to interpret his words. Black Deer thought to himself, "You Pawnee dogs can't speak a decent language yourselves, so you profane the beautiful Nehawka tongue," but he had no choice: he listened. "We people of the village on Plenty Potatoes want to thank you fine young Nehawka fellows for coming to visit us once again this harvest season. We look forward to your annual visits because you always give us so much laughter, especially our young women. Their minds might once have been on men of another village, but you have shown them why we Pawnee are famous for being the handsomest people. For many years, for many generations our people will tell stories about your little visits and what amusement they have brought us. Especially this one. We will name this winter 'The Winter Our Nehawka Friends Came to Visit and Made the Girls Laugh.' "

The old man paused until the laughter of his audience quieted and then, looking directly at Black Deer, said, "Please accept our gifts and take greetings to all our friends in the Turtle Creek village, especially your father, Big Elk."

Black Deer's mouth fell open and he surged forward in the arms of the men holding him. The old man laughed and said more words. "Yes," the interpreter laughed. "We know your father, Big Elk. He is a fine warrior, for a Nehawka. He deserves an obedient son. Or at least a handsome one. Perhaps some Pawnee paint, robes, moccasins, and food will improve you so that you can find yourself a woman, even though the girls of our village assure you that it will never be a Pawnee beauty."

At that point the village formed a long parade behind Black Deer, Ribs, and Digger, and singing led them out into the grassland toward where Early Cry and Birch Bark wept in fear for what had happened to their brave companions. Later Early Cry and Birch Bark would tell the people of Turtle Creek how terrified they had been when they heard the screams of the Pawnee in the village. And then, when the three warriors of their group hadn't returned for so long . . . None of which made Black Deer, Ribs, and Digger feel the least bit better about their humiliating ordeal.

As the caravan neared the creek bank where Early Cry and Birch Bark were still hiding, a small band of Pawnee warriors stood from their hiding places behind the boys where they had been waiting since almost dawn and seized them by their arms before they could so much as stand up. The Pawnee led the boys out onto the grassy plain to meet their captured companions. They were taking no chances: they wanted to be sure that Black Deer, Ribs, and Digger would not have a chance to conceal their humiliation. The Pawnee wanted the younger members of the raiding party to witness the full glory of the Nehawka warriors' return, complete with Pawnee clothing and food, surrounded by Pawnee girls.

With exaggerated ceremony and another long, interpreted speech, the boys were reunited. As they walked back eastward the Pawnee waved at them and shouted wishes for a safe journey and for a prosperous winter in Turtle Creek village. The boys walked what seemed to be half the distance back home before the sounds of the Pawnee girls' shouts were no longer in their ears.

When they were sure they were well out of sight of their well-wishers, they tore the Pawnee clothing from their bodies and washed away the paint from their faces and the oil from their hair. They would prefer to travel and return home naked than to wear Pawnee clothing one moment longer than necessary. That night as they lay naked on the grass, Black Deer, Ribs, and Digger wept. They spoke of not returning to the Turtle Creek village, but realized that would do no good, because everyone would know what had happened to them in the Pawnee village this terrible day. Even if they took Early Cry and Birch Bark with them and started a new Nehawka sub-tribe, or went to war against the Cheyenne and died, someone would tell their story in the Turtle Creek village after the first trading meeting with the Pawnee. The boys had only one brave deed left in them—going home.

When they reached the village, they told the story themselves. Whatever the older boys forgot, Early Cry and Birch Bark managed to remember and report in detail. The humiliation was so complete the elders decided no disciplinary action would be necessary. The Pawnee had done enough to the fractious boys.

Besides, there were other important concerns to attend to. Most important, it was time to make plans for the harvest dance of the Buffalo Clan and the winter buffalo hunt. When the buffalo began to come near the river valley, their hides heavy with winter hair, it would be time to gather meat and robes. Although the hunt was still a few months away, there was already anticipation. It was a big event for the village—not as important as the main hunt in the summer, but exciting nonetheless. Of course there would be fresh meat in the village, they thought, hoping that Father Buffalo would be as good to them this winter as Mother Corn had been in the preceding summer. The elders and full warriors would need to renew the rituals and prayers of the Buffalo Dance to perform it perfectly and ensure prosperity for the people.

There were many other preparations to be made—food for the feast at the Buffalo Dance, arrows and lances to be readied for the hunt, flint knives for skinning the slain buffalo, tipis for camping, skin pouches for carrying meat, pack racks for the dogs, pouches of corn, squash, and beans to eat on the hunt. And plenty of clothing, for hunting was hard on clothes—for the men when they killed and skinned the animals, for the women when they cut the meat and scraped hides.

As the day grew warm, more of the elders of the village came out to sit in the sun, out of the wind, and discuss all that had to be done. This was one of the last warm days of fall, and there was time to enjoy the season, too. Some of the older boys began a vigorous game of spear and hoops, dashing in and out among the lodges, throwing lances at the hoops, falling, arguing, whooping, cheering. It was better that they use up their energies like this than in making ill-timed raids on the Pawnee. Springtime would be plenty soon enough for warfare, and chances for success would be better then, the old men assured them.

The afternoon became warm enough for a few young women to brave the cold waters of the Smokey River backwaters to fish in the shallow ponds for arrowhead roots. Young men sat along the banks, throwing pebbles and suggestive remarks at them, but the girls just turned their backs and ignored them.

At last the girls threw back sharp words of annoyance, but the smiles on their faces betrayed the reality that the attention of the young men was not altogether unwelcome. "You women will have to stand in someone's robe tonight to get warm again," Black Deer shouted, becoming in turn the butt of his comrades' laughter when Afraid-of-Bird shouted back, "You'll be an old man before you are rid of the smell of Pawnee robes and a Nehawka girl will stand in a robe with you, Black Deer!" The other girls laughed and mocked Black Deer as he rose and walked back toward the lodges. He had hoped to win favor with the young women of the village with his raid on the Pawnee, but instead they laughed, just like the Pawnee girls.

Within the village, ever more pale blue smoke rose as the women took advantage of the warm, still day to finish the smoking and drying of meat from the buffalo cow and rings of squash and pumpkin from the last harvest. As they tended the smoldering fires under the drying racks, they leaned against the warm south walls of the earth lodge and repaired moccasins, decorated new winter clothing with colored porcupine quills, and exchanged gossip about the other lodges.

The women also had to be on their guard to watch the drying

racks, for it was part of the young boys' war games that they mounted raids against the racks, and with long sunflower stalks tried to steal rings of squash or—better yet!—pieces of drying buffalo meat. The women threatened and scolded, but as was the case with the girls at the pond, the women's smiles betrayed their tolerance for boys' pranks on such a beautiful fall day.

One party of men worked at replacing two rotting beams in the lodge, while others flaked flint tools and fashioned weapons, quietly singing to themselves. Village dogs ran with the sunflower-stalk warriors; one risked the blows of lances while he chased the sliding hoops. Still other dogs lazed in the sun, their eyes narrowing, their chins drooping ever closer to the dust.

As the sun began to throw long afternoon shadows into the village, a sudden, cold north wind blew flurries of cottonwood leaves between the lodges. Before long, sullen gray clouds hid the sun and the old men began saying they smelled snow. The dogs moved to the entrances of the lodges and whined, as if they too smelled the approach of winter. Women moved babies into the lodges and left them in the care of the grandmothers as they returned outside to clear the drying racks.

The boys had grown tired of the spear and hoops game and went to the pond to help the girls bring back the baskets of arrowhead roots. The water was cold enough this late in the year to make the harvest a chilly task, but now the crisp wind had made the wet chore very uncomfortable. Little matter. The baskets were full, and since the tubers do not store well, they would be eaten in that very night's soup. The girls had found a few freshwater clams in the shallow water too, and those who did not share the dietary prohibition of the Wind Clan against shellfish would savor them. You can be sure no one would risk violating those prohibitions, especially today when there was some question about whether the traditions of the Sacred Rain-Fire Bundle might have already been broken by Black Deer and his friends! As it was, some thought the approaching storm might just be punishment for the transgression.

Some of the youngest boys who had no baskets to carry gathered bundles of sticks for the evening cooking fire. Some of the girls carried water for the soup. No one returned to the village empty-handed. It was rarely necessary for a woman of the village to ask for water or firewood for her cooking. One of the first courtesies learned by the young of the Turtle Creek village was that a Nehawka does whatever needs to be done. No commands were given, for taking care of such problems was part of being a member of the village, a part of being one of the People, the real people, the *only* people.

Even as the women of the south side of the lodge began cooking the evening meal of fresh buffalo soup with arrowhead tubers and slices of roast pumpkin, the north wind blew harder, and colder. The warmth of the lodge felt good, and the pouches of dried food hanging throughout the lodge were reassuring. The smell of cooking was welcome too after the long day, but now it would be a race between finishing the meal's preparation and the children's going to sleep.

The day's games, the memory of the warm sun, and now the warmth of the bed robes combined to make everyone's eyelids heavy. Only the elders who had lounged and napped away a good part of the day in the sun had any energy left.

The evening meal was quieter than usual because of the general weariness, but a proper Nehawka always ate quietly. The subdued mood was broken only after the meal, when the young women and their mothers went back to the pond to get water for the evening, and those who stayed behind at the lodge heard the subtle notes of a love flute over the rustling of the wind.

Some young man, they knew, was hiding along the path to the water, hoping that the notes of his magic song would carry his message to the heart of the woman who heard it. Whether there was magic in the song or not, it was hard to conceal such things in the small village, and the woman for whom the song was being played, Afraid-of-Bird, knew that it was for her. She was grateful that it was dark along the water path so her sisters and mother could not see her blush or sense the quickening of her heart.

Afraid-of-Bird knew the song as Black Deer's, and the thought of it made her heart beat harder and faster. If only Black Deer hadn't been such a fool. She couldn't be sure herself if she was uneasy in her heart because a man was courting her so shortly after she had gained her womanhood, or because it was Black Deer, the joke of the village tonight.

What was worse, Afraid-of-Bird had heard the gossip that before Black Deer left on his foolish raid against the Pawnee an old woman had overheard him as he sang quietly, while working on arrow shafts, the song "My Thoughts Are on the Other Bed." She had scolded him and told him that he was too young to sing such songs, and maybe that was why Black Deer had gone on the war-path—to prove to others, even himself, that he was a man worthy of thinking about the other bed. Now he had proven only that he was still a boy.

In a lodge, the little girl named Willow giggled at the sound of the flute, recognizing it as her brother Black Deer's courtship song. Older men in the lodge smiled too, remembering the times they too depended on the sounds of the love flute to express their feelings. Surely this spring there would be intermediaries going from lodge to lodge, family to family, making arrangements for the young couple, ironing out the problems of clan politics and family disagreements.

Some time later Black Deer returned to his lodge, trying to conceal the flute in the folds of his robe, hoping to avoid the eyes of his family. Willow began to ask him where he had been, knowing of course the answer full well, but her mother quickly sent her on an errand to the other side of the lodge to avoid an embarrassment for Black Deer. His abortive raid against the Pawnee village had humiliated him enough for a while, his mother thought. It was not a good time for him to press his courtship. It would not be easy for him to find a family in the village willing to have him for a son-in-law.

Outside there were ever more signs of the approaching winter, although there was little of it in the warm, quiet lodge. Now and then there was the sound of a smoking rack or some tipi poles blowing to the ground and the dogs barking from every lodge. Winter was here. Those who stepped outside to relieve themselves brought back with them the chill of winter.

An elder from the neighboring lodge, Strikes-the-Ree, entered through the door flap, shook a few flakes of snow from his shoulders, and greeted the family, both sides of the lodge. He sat with the other old men in the west quarter of the lodge, with the fire between them and the door. The women went on about the tasks of putting the children to bed and getting the cots and bedclothing ready for the night.

Strikes-the-Ree opened his pouch of tobacco and filled his pipe. He gave the oldest woman of the household, Black Deer's grandmother, a small gift of sunflower oil for the hair of the women. There were sounds of thanks throughout the lodge. Strikes-the-Ree was not a rich man and his family was small, so his gift was particularly generous.

Strikes-the-Ree had been the last to leave the storytelling session the previous night, so the rest of the people of the lodge wondered if the warmth of the day had restored him sufficiently that he was back for more stories. Or was he here to discuss Black Deer's disgrace? Grandmother offered him a small piece of meat from the supper pot, and he accepted it in the horn spoon he had brought along. Nothing was said as he ate.

Finally Strikes-the-Ree lit his pipe, passed it to the man seated at his side, and broke the silence. "It is winter. Tomorrow we will be wading through snow from one lodge to the next."

There were nods of agreement around the lodge. Had the visitor come only to talk about the weather for a few moments? "But it is time for the snow. We shouldn't be surprised that it is finally here."

Again there were nods. Apparently the garrulous old warrior was here to speak about the weather. "And we should be grateful too that our winters are not as hard as they used to be long ago." Strikes-the-Ree paused, puffed at his pipe, and looked at the flakes of snow blowing in the lodge's smoke hole. "Long ago, you know, before we had the Rain-Fire Bundle"—he pointed to the tattered white coyote-skin packet hanging from the blue pole—"the people had no protection from the cold and the wind and the snow. You young people have to remember the old songs and words, so your children and grandchildren will have easy winters, too." He threw a pinch of cornmeal at the bundle, and blew smoke toward it from his pipe.

Perhaps Strikes-the-Ree was indeed here to talk about Black Deer. "We were given the Rain-Fire Bundle by Coyote when he killed Father Winter. Yes, kinsmen, winters were once much harder. And longer and colder, before Coyote killed the giant called Father Winter. Now we have only Mother Winter to deal with. Coyote, you see, was living with his blind grandmother, and she said to him, 'You filthy, ragged no-good! You never bring food or honor to our lodge. Go out there and bring us some food. But don't you go to where the giant Father Winter lives.' As usual Coyote paid little attention to his grandmother and he started off . . ."

Around the large lodge there were smiles. Tonight there would be stories. Good stories.

Mother Winter or not, that winter was hard and long. The snows piled up around and between the lodges and the supply of firewood grew short. The supply of food was not adequate and the snows were too deep for the people of Turtle Creek village to venture out onto the hills in search of buffalo. Bellies grew thin and babies cried.

The elders held councils and decided that the difficulties of that season might be a result of Black Deer's unauthorized war party with the Rain-Fire Bundle. Perhaps the power of the Bundle was displeased. And yet there was no one in the village more suitable to become keeper of the Rain-Fire Bundle than Black Deer. If the harsh winter was indeed Black Deer's fault, then, they reasoned, the solution might be Black Deer, too.

Black Deer was called into the elders' meeting and told that while he was overdue at any rate to become a man—or at least to behave like a man, to take on the obligations of a man—the matter had become a good deal more urgent now: the people could not wait for him to mature, because he might have offended the Rain-Fire Bundle. To save his people, he would have to become a man. Now.

The village was told they must aid Black Deer to become a man so they could avoid winters like this terrible one, and Black Deer, *despite his foolish past, was never again addressed as a boy. His name became Elk, and the Turtle Creek Winter Count called this "The Winter So Hard, Black Deer Became Elk."*

▸ ▸ **PART II:** *Visions and Dreams*

Through the winter Elk sat with the old men, learning the stories, rituals, ways, secrets, customs, words, and names of the Rain-Fire Bundle followers. When he had learned everything the elders could remember, they took down the ancient Rain-Fire Bundle from the blue support post in Elk's lodge, prayed the prayers, burned white cedar, put powdered meat and cornmeal on the sacred buffalo skull at the west end of the lodge, threw meat and corn to the four directions, to the sky and the earth, expressed their understanding of their complete helplessness and ignorance before the Thunderers, asked the women of the lodge to leave, and opened the Rain-Fire Bundle.

Elk was full of fear as he saw for the first time the sacred and powerful objects of the Bundle. He knew that the Bundle could cause tornadoes and blizzards, or blow away mosquitos with a gentle breeze. He knew that water creatures were its kin and lightning its sign. He understood that Rain-Fire Bundle followers could not eat shellfish because they are children of the sky, just as lightning is a child of the sky, or touch the blue-green war paint that came from certain rocks, for fear of bringing storms or worse.

Elk struggled to push thoughts of Afraid-of-Bird from his mind as he wrestled with the crushing complexities of becoming a man and mastering the secrets of the Rain-Fire Bundle, both in the same winter. His struggle with himself was not simply from his new feelings of responsibility toward his people, but because the sixteen seasons of youthful arrogance he had enjoyed to their fullest limit had actually ended in the Pawnee village on Plenty Potatoes River. His embarrassment was more than most of his friends and relatives knew. He found that the pain of humiliation in this one failure far exceeded the pride he had previously felt in all his victories.

Elk heard nothing, of course, but he knew that the villagers still spoke of his failed raid and how the Pawnee had mocked him as a warrior. He knew that he could not ask a woman to stand in his robe with him, nor offer her father horses for her, because he would bring the shame of his immaturity with him to the girl's family and lodge. Afraid-of-Bird spoke to him, kindly, and he felt that she respected his work with the Rain-Fire Bundle and his apprenticeship with the elders during that long winter, but his penance was not, in his own mind, complete.

For one thing, Elk needed a vision. To some, a vision came easily. Others—his uncle Otter, for example—never had a vision, though they went to Holy Hill, the center of the earth, many summers in their youth. A vision did not guarantee community respect or admission to tribal societies, nor was the lack of a vision a handicap, but it was important for every young man to prepare himself for a vision and offer himself to the Thunderers for their gift.

Every young man, about the time he was ready to become a warrior, would take a robe and climb the steep path up Holy Hill. For four days the boy prayed on the hill, concentrating his thoughts not on his hunger or thirst, not on his loneliness or the mosquitoes or the heat of the sun or the cold of the night or his fear of the night spirits and Thunderers, but only on his awe of the Thunderers and of the other mysteries of which he was becoming increasingly, and quickly, aware—life, death, the passage of the seasons, the gifts of buffalo and corn, the beauty and power of the Nehawka people.

If the Powers gave him a vision, he would come down from the hill happy, although exhausted, afraid, and maybe even sick, because he had had a glimpse of the world beyond, like those whose spirits made short journeys to the other world before their bodies died. It was not necessary or even common for the boy himself or even the elders to understand the vision. "We are too small, even the entire village, even the entire Nehawka tribe, to understand the smallest part of the Powers," Strikes-the-Ree had told him. "And the smallest part is all we *can* see in our visions. All that is important is that we see and remember."

Strikes-the-Ree showed him the small black arrowhead, made by the little people who lived on the earth before the Nehawka lived here, he had been given during his vision many winters before. Strikes-the-Ree wore the arrowhead in a small deerskin pouch tied in his hair behind his left ear, just as he had seen in his vision. Most of the men of Turtle Creek village had small, sacred objects they had been given in their visions; a few considered their gifts to be luck-bringers or powerful weapons, but most knew only that the gifts were given to them with no explanation, no instruction.

And there was the vision-gift of Elk's father, Big Elk. Under his wolf-skin pillow, he carefully protected a soft deerskin pouch about the size of his fist. In it was a shiny white tooth of a Thunderer that he had found while climbing Holy Hill for his vision quest. The Turtle Creek villagers had always thought it particularly auspicious that Big Elk had not even reached the crest of the hill before he was given his vision-gift. The sacred object was obviously a tooth, but a tooth larger than anyone had ever seen before; it was the tooth of a Thunderer, perhaps a first tooth that was lost when the Thunderer was only a child.

When the winter was gone and the willows had become yellow-green, though the nights were still cold enough to leave ice on still water, Elk announced to Big Elk and Otter that it was time for him to go to Holy Hill, and the two old men agreed. They helped him tie his robe with deerskin thongs and painted him with symbols of wind and sky, the signs of his family and lodge. They helped him pray and walked with him to the foot of the high hill overlooking the river.

When he reached the top of the hill, he looked back and saw that the two old men were still watching him from far below. He turned his back to them and sat on his robe. He sang his strong-heart song and prayed:

Hey! You Thunderers who shake the sky,
 I, Elk, your kin, am here.
Hey! You Powers who gave us corn and buffalo,
 I, Elk, your kin, am here.
Hey! You mysteries who fill women's bellies with our young,
 I, Elk, your kin, am here.
Hey! You creatures of the sky,
 I, Elk, your kin, am here.
Hey! You creatures of the water,
 I, Elk, your kin, am here.
Hey! You creatures beneath the earth,
 I, Elk, your kin, am here.
Hey! You creatures of four legs,
 I, Elk, your kin, am here.
Hey! You Powers of the Four Directions,
 I, Elk, your kin, am here.

He offered some of the small pouch of blessed cornmeal Big Elk and Otter had given him to the four directions, to the sky, the earth, and the river far below the hill.

Hey! I, Elk, am here, seeking a vision.
Hey! I, Elk, throw aside the games of boys and wait to take the secrets.
Hey! I, Elk, will kill our enemies.
Hey! I, Elk, will lie with a woman . . .

Elk struggled with all his strength to keep his thoughts focused on the Powers, not to let them stray to images of Afraid-of-Bird's black eyes, shiny hair, and firm breasts, so beautiful when she came out of the ponds after picking arrowhead roots or cattails . . .

"Hey! Elk shouted loudly. And again,

Hey! It is I, Elk.

Through the day Elk prayed and sang his songs, rejecting thoughts of his family, friends, lodge, and Afraid-of-Bird. As night fell, he could hear sounds from the village—the barking of dogs, the laughter of women on the way to the ponds to collect water, the shouts of children at play. He sang his songs again, to drown out the sounds that might divert his attention. He smelled smoke from the village's fires, and his stomach reminded him that he had not eaten that day. He laughed at his stomach and told it that it might as well put its mind to better things because he, Elk, would not eat for the next three days either, unless a vision came to him earlier.

But it did not. He did not sleep that night so he would not mistake a dream for a vision or a vision for a dream. His discomfort, the cold of the night, his loneliness, his fear made the task easy. The next day was warm and sunny, however, and his eyes fought to close. He pricked at his arms and legs with a small, sharp rock to keep himself awake, and rivulets of blood mixed with his sweat and Big Elk and Otter's paints.

The second night on Holy Hill it was harder to keep awake because the pain of hunger and thirst began to dull. Elk fell asleep several times but he could tell from the movement of the stars that he did not sleep long, and fortunately he did not have dream-visions that might leave him uncertain of what had happened on his quest.

The third day rain fell on Elk, washing away the blood and

paint. He shivered in the cold, thanking the Thunderers for this help in his struggle to stay awake. The rain eased as night approached and Elk knew that he couldn't fight sleep much longer. The first time he dozed off, he awoke with a jerk when a coyote approached him and said, "You may sleep now like a boy and come back next year to seek a vision, or you may listen to my songs and receive a gift."

Elk sat bolt upright with a jerk. He looked around him but could see no coyote. Had it been a dream? Had it been a vision? He heard a coyote singing on the river bottoms before him. He sang a line from his strong-heart song and the coyote answered with its own song. The exchange encouraged Elk. He found new strength and was still awake when the sun rose the next morning. He wondered if Coyote would be his lifelong ally, as he had been his father's.

The fourth and last day of his vigil Elk slept. He tried, but his strength was gone. He was so weak from hunger he wondered if he could stand and walk back to the village at the end of the day, when the sun set and vision time ended. His tongue had swollen in his mouth, for he had not had water since the rain the day before. He couldn't tell whether the blurring of his eyes was from hunger or exhaustion. Most of all, he felt the disappointment of his failure in a vision quest. Perhaps even the Powers felt contempt for him as a result of his humiliation at the hands of the Pawnee the previous harvesttime.

When the sun went over the hill far to the west, over the Turtle Creek village behind him, Elk wept women's tears. At least he had been a man in his endeavor. He had stayed the full four days; he had not retreated, had not crept back into the village for food and the shelter of his mother's lodge. He would come down from Holy Hill more a man, although this year he had had no vision.

Elk gathered up his robe, bound it with Otter's deerskin straps, and slowly, painfully began the long walk down the hill into the dark night. Three times he stumbled and fell, the last time cutting his knee on a sharp rock projecting from the hillside. He lay there on the hillside, covered with dirt, more tired than he had ever been in his life, disappointed, hurt. For a while he considered unrolling his robe and spending the night where he had fallen, rolled up into a clump of plum bushes.

No, if he did not return, his father and Otter might come looking for him. It would not be disgraceful to come down from the hill without a vision, but it would be unlike a Nehawka man to lie in a pile where he fell, like an opossum. Elk struggled to his feet and started again down the hill, but not on the path that young men had followed for generations. In his fall, Elk had lost the path and in the dark, cloudy night, he could not find it again. He staggered back and forth, hoping to intersect the path, but did not. He knew that he could get down the hill without it, but the trees, bushes, canyons and drop-offs would complicate the descent, especially in the dark, especially in his weakness.

He stumbled and slipped his way down the hill for what seemed like most of the night. He should have reached the village long before. He was lost. In the light he could surely find his way—Elk knew the land for a day's travel in every direction from the village as surely as he knew precisely where every post and pole of his lodge stood—but still, he hoped for the dignity of a proper return to his village tonight.

Again and again he fell into the gullies and washes that raked Holy Hill's flanks and had to crawl his way up the steep scarps of the other side. It became increasingly clear to Elk that not only would he not make it to his village tonight, if he didn't find his way home soon, he might not be able to make it at all. He began to consider the very real chance that he might die tonight. He sat on a small hummock of dirt and again wept. This would be the final humiliation for his family, for him to die while trying to walk home from his vision time. He sang his death song, just as he had done in the Pawnee village when he was still a boy the fall before:

Hey! My friends, I, Elk, know this: every bird comes at death to earth.
Hey! You Thunderers, I, Elk, know this: every summer wind that blows north, again blows south in the winter.
Hey! You Powers, I, Elk, know this: a man leaves his lodge by its door and returns by the same path.
Hey! My enemies, I, Elk, know this: it is good to live, but it is fitting to die,
And this is a good day to die.

In his confusion he wondered if he was close to the village and his friends and relatives would hear him, and laugh at him for losing his way, magnifying his disgrace. He sang the rest of his song quietly, to himself and the Powers.

Elk rose and felt a steep hill before him. He looked at the sky and for a moment the clouds cleared enough that he could see a sliver of a moon before him. He was headed in the right direction. His confidence restored, Elk clawed his way up the hill and when he reached the top, he stood and peered around him to see if he could spot a landmark. He saw little, and what he did see told him nothing.

Then he heard voices. He paused and listened, but his gasps and the beating of his heart drowned out the faint sounds he was sure he had heard. Elk held his breath. The voices came from beneath his feet. He looked down. He saw light deep in the ground, fire. He heard the voices again but could not understand what they were saying. A blue-green flash exploded in his face and he saw a bird with brilliant plumage, just like the bird of the Rain-Fire Bundle, except the feathers of this bird were not dulled by death and time.

The bird flew at his face repeatedly until Elk lost his balance. Elk began to fall—not to the ground but as if from high, high above. Elk was flying, and the blue-green bird flew alongside him. "The sky," the bird said to Elk. The bird pulled a feather from its breast with its beak and handed it to Elk with its talons. "The sky," it said again. Elk took the small feather and was surprised that it was so heavy. Elk flew on with the bird. The heavy feather made him fly even higher and faster. Despite the feather's weight, it continued to give Elk the power to fly. Elk was confused, ecstatic, frightened—all at once.

"The sky," the bird said to Elk, flying again into his face.

"The sky," and suddenly Elk slammed into the earth. The bird was gone and there was no longer the lightness of flight, only the pain of a heavy fall. Screaming filled Elk's ears, and fire was everywhere. "Elk! Elk! Elk!" voices howled. "Elk! Elk! Elk!" Had he fallen into the secret lodge of the animals, where they decide the course of man? Was he in the bowels of the Hill-That-Eats-People? Had he been seized by the River Monsters and carried to the fires of their home?

When Elk awoke he was in his own bed. His mother and father, Otter, Willow, others of his lodge and the village were sitting about the lodge, watching him. He tried to sit up. Pain filled his every movement. He saw smiles of relief as his kin and friends saw that he was alive.

"Welcome back, Son," Otter and Big Elk, both spiritually his father, said in unison.

Elk tried to talk, but his mouth was still so dry and swollen he could make only small animal sounds. At least he had not dreamed the part about going up to Holy Hill for a vision. He could be sure of that.

Otter pushed him back onto his bed and held a wad of wet cattail down to his lips. Elk sucked at it. Elk struggled to speak and tell Otter what had happened, or more accurately, to *ask* Otter what had happened; Otter knew more about visions than anyone else in the village because he had not had one and had therefore spent more time and energy considering them. Elk haltingly told him of the long, fruitless wait for a vision, and the words of the coyote. He told Otter and Big Elk about being lost on the path down from Holy Hill and climbing the last, steep hill between him and his home. He told them about the blue-green bird, the one from the Rain-Fire Bundle, and what the bird had said. Elk spoke of flying and falling.

Then Otter and Big Elk told Elk what had happened at the end of his journey. Elk had fallen through the lodge's smoke hole, directly onto the cooking fire. Miraculously, he had fallen the distance of three men's height but had only a few bruises and burns to show for the tumble, and a lame hand.

Elk squeezed back tears of disappointment. On his return from a search for a vision he had gotten lost in his own village and fell into his own lodge's smoke hole. He would leave the village at once and become a lone man on the Plains—certain death—he cried to Otter and his father. No, no, they assured him. His story of the blue-green bird and flying, the strange message "the sky," and the miracle that lost in the night he had stumbled into the buffalo-head-size hole that returned him to his family's lodge was the kind of thing Coyote would do to an ally (or perhaps not, they admitted) but scarcely the circumstances of disgrace. This, Otter and Big Elk agreed, was precisely that of which visions were made—profound truth easily confused with buffoonery, discovery that might as easily be error, blessings that are half curse, mysteries, questions, doubts, and fear. Otter and Big Elk talked about Elk's experience while he listened, his tongue still too heavy for talk.

"It's our death song!" Otter sputtered. "Elk's vision is about the Nehawka death song. Coyote came to him and sang with him, and like Coyote, every word of the death song was twisted, changed, mocked. Hey! My friends, I know this: every bird comes at death to earth, we sing, but Elk has learned that the Sky Bird in the Rain-Fire Bundle did not come to earth when it died. It not only lies in the Sacred Bundle, where it has been above the ground many, many generations since it died, but Elk's dream says that the bird's spirit still flies over this lodge."

"Hey! You Powers, I know this, says the song we taught Elk when he was only a child, a man leaves his lodge by its door and returns by the same path. Elk is now the only man of his people who will die having left his lodge and not returning by the same path!"

Big Elk laughed at Coyote's devious sense of humor. "But what of the certainty of death our song speaks of? What of the return of the winds? Hey! You Thunderers, I know this: every summer wind that blows north, again blows south in the winter, we sing. Hey! My enemies, I know this: it is good to live, but it is fitting to die. What of these parts of our song and Elk's vision?"

"Perhaps the Powers are telling us Elk will not die. His shame may become his immortality. The story of his raid on the Pawnee village—" Elk groaned, not in the pain of his body but the pain of his spirit. Otter patted his shoulder and pushed him back on his robe. "His story is known throughout this village and I suspect that the Pawnee are making the most of it, too. Even when Elk is dead, his story may live on with our people like the stories of the Orphan."

Elk groaned again and protested.

"Of course you don't want to be remembered like that, Elk, but Coyote mocks those he loves. And Coyote is a powerful ally. And as it should be in a vision, Coyote is most easily understood when he is impossible to understand, most often misunderstood when his message is obvious."

"What about the constant exchange of winter and summer winds we sing about in our song?" Big Elk wondered.

"That may be a mystery we will have to wait to understand, or that we will never understand," said Otter, looking at Elk and checking the cuts and burns on his face. "Think about last night, Elk. Think about what you might have forgotten. Think about your vision whenever you can. Try to remember every detail about it. Tell us, your fathers, what you remember. We will try to help you understand it, or accept not understanding it. Did Coyote say anything more to you, or sing anything that you might have forgotten to tell us?"

Elk thought a moment and shook his head.

"Did you see anything else? Other animals? Did you hear any more voices?"

"Voices in the Animal Council, in the ground. Probably only voices here in the lodge," Elk said through swollen lips.

"Otter and I will pray for understanding of that," said Big Elk. "Did the Sky Bird say anything more?"

Elk quickly sat up on the bed. He groaned at the agony that shot through his tortured body. "Yes, yes," he said through the pain. "Took feather from breast, gave it to me so I could fly. But it was very heavy, even though it helped me fly. I held onto the feather. It was heavy and yet it took me higher into the sky. I . . ." Elk looked down at his right hand, clenched in a taut fist as it had been since he fell through the lodge's smoke hole earlier in the night.

Otter and Big Elk took his hand. They had assumed that the fist they could not open was the result of a broken bone or torn tendon Elk had suffered in his fall. Big Elk pushed Elk's fingers open slowly, firmly. Elk flinched in pain. Otter began to sing Elk's strong-heart song, and Elk joined him—

Hey, I am Elk, and I water the grass with your blood.
Hey, I am Elk, and I make your women cry and dream.

Elk's mother brought warm water from the cooking pot. Big Elk hoped it would soothe and loosen Elk's fingers, clenched so tight Big Elk could not pry them open. They did not open. Strikes-the-Ree joined the group and considered the problem of Elk's clenched fist. He heard Elk's vision and listened to Otter and Big Elk's interpretation, nodding in agreement all the while. "Sing Rain-Fire Bundle songs," Strikes-the-Ree advised. "Sing Rain-Fire Bundle songs. Everything here is about the Rain-Fire Bundle. Elk's vision is about the Rain-Fire Bundle. Coyote changed our death song into a Rain-Fire Bundle song. The Sky Bird, the coyote, the feather. It is all about the Rain-Fire Bundle, and Coyote will be Elk's ally."

Big Elk began to sing Rain-Fire Bundle songs, Otter joined him, and then Elk. Strikes-the-Ree, not a member of the lodge, was not entitled to sing Rain-Fire Bundle songs but he jerked his right hand in rhythm, as if striking a drum, as the Rain-Fire Bundle people filled the lodge with their sounds.

Elk's hand slowly fell open. Clenched in it was a small blue-green stone about the size and shape of a baby's finger. It was like stone but it was heavier than most stones. As Elk had reported, the pebble was exactly the color of the feathers of the bird in the Rain-Fire Bundle. It was a sky rock. A rock that flies. A feather-rock. Elk had had his vision, and, as was always the case, the Powers had given him a gift to sweep away all doubt.

Otter, Big Elk, Strikes-the-Ree, and Elk stared at the stone in Elk's hand. Otter renewed the singing of the Rain-Fire Bundle songs, and the others joined him. Tears ran down the men's faces as they realized the mysteries that had just passed over them and through them. When they finished their singing, they sat silently together, tears streaming down their cheeks. When the women of the lodge knew the singing of the sacred songs was finished, they came back into the lodge and found the men still sitting, still crying, still staring at the heavy blue-green stone.

Knowing and yet not knowing, not knowing and yet knowing, the women screamed their trills of victory. If the men could not know, the women certainly would never know. But Elk had had a vision, and brought home a dream and a gift to his people, the Nehawkas of Turtle Creek.

"Bring your Rain-Fire Bundle to him," Otter told Big Elk, but Elk rose from his bed and said, in a loud, firm, full, man's voice, "No!" The people stopped and looked at him for direction. "*Sky* Bundle. It is no longer the *Rain-Fire* Bundle. It is the Sky that the bird of Elk's dream spoke of. Now it has become the Sacred Sky Bundle of the Nehawkas. It is a gift to our people from the Thunderers. It is Elk's vision-gift."

Without hesitation, Big Elk took the sacred bundle from the blue pole, handed it to Elk, and said, "And you, Elk, are its keeper." Elk opened the white coyote-skin pouch and added the blue-green sky stone of his vision to the fire shell, the corn, and the Sky Bird inside.

Big Elk was slow to approach Elk as he worked at the bundle. Everyone could see that Elk was acting in a sacred way, that he was doing what he knew how to do by virtue of his vision, not his training. When people are controlled by the Powers, like the Buffalo Dancers when they are buffalo and no longer people, it is not wise to move too rashly: such powers are dangerous, even when they are in the souls of friends and kin.

Big Elk moved slowly toward Elk, hunched over the Sky Bundle, working with its contents, singing its songs. "Elk, my grandfather"—Big Elk used a rare term of respect for his son— "I beg your consideration to add to the sacred objects of the powerful Sky Bundle this gift of my vision." Big Elk handed his son the leather pouch with the Thunderer's tooth he had protected under his pillow since the day of his own vision.

Elk smiled at his father but said nothing. He took the heavy pouch and added it to the contents of the bundle when he again folded it.

That day the people of Turtle Creek sang and feasted and celebrated their good fortune. Today there was not only a new man in the village, but a new and obviously powerful gift: the Sacred Sky Bundle of the Nehawkas.

WINTER COUNT

On the hunt that winter the elders decided to record the name of that year in the winter count as "The Winter Elk Flew."

► ► **PART III:** *Wind and Sky*

The renewal of the power and rites of the Rain-Fire Bundle as the Sky Bundle was not welcomed by everyone. For several generations, as the Rain-Fire Bundle had faded in its influence within the village's daily life and ritual, the Buffalo Dancers had grown ever stronger. More and more Nehawka throughout the tribe and not just at Turtle Creek came to believe there was power in dancing as a buffalo, in taking on the body and soul of the great creature that provided home, clothing, tools, nutrition, indeed, life for the tribe.

It was intoxicating to become for a night one of the mighty Father Buffalo, to feel the strength of those great shoulders and the sacred pulse of the noble beast's heart in one's own breast. The Buffalo Dancers were not happy to see their followers turn back to the Sky Bundle.

Elk, who had himself become a Buffalo Dancer, insisted that his own allegiance to that proud society was as strong as it had ever been, that there was no reason at all why a good Nehawka should not have room enough in his heart to hold many sacred paths to knowing. How could anyone possibly reject this gift? Why would anyone insist that the people should have only one cache of dried meat when they could have two, have only five braids of turnips when they could have twenty, have only half a parfleche of dried corn when they could have a hundred? Similarly, why would the people want only one sacred gift, the Buffalo Dance, when they should take all the gifts that the Powers offered—the Sky Bundle, the Orphan stories, the Crazies Society, the Soldier Society?

The Buffalo Dance?

Elk had worked hard to erase the disgrace of his disastrous raid on the Pawnee village, and no one laughed at him any longer in his presence. Still, many of the old people felt that the disgrace of his youth lived on and that this popular rush to a new Sacred Bundle was only another example of his family's bad habit of moving too quickly without appropriate consultation with the people or the Powers. Most of the people in the village did not spend a lot of time considering such political and theological problems; all they knew was that this new concern with the Sky Bundle was causing trouble, and the village did not need trouble.

But there is no life without trouble. The arguments went on through the summer hunt and harvest. Elk's life was filled with Sky Bundle rituals and debates with elders about the Buffalo Dance. His newfound maturity and responsibility were most threatened the day that two elders confronted him and said, "You have brought the Sky Bundle to us, Elk, and you have had a powerful vision. But you are young and strong, too, and you should take a wife. How can it be that you are powerful enough to be a Buffalo Dancer and Keeper of the Sky Bundle but not strong enough to take a woman into your robes?"

Elk smoldered. "If I could take just a little time out of atoning for the stupidity of my youth, a few moments from the burdens of the Sacred Bundle, a day or two from arguing with the Buffalo Dancers, and maybe a morning now and then from having to explain why I have not taken a wife, there is every chance that by now I would have taken two or three wives."

The old men looked at him, thought a moment, snorted, and shuffled off toward their lodge. He had apparently answered their questions, but that still didn't give him the time to begin a courtship of Afraid-of-Bird, who was well into her marrying age and growing more beautiful every day. Still, Elk had to erase his shame and take care of his duties to the tribe and the Powers before he assumed the responsibilities of a woman. And children.

Soon. Soon.

Elk's old friends and raiding companions watched him at his labors. They had had their visions, were successful hunters, and had gone on some victorious war parties. They sympathized with Elk's struggles, but there was nothing they could do. Though they too had carried away the gifts of the Pawnee on that terrible day years before, they had not been the leader of the abortive war party and were therefore not burdened with its consequences like Elk. Nor were they born to a responsibility like caring for the Sky Bundle. Nor had their visions complicated their lives, as Elk's had his. They had to go on with their lives, and they did.

They too watched Afraid-of-Bird mature, a fine, beautiful Nehawka woman. At the games, games Elk was too busy to attend, they watched Afraid-of-Bird dance. They saw her hips sway rhythmically under her soft deerskin dress. They saw the firelight shine on her black hair, made all the shinier with sunflower oil. They watched her white teeth as she laughed, and her black eyes. They knew Afraid-of-Bird would be a prize for any man, and they knew that Elk hoped to take her to his lodge. They suspected that she hoped the same.

It was also clear to them that this was not likely to happen. Not very soon at any rate. Elk was preoccupied with matters of politics, the Sky Bundle, and the Powers, and as a result, a fine Nehawka woman was sleeping alone, and beautiful Nehawka children were not being born, as was fitting and proper. Elk's two old friends developed a plan to correct this matter.

It was Digger who first approached Afraid-of-Bird. Afraid-of-Bird was in large part attractive because of her strong virtue, which made approaching her all the more difficult. Like a good, moral Nehawka woman she was never alone away from her lodge, since it was understood that any woman who wantonly walked alone was inviting a man to pull her onto the grass and be a man with her. Afraid-of-Bird issued no such invitations.

Digger watched her in her daily routines, learning and remembering where she went and when and with whom. He watched for times when she might be caught alone, even for a moment, times when he might whisper five or six words to her, or even catch her eye. He followed the women to the creek morning and evening when they went for water. From behind trees and plum and chokecherry bushes he watched Afraid-of-Bird gather wood for her lodge. Lounging at the entrance of his own family's lodge, Digger watched Afraid-of-Bird visit her relatives in other lodges.

There was no opportunity for him to talk to her, but the very act of his seeking her out was a sign to her. Others told her that Digger was watching her. She caught glimpses of him. She began to think of ways she could make herself available for a word or two, to learn what he had to say or ask. Was he planning to court her? Digger was a pleasant enough boy but she wanted to wait a bit longer, in hope . . . Well, in hope.

Or was Digger approaching her as a representative of another suitor, an old friend who was too shy or perhaps a bit out of favor in village politics? Perhaps . . .

Afraid-of-Bird was gathering wood with the women one day when a rainstorm broke and everyone made a mad dash for the village, and for the brief moment that she was running alone, unwatched by her mother and her aunts, Digger sprang from his hiding place in the brush and ran alongside her just long enough to whisper to her: "The man you want will meet you where the creek flows into the Smokey River the night after the next full moon. I will help you." And Digger fell back into the brush before any of the other women could see him.

Afraid-of-Bird could scarcely contain her excitement over the next days. She watched Elk as he moved through the village, to see if he might glance her way or even give her a sign. Perhaps she could give him a sign that she would be at the meeting place, although it was clearly a risky venture.

Eloping was like Elk—or at least the old Elk. She was a little surprised that in the midst of his long struggle to regain favor with the people, he would again move rashly, in violation of village modesty. A proper warrior stood in his robe with the woman he was courting, at her lodge, where the village could see and assess his intentions. He sat at the woman's father's fire so her family could come to know him and measure his worthiness as a household member.

Young people of Turtle Creek did occasionally elope, and when they returned a few days later they were accepted back into the village as a married couple, because the very act of a woman leaving her lodge to join a man at night, unaccompanied, was a commitment to marriage. This hasty flight, while it would be typical of Elk and his family, would not help him integrate the ways of the Sky Bundle into village life. But she knew he had watched her many years, and that he had little time to follow the deliberate, elaborate patterns of village life, and had not yet recovered his reputation enough to be accepted into her family through the normal paths of courtship.

The day after the full moon Afraid-of-Bird was sure that her family must know what she was up to. Her heart pounded all day long. She spilled water, dropped wood, stumbled over children, hit her head on the lodge door, laughed and cried without explanation. If the people of her lodge did notice her curious behavior, they said nothing. It would not have been the Nehawka way to interfere in her life and thoughts. If she had something she wanted to talk about, she would talk.

Afraid-of-Bird lay in her robes that night hoping that the pounding of her heart and the roar of her breathing would not wake the others around her. When she was sure everyone had fallen asleep, she rose deliberately from her bed, picked up the small packet of clothing and food she had hidden under her pillow, and stepped from the lodge. Even if someone noticed her leave, no one would say anything, because she might only be stepping out to relieve herself and this was not something one asked about.

Outside the door of the lodge she pulled her dress down over her shoulders and slipped new moccasins on her feet. She quickly combed her hair and braided it and hurried down the path to the creek. She was frightened, because she could not recall a time when she had ventured out of the village alone. It was not the sort of thing a Nehawka woman did. Afraid-of-Bird was relieved when after she had taken only a few steps Digger rose from the bushes and came to her side. He smiled at her in the moonlight and took her arm. Without a word they both set off at a soft, quiet lope along the banks of the creek toward where it joined the waters of the Smokey River, far enough from the village that no one would see or hear them or smell the smoke of a fire.

As they neared the union of the rivers, a traditional place for such elopements, Afraid-of-Bird saw the faint flicker of a fire and the pale brown shape of a small camp tent. Digger went a few more steps with her and then stopped. She turned to him and thanked him. He nodded, looked away, and began the long run back to the village.

Afraid-of-Bird approached the camp slowly but not quietly. Softly, she sang her virgin's song, the song she had sung while gathering sage for the Sacred Sky Bundle and when butchering the first buffalo of the winter hunt, the song she had learned for her marriage night:

> I am Afraid-of-Bird, once alone;
> Now I am Afraid-of-Bird, forever a part of another.
> It is better to be together.

As she approached, a young man rose from beside the fire and turned toward her, the fire at his back so she could see only the light on his shiny black hair. She walked in fear and joy, both together, both at once. He opened his robe so she could step into it. He closed the robe around her.

Inside the robe it was warm, in contrast with the night air. In the robe she could smell his man smells, clean man smells; as was proper, he had bathed in the river and rubbed himself with sage. She could feel the hard pressure of his manhood against her dress, insistent and unfamiliar. She pulled at the string securing the front of her dress so it could fall open. In the restraints of the robe, her dress fell only far enough that one of her breasts was free but it was, for the moment, enough. When her bare breast pressed against her lover's chest, she almost fell from the ecstasy of the feeling that filled her. She felt her man's body shudder with the same ecstasy.

The only sound in the deep, dark robe was the pounding of her heart—no, it was not *her* heart; it was his. She laughed softly aloud when she realized that she was not the only one here tonight who was frightened and excited and full of joy, too long delayed. Her lover jerked, as if startled at her laugh.

"I laugh only at myself and because of my joy," she whispered, her voice almost lost in the dark warmth of the robe.

"I cry because of myself and my joy," Ribs said.

Ribs! She stepped back from the robe and pulled her dress across her breasts. She took his shoulders and turned his face toward the fire. It was Ribs. She pulled her hand back and slapped him so hard he reeled backward and fell over his robe into the campfire, sending a shower of sparks into the night sky.

Afraid-of-Bird, with her quick laugh, would have found this funny in another circumstance, but now she was overwhelmed with the consequences of this night. Still, she might have laughed, but when she slapped Ribs, her hand had met a face wet with tears. As she sank to her knees to cry, she looked across at Ribs, his robe still smoldering from where it had caught fire, and she could see that he too was crying.

Afraid-of-Bird had known Ribs all his life—but then everyone in the village knew everyone all their lives. Ribs was a good, brave, kind man. He was handsome, a good hunter, and a good family member. He was welcome at any cooking fire. He would have been welcome as a suitor in any lodge. Any other young woman in the Turtle Creek village would have gladly stepped into Ribs's robe for a few moments of courtship.

Both Ribs and Afraid-of-Bird knew what he had done this night. Afraid-of-Bird could not go back to the village the same young girl who had left it. She had compromised her virtue completely by coming here and she could only go back a cheap woman available to anyone who needed a woman, anyone who couldn't get any other woman. Or she could return to the village a woman and a wife. Ribs's wife.

She could have thought about Elk but it was too late for that now. Elk had moved too slowly and now she was Ribs's woman, not Elk's. There was no sense in lamenting what might have been because she knew that this was what was. Afraid-of-Bird looked across the smoking remnants of the fire and considered Ribs, sitting there with tears of shame running down his face, coals still glowing and smoking on his best robe. And she laughed. Ribs looked up at her in amazement. "You're not angry?"

"Yes, I'm angry," she snapped. "You behave like Coyote instead of a Nehawka. You and Coyote get your women by lying and cheating."

"I have no women, Afraid-of-Bird. I have been alone until now," Ribs said apologetically.

"And you look like Coyote, sitting there with your robe on fire." She said through her sobs. "You are a mess." She wet her finger with her tongue and extinguished some of the small glowing spots on his robe.

"You smell like Coyote, too," she said. Ribs knew that Afraid-of-Bird was thinking of the old tale in which Coyote instructs his anus to watch his cooking supper while he sleeps; when he awakes, he finds that Rabbit has stolen his food, so Coyote punishes his own anus by stabbing it with a firebrand. Angry and in pain, Coyote falls into his own campfire, catching his fur on fire and smearing himself with the remnants of his stolen supper.

Ribs wiped at his tears, looked at his sorry condition. He was not much of a suitor for this beautiful Nehawka woman, his robe smoking, his face covered with tears. He threw the robe aside and fanned at his fire. Once it was burning again, they could see that he had also fallen on and broken the pot in which he was cooking wasna soup for their wedding feast. The only reason his robe hadn't been burned even worse was that it was soaked in soup and covered with bits of cooked meat and berries. Ribs *was* a mess. He *was* indeed like old Coyote.

Ribs laughed. A little at first, and then more. And for the first time he was happy that he had done this terrible thing. Afraid-of-Bird was still angry with him, and still heartbroken that Elk would not be hers, and embarrassed that she had not been married like a proper Nehawka girl. But when she had salvaged some of Ribs's wedding feast and eaten, when she had extinguished the last of the smoldering embers in his robe, when she had seen his chagrin and heard him talk of his love for her, when they had laughed together for the first time as man and woman, her heart softened.

That night as they lay in Ribs's small tent, he was so timid and gentle that Afraid-of-Bird was happy, too. Ribs was astonished that, though he had dreamed of this night a hundred times, and whenever he saw Afraid-of-Bird in the village his manhood was embarrassingly independent, now, when it was his obligation to be a man, his manhood failed him.

Afraid-of-Bird sensed his embarrassment and frustration and, somehow, almost against her will, suddenly loved this man who had stolen her virtue. He would be a good husband. He could not be cruel when he was so fragile. She vowed to herself right then, before their marriage had been consummated, that she would let the village have his hard warrior side but make his softness, his gentleness hers. "Don't worry, Ribs. I will be a good wife for you and I know you will be a good husband."

"I will be a good husband, but perhaps not tonight," Ribs said.

"Tonight is not important as long as we are together. There will be many other nights." And Ribs was at once again a man.

Ribs and his new wife returned to the village the next day. A few women clucked their tongues but others trilled a victory cry. Afraid-of-Bird had slept alone far too long. And Ribs would be a suitable husband.

Elk was one of the first to congratulate Ribs. Ribs started to explain but Elk put his arm around his shoulders, as young men who had been childhood friends. Ribs knew that Elk's heart was aching, and Elk knew that Ribs had not acted out of spite or cruelty or thoughtlessness. They would remain friends, but Elk did not speak again with Afraid-of-Bird, or exchange a glance with her, for almost four years.

Instead, Elk poured even more energy into the Sky Bundle. He prayed and sang and talked to others in the village about the powers of the Bundle. He smoothed the way for the Bundle and its powers with the elders and the leaders of other clans, families, societies, and tribes, until the last resistance lay within the Buffalo Dancers, and Elk could think of no way to ease their minds about the Sky Bundle.

As anyone who knows Coyote and his ways should have known, the moment of the Sky Bundle's death and its rise to prominence came within almost the same moment and in a way no one could have expected. It happened on a hot day well after harvesttime. The crops had been taken from the fields and the tribe was already making preparations for the long winter hunt, the hunt that would provide them with food, clothing, and shelter for another brutal Plains winter.

All the tools, weapons, and supplies had been assembled for departure for the hunt. Everyone hurried, because it was important to be well onto the buffalo range before snow flew, and yet here they were, sweating in unaccustomed heat. They would leave in a few days, taking the Sky Bundle with them in the hope that it would protect them from severe weather. The Buffalo Dancers did their dance, their bodies covered with full buffalo hides and buffalo heads over their own faces, protected by the fact that they became mighty buffalo while they danced and therefore were unaffected by the heat. Everything that could be done was done to ensure a successful hunt.

The sun was still high in the afternoon sky when four young boys who had been playing at a hunt on top of the hill to the west of the village came running down the hill as fast as they could, falling, tumbling, running, screaming. "The Thunderers! The Thunderers!" they howled in terror, pointing back toward the hill behind them.

And behind them, from over the hill, came the Thunderers. A tornado as wide as the entire village roared into sight, lifting oak trees roots and all into the sky, tearing the grass from the ground, blackening the sky with its destruction, sucking water and fish from the creek, dust and gophers from a buffalo wallow.

The people of Turtle Creek had only moments to throw themselves into the lodges before the tornado roared into the village. The children screamed as air was sucked out the narrow doorways of the lodges, tearing bedding, sacred objects, food, tools, cooking pots, clothing, everything up through the smoke holes. Dust and the power of the wind made it almost impossible to breathe. Dogs howled as they died, flung against walls, torn apart by wind and wood. Timbers creaked and groaned. Trees slammed into the lodges. One lodge leaned slowly to one side and collapsed, crushing three old women who had hidden under their bed robes.

And then suddenly all was quiet, except for the screams and cries of the people and animals who were dying or afraid of dying. Elk crawled from under the rubble where he lay protecting the Sky Bundle with his body. He looked around his lodge. The smoke hole had been torn open so there was almost more sky than roof above him. A dog was impaled on a pole at the smoke hole, still screaming. His people's possessions—their sacred objects—were scattered. He moved quickly around the lodge, touching each of his people; as soon as he determined that one was alive and not badly injured, he moved to the next. He stepped outside, over the rubble of the entryway. All around him was destruction: people crying and bleeding, supplies for the hunt torn, destroyed, burning, scattered, ruined. People were already mourning their dead and attending to the wounded.

There were suddenly so many feelings, it was hard to sort them out or even consider them in a meaningful order. How could the people leave on the hunt with so many people dead and hurt, buried in the ruins of the lodges or blown away and lost? Even if they could leave on the hunt, there was nothing to take by way of tools, weapons, and supplies. Everything was gone—spears, baskets, bows, robes, ropes, knives. How could they survive the winter without meat from the winter hunt?

And if they salvaged enough tools and energy to make a hunt, who would repair the lodges so the people would have homes to return to, shelter from the hard Plains winters?

Why did this happen? What had happened to the Sky Bundle? Wasn't this precisely what its powers were for? Wind and Sky?

That there were no injured people in Elk's lodge did not help Elk's situation. Someone was seriously hurt or killed in every lodge but his. Was the Sky Bundle simply a family talisman that didn't speak to the rest of the village or tribe? Was all this disaster a result of the people not paying enough attention to the Buffalo Dance? Were the spirits of the buffalo angry? Or were the spirits of the sky angry because the people were still doing the Buffalo Dance? The confusion in the people's minds matched the confusion of what was left of Turtle Creek village.

The angry people of Turtle Creek surrounded Elk and wanted to know why he hadn't been atop one of the lodges when the storm hit. Why hadn't he held the Sky Bundle toward the sky and sung its songs while the storm was going on? Why hadn't he used his knowledge, his visions, his influence with the Powers and Thunderers to save his village?

Elk had no explanation. He had been in his lodge attending to the Bundle and praying when the storm hit. He was asking for a good hunt for the people and for a winter that would give them good food and shelter so even on the hunt they could consider the power of the Sky Bundle. The people laughed at him. Not just the most conservative of the elders now, but even those who had previously supported Elk.

They turned from him, all except some of his old friends like Ribs and Digger, his father and mother, Early Cry and Birch Bark. And Sand, Afraid-of-Bird's younger sister; Sand came to Elk's side. Disheartened, Elk climbed to the top of his family's ruined lodge with the Sky Bundle and prayed. He didn't ask for anything. He never did. That would have been an unforgivable arrogance. He simply prayed. He was grateful that so many had been spared, that the Bundle was safe, that the Thunderers had decided to visit Turtle Creek village. As much as he wanted to ask, to beg, atop his family lodge, he could only offer thanks.

It did not help that several people shouted at him, mocked his prayers from below, in the village. Mocking was not a Nehawka way, he knew, but he also knew that the people were hurt and angry, and some of them blamed him for their pain and anger. For all Elk knew, they were right. All he could do was what he had to do. So he prayed and sang. And offered up his thanks, through the night and into the next day.

Then, at almost exactly the same time the next day, the Thunderers came again. Elk was still sitting atop his lodge so he was probably the first to see them. He couldn't believe his eyes. For the first time in his life since he had been marched from the Pawnee village in Pawnee finery, he wished he could die. Despite his prayers and his people's pain, over the hill to the west came another tornado, at least as big and dark as the one from the day before. He tried to shout but his pain killed his cry. He thought of his people.

"The Thunderers!" he screamed as loud as he could. He sprang to his feet atop the lodge, pointed to the west, and screamed again, "The Thunderers!" And the people began their mourning cries and strong-heart songs even before they had retreated to what was left of their lodges. Elk stood on his lodge and raised the Sky Bundle to the sky. He would prefer to die and lose the bundle, he thought, than face his people's pain again.

He watched the huge, roaring horror bear down on the village. Once again the ground exploded as the winds hit the creek and the buffalo wallow and the trees. The Thunderers came directly at the village. Tears ran down Elk's face but he stood solidly, holding the Sacred Bundle of his vision to the sky. Again, for the third time in his life, he began his death song—

Hey! My friends, I, Elk, know this: every bird comes at death to earth.
Hey! You Thunderers, I, Elk, know this: every summer wind that blows north, again blows south in the winter . . .

Elk closed his eyes. Wind battered him. Pebbles, sticks, limbs, birds hit him. He heard the screaming and bellowing of great animals and felt the ground shaking. As in his vision he was again flying. He was battered by things of the prairie that the winds threw at him. And then, just as had happened the day before, but long before Elk expected it, the wind stopped.

Much too soon.

He felt more surprise than relief. For one thing, he was still alive. He opened his eyes. He looked around the village. Nothing much had changed, but it would have been hard for him to tell the difference between the ruin of yesterday and that of today. The calm was a relief for Elk, but then again, it was something of a letdown after the drama of yesterday.

He looked at the Sacred Sky Bundle in his hands. It was unharmed. His arms were covered with streaks of blood, and so was the rest of his body. Nothing serious, but he had obviously been pummeled by a lot of small, fast-flying objects that had inflicted a thousand cuts on him—like the ritual of a hundred cuts that wives or parents occasionally performed when a husband or child died.

He crawled down from the crest of the lodge, the first time his feet had touched the ground of the village in a full day. His people were coming out of their lodges. Like Elk, they looked around them. They too were amazed as they surveyed the damage—or rather, lack of damage. Aside, that is, from the massive destruction of the day before. The people looked at Elk, wondering, since they had blamed him for the previous disaster, if they should now thank him for whatever he and the power of the Sky Bundle had done to protect them.

Elk decided it was time to speak. He stood at the base of his lodge until Badger passed by. Badger controlled announcements in the village and Elk needed to speak through him. He raised his finger to Badger and Badger came to him. "I need to speak to the people," Elk said quietly.

Badger raised his staff and called for attention. Elk wanted to speak and he, Badger, would repeat his words. The people turned to Badger. Elk said to him, "I am a Turtle Creek Nehawka and I know what the Turtle Creek Nehawka think. I understand the questions and confusion of this moment. But I have some words I must say."

Badger turned to the people and shouted Elk's words: "Elk is a Turtle Creek Nehawka and he knows what the Turtle Creek Nehawka think. He understands the questions and confusion of this moment. But he has some words he must say."

Elk spoke to Badger's ear again. "The Sky Bundle is not something to worship or believe in. It is not a thing we can ask for favors. It is not something that will protect us from storms or from the Pawnee. It will not give us life or victories. It is only powerful. It asks nothing of us. It gives us nothing. It is simply here. It is powerful and it is the Sky Bundle. It is the Sky Bundle and it is powerful. And it is ours."

Badger shouted Elk's words to the people standing in the rubble of their village, and with both hands Elk raised the Sky Bundle over his head.

"I do not understand the Bundle. No one can understand the Bundle. All I know is that the Bundle is a gift to us from the Powers. You want me to tell you what the Sky Bundle means, but it is like a man's vision. I don't know what it means," Elk said to Badger.

Badger again echoed Elk's words.

"The Sky Bundle may have brought this terrible destruction to us from the Thunderers. I don't know. It may have nothing to do with these matters. I don't know. I do know that the Sky Bundle is a gift and it is powerful and it belongs among us. It requires nothing, it threatens nothing. It is a *gift*. I do not know what it means." Elk stopped. He was filled with the anguish of his people, owned by the power of his vision gift.

Badger repeated his words, and added, "Elk serves the Sky Bundle and speaks from it. He is a holy man and the words you hear are from the Sky Bundle, not from him. I am Badger. I am your crier, and I know whose words I hear." This was an unheard-of license for a crier, but everyone's respect for Badger was so immense that no one doubted his judgment. He could say such things, and what's more, he was surely right in this judgment. People nodded in understanding and agreement.

The sun was high in the sky again and the people were still arguing throughout the village about the meaning of the two days of storms and their relationship to the Sky Bundle—not to mention the continuing mourning and fear for what was to become of the people without a winter hunt. Then a man came with news from the creek. As it happened, the man was Ribs.

He came running easily up the trail from the creek below the village, carrying something in his hand. He ran to the center of the village and held it high, saying nothing. The people gathered around him and saw that it was the beard from a bull buffalo. A *big* beard, from a *big* buffalo. He held the hair up to his old friend Elk, and gave the buffalo beard to him.

Ribs grinned and without words waved for the people to follow him. He returned down the creek path, the trail the women usually followed to reach the water. He stopped and swept his hand across the wash below him. Women who had only moments before been lifting the mourning cry to the skies now made the trill of victory. Below them were dead buffalo, driven off a cliff into a narrow canyon by the storm. A hundred buffalo. More than the village could possibly use in a winter.

Out of the disaster, as a gift of the disaster, the village that yesterday had no hope for food, today had more food than it could use. The storm that had destroyed the means for gathering food had given the people more food than they could possibly cut and dry. Denied the tradition of going out onto the high plains for the winter hunt, the people suddenly had no need to go out onto the high plains for the winter hunt. The disaster had become a blessing. From death came life. It was Coyote at his best and worst, right where Coyote always is, at his best, which is his worst, at his worst, which is his best.

For days the village was in a state of Coyote-like contradiction. As the people buried their dead, they celebrated their good fortune. As they harvested the buffalo gift, they struggled with the damage to their homes. Although they were grateful when the weather turned bitter cold, giving them time to cut and dry the buffalo, they fought to stay warm in their homes and at their work on the buffalo kill. As they worked to repair the wounds of their relatives and friends, others injured themselves in the frenzy of butchering at the creek. Although they were thankful that the buffalo were at the creek where the meat could be cleaned more easily, they worried that the women had to walk longer distances over the hill in the cold to get clean water upstream.

Everywhere in the village people wept and laughed, and turned to each other and said, "Coyote!" That's all anyone needed to say: "Coyote!" Who else could so completely confuse good and bad? Coyote. And Coyote had obviously become an ally of Elk, and the Sky Bundle. And of the Buffalo Dancers, whose task it was to provide the village with a good spiritual setting for a successful winter hunt. Coyote had brought the Sky Bundle and the Buffalo Dancers together. The result of it all was an alliance between the Buffalo Dancers and the Sky Clan.

Elk's reputation among the Nehawka grew, and he was asked to be the chief of the winter hunt for fourteen years in a row, an honor that had not been conferred within the memory of anyone in the village. But what could be more obvious, after all?

That winter was known as "The Winter of the Buffalo Rain." There was no discussion. The matter was not even considered by the elders. That was the name by which the winter was known to everyone. That too was obvious.

► ► **P A R T I V :** *Full Circle*

Years of peace followed the Winter of the Buffalo Rain. There were no battles with the Pawnee or Mandan or any other tribes. There were rumors of problems with the increasing incursions of the Long Knives from the East, but life in Turtle Creek was easy. Best of all, there were few problems in the village. Everyone got along in the lodges. Beautiful babies were born and young people grew strong and handsome. Old people died, of course, but then old people always die. That's what old people do! That is what life is about.

Elk found his own peace with his young wife, Sand. She knew that she was not Elk's first choice for a wife, that she could never have Afraid-of-Bird's place in his heart, but she knew that he loved her. Elk knew that Sand understood his pain, and he loved her all the more for her understanding. He was happy, especially when they were on the hunt and he could sleep beside his Sand in the relative privacy of the tent instead of in a crowded earth lodge. Sand gave him two fine sons and Elk adored them. He loved them in part because he knew that they would inherit his responsibilities toward the Sky Bundle, and he loved the Sky Bundle, and feared it, because he knew its power. From the turmoil of his youth came a serenity in his manhood.

Death was a part of village life, but two deaths affected Elk more than he expected. Within a few days of each other, Elk's father Big Elk and his old friend Ribs died, both of a mysterious illness. Travelers bringing pipestone from the east told him this new death was happening to many people in their homes, that it was a death carried by the white people they had met and traded with at the Smokey River.

Well, Elk thought, there is no escaping death.

His father, Big Elk, had lived a good life. His funeral was traditional. While the women keened and cried, many of the men told tales about Big Elk and his exploits. They told about the Pawnee he had killed, and his travels far to the west to bring back flint and to the east for pipestone.

To Elk's surprise, he heard that his father had had a way with women in his youth. Elk laughed when elders said that despite his late start, he might have the same talents. There was some talk about Big Elk's impetuous youth, his time of exile, his problems with the Ponca woman, but the stories were left untold when an elder poked the storyteller and pointed toward Elk. Apparently the family was not ready to remember all of its past. Elk spoke on the occasion of his father's death, and reminded the village and his kin of all that Big Elk had done for them during his long and powerful life.

Elk spoke too at the death of Ribs. He spoke of his own pain at this loss of an old, good friend; and he spoke of the pain of Afraid-of-Bird, his wife's sister. He watched Afraid-of-Bird slash her arms with a flint knife, and he asked his own mother to nurse her back to health from her sorrow and her injuries: she was after all his wife Sand's sister, and therefore it was his obligation in accordance with the customs of the Nehawka to take her into his lodge as a second wife so she would not be without food, without a man, without a family.

The new arrangements were not going to be easy for anyone. There were Sand's feelings, and Afraid-of-Bird's. How could Elk comfort Afraid-of-Bird in her loss of Ribs and conceal his own joy that she would soon lie beside him in his bed? How could he excuse the foolishness of his youth and his delay in courting her? Sand had been a good wife—and she loved her sister—but she always knew that she was second in his heart and now would she be second in his bed? Of course Elk remembered the old men's jokes about the unfortunate warrior who wound up with two sisters as wives, both of them close and supportive against this male outsider who demanded, abused, forgot, neglected, ignored, and expected. One wife is hard enough to deal with, the men laughed. But two? Two *sisters*?

Sand, Afraid-of-Bird, and Elk worked hard at making the situation in the lodge as comfortable as they could, and they lived together many years, until their deaths, as a loving family. They laughed together far more than they argued. When one of them grieved, they all grieved. Their children were beautiful and happy and never knew unhappiness while they were children, and that, in Turtle Creek village, was understood to be what childhood should be. The little ones had a good father, two good mothers, and relatives enough that it took them the rest of their lives to sort their relationships out.

Elk's life was a good Nehawka life, in that he was admired and honored by his people as a generous and wise man, a generous husband, a firm but loving father; but his life was also full of questions, because along with everything else, Elk was a Nehawka holy man. He thought long and hard about the ways of the Buffalo Dance and the Sky Bundle. He prayed and pondered his vision. He considered each item in the Sky Bundle, wondering about its power and significance, curious about why the Thunderers had included these things in the Bundle.

He wondered about himself and his life. He appreciated his people's affection and respect, but he sincerely wondered if he was worthy of it. At last, however, the time came when he truly became a Nehawka man, when he no longer had doubts about his own worth. His heart was especially full because Afraid-of-Bird and Sand both understood the event and loved him all the more for his strength.

It was not a stirring moment, not a time in the heat of battle or the hunt, nor in storm or fire. It was a quiet evening around the fire. Some old men came to Elk's lodge one evening to tell stories. The children gathered in their mothers' laps and visitors from other lodges joined the audience as the old-timers told story after story, about Coyote and Orphan and raids against the Pawnee and water monsters and efforts to steal the eggs of the Thunderers.

Big Belly, however—whom everyone loved but mostly tolerated because he was a little dull-witted and difficult—began to tell a story about a long-ago raid against the Pawnee. A raid by some young Nehawka warriors who were acting without the permission of the elders. They set off to the west for the fourth year in a row to insult the Pawnee, Big Belly told his eager audience, but things didn't go well on this raid and they were humiliated in a way that no one ever forgot, the old man told them. "I will tell you the story of that raid and its disgraceful end," Big Belly laughed.

Then Big Belly stopped short in his narrative, sensing the uneasy silence that suddenly came over the room. He stopped and looked uncomfortably around the lodge. It was obvious even to him that he had said something wrong, something stupid. Everyone sat silently, looking at their hands. In embarrassment, Sand and Afraid-of-Bird covered their heads with their robes. Elk, Big Belly's honored host, sat absolutely still, not moving a muscle; he stared into the fire without blinking. Old Man Big Belly sat in silence a long time and thought about what he had done. No one said anything. Big Belly tried to remember what he had said and why it had caused all this embarrassment among his friends and kinsmen. And then he remembered.

Finally he said, "I have forgotten the rest of the story. I am old and foolish and forget. Sometimes I say things I shouldn't say. I must excuse myself and go back to my lodge. It is not a good story.

I forget how it ends. I am sorry for keeping you up so long. I am an old fool sometimes."

Elk put his hand gently on the old man's shoulder and pulled him back to his seat. "Here, Big Belly, my uncle. Have some more meat. It is fat and soft so you don't have to chew so hard with those three teeth you have left. I remember that story you are telling about the foolish young boy and the Pawnee. I remember it well, my old friend. The young boys raided the Pawnee village, counting coup three years in a row, and then they decided to make another raid, but, just as you said, things didn't turn out quite as they had expected. They left early one morning, before anyone else had awakened, making the mistake of taking with them the Sacred Rain-Fire Bundle. They traveled one full day toward the west . . ."

Big Belly almost spoiled the story when he rose from his side of the fire and embraced Elk. He sat back down and mumbled something about what a fine man Elk had become and how fortunate the Nehawka were to have him and what a fool he was, but Sand and Afraid-of-Bird calmed him and began to comb his hair, a sign of respect reserved for the wise. Elk finished the story about the foolish boys and their encounter with the Pawnee, and everyone in the lodge agreed that no one had ever told the tale better.

That winter the elders argued at length about what the winter count should say about the year. Most felt that it should be "The Winter that Elk Became a Nehawka Chief," but Elk, one of the elders, spoke against that choice. He felt that they should call it "The Winter an Elk Became a Man." He insisted, and that was the decision of the council of elders.

Beginnings

G host Elk turned and looked back from the top of the hill. He knew that this would be the last time he would see the village of his parents and grandparents and all of his family for all of time. In the village below, his brother Snake raised his hand in farewell, and high on the hill Ghost Elk raised his hand, too. One last look at the lodge he had lived in all his life, one last look at his old neighbors and friends, one last look at Mother Corn village.

Ghost Elk was grateful that they were still his friends. His departure had not been easy. The argument had been long and bitter. Would the people, the Nehawka, stay in hope that it would eventually rain? It always had rained, but now the streams were dry. The fish were gone and the crops died. Not even the usually abundant deer and elk came to the hunting grounds. Ghost Elk had argued that it was time for the Nehawka people to move on, to seek a new home closer to the home of rain, away from the sun and the hot winds of summer; Ghost Elk's brother Snake argued just as passionately that this was the land of the Nehawka and there could be no other home. The land, the sky, the Powers had always been good to the people and would surely reward their patience. Ghost Elk said there was no choice, they must leave; Snake said there was no choice, they must stay.

So it had come to this. Ghost Elk and fifty-two of his followers had packed their goods and were setting off into the unknown, toward the home of the rain, the place from where the rivers came. Snake and eighty-six others, many of them sick, elderly, and children, were to stay in the ancestral village on the Big-Fish River, where there were no longer plenty of fish, but where they still had hope.

The argument in the village had grown heated because each side believed passionately in the truth of its position. Even more important to everyone was the terrible thought of the people being split, of losing friends and relatives forever. Moreover, life was always hard and there were always dangers, both in the village and on the hunt; both the travelers and the village would be endangered by the loss of half their number. A hard time was certain to follow.

Once the decisions had been made about who would go and who would stay, there was no longer anger in the village, only sorrow and fear. Those who had decided to stay behind at Mother Corn village helped the travelers assemble the moccasins, dried meat and berries, arrows and flint knives, all the tools, supplies and weapons they would need to travel the long distance into strange land to establish a new home.

The last night the village was whole, there was a Buffalo Dance, filled with hope and fear, love and despair. There were gifts and tears. Families divided; life would never be the same again for the people. Snake gave a long speech, urging the people to pray each for the other. He gave his brother two large clam shells joined together for carrying fire, shells that had been traded up the river to the village from far, far below in the warm lands. He gave Ghost Elk's band a small supply of the precious smoldering wood from the water trees. He gave Ghost Elk a white coyote skin to protect him from enemies, and tobacco for his pipe. He gave him some seeds of the sacred blue corn to plant at the place of the new home.

And Snake gave his brother a bird, a bird the color of deep water, because there were many who believed that it was this bird that brought rain. This was a powerful gift, the sort of gift one expects a brother to give a brother, even when there have been angry words. Ghost Elk knew that the people who were staying at the village needed rain, too, and this sacrifice of the Rain Bird might cost them their lives while it saved the lives of the travelers. Ghost

Elk accepted the gifts and wrapped the thin cord tied to the bird's leg to his own wrist.

Ghost Elk tried to find the words to thank his brother but he could not find them. He wanted to speak of the pain in his heart, and of his fear. Snake understood his brother's thoughts: everything they were doing this night was for the last time. Every word, every embrace, every smile, every tear—the last time. They would never see each other again. The people who had been together through all time would now be two people, the people of Mother Corn village on the Big-Fish River, and Ghost Elk's band, going elsewhere, to be another people.

"No," Ghost Elk insisted. "We will always be Nehawka. The great bull bison is always a bull bison, wherever he is, even when he is dead. We will always be Nehawka. Perhaps you will hear stories of us from the Land from Where Winter Comes. Wherever we are, we will dance the Buffalo Dance, and we will speak of our relatives and friends in Mother Corn village. Now there are two bands of the Nehawka and we will be even stronger." Not even Ghost Elk heard his own words without doubting them. Ghost Elk's travelers passed over the hill toward the summer sunset and away from the home village of the Nehawka people.

Many days, more than the period of a full moon, the travelers moved away from the sun, toward the home of winter, rain, and the rivers. Twice they saw the smoke of villages and camps but they were careful to avoid any contact since they did not know the ways of the people in this distant and less civilized land. They kept the fire glowing in the smoldering wood, held in the two halves of the fire shell they carried with them, but they did not have the courage to build a fire over which to cook.

They reached a big river, far too wide to cross, and they followed its banks since they led in the direction of the home of rain and rivers. There was still no rain. Not a drop in the thirty sunrises they traveled. There was no game, no food, nothing but parched grass and a burning sun. The only sign of hope they had was that the great river they were following was full of water, more water than they had ever seen before. Unfortunately, there was also so much water, moving so fast, that they could not hunt for fish or clams in its waters, and while they saw a few tracks of deer, elk, and buffalo, they did not see the animals that made them.

Ghost Elk could see that the situation was reaching the point of disaster. His band could not go much further, and yet he saw nothing to recommend a site for a new home. He wanted a good, clear stream; some low, flat ground where the women could plant squash and corn; some still water for clams and cattails; a protected place for lodges, wood and game. It was not as if he saw land where two or three of these necessities were missing; he did not see a place where more than two or three of these requirements were present. They traveled on toward the setting sun.

The end of the long trek came the day the travelers crossed a high, broad, flat plain, exposed to the sun and wind, barren and empty. It was a frightening day, because Ghost Elk and all the others knew that they were vulnerable while moving across the plain, open to attack from any direction. There was no wood here, no water, nor had there been good water or wood for many days. Far from improving, the land was getting ever more barren, drier, less hospitable. There was talk about turning and trying to reach the old village, but Ghost Elk cautioned that there were no longer enough supplies for three days, yet all the days of a moon it would take to return to the village.

Lame Bear, the old man who kept the fire, approached Ghost Elk that day with tears in his eyes. He tried to talk but could not find the words. "What is it, Lame Bear?" Ghost Elk asked, trying to understand what the old man was struggling to say. Finally Lame Bear reached into the skin pouch at his side and pulled out the fire shell. He opened the two halves and held them out to Ghost Elk. Ghost Elk understood: the fire had gone out. In the long trek across the open plain Lame Bear had had difficulty finding fuel to keep the fire smoldering. He had said again and again that fire needs to breathe, to eat, and that they should stop and build a fire, but conditions had not permitted that.

Lame Bear had not been able to fulfill his obligation and now the band's fire was dead. Given enough time and the right tools and dry tinder and wood, Lame Bear could make fire again, but not here, not now.

Nor would the new fire be the old fire of the people. The fire they had brought with them from Mother Corn village was a fire that had burned continuously for generations. The word "Fire" was not used for the fires that came across the grass from the sun's home or from the burning trees that had been struck by lighting. "Fire" was a word reserved for this one fire, the fire that the Nehawka people had always had, had nurtured for so long, the fire of Mother Corn village on Big-Fish River.

Without the old fire they would no longer be the same people. Ghost Elk looked to the sky and wondered what his people had done so wrong that they had become cursed? Or was it all his mistake? He held out his arms to the clouds, always promising but never giving, and asked the Thunderers to help him and his people find a new home.

And then, at the moment he learned the fire was dead, Ghost Elk also sensed a small weight on his arm, where the Rain Bird had traveled this long trip, but not the same weight. Ghost Elk turned his face to his left arm, and there, dangling from the light cord at his wrist, was the Rain Bird, dead.

The old fire had died, the Rain Bird had died, and now Ghost Elk's band would die too. His heart no longer was full of hope and courage; Ghost Elk had failed and he felt nothing but surrender and despair. And a raindrop.

Ghost Elk opened his eyes. He had felt a raindrop. And then another. And another. Then Ghost Elk's face was filled with rain, and cold water ran down his breast for the first time in many moons. The people of Ghost Elk's band began to laugh and sing. This was the sign they sought, and the death of both the fire and the Rain Bird no longer seemed important now that they had rain again.

Suddenly a bolt of lightning struck at the ground only a short distance from where they stood, and they recognized the sound of a great tree exploding, and yet they had seen no tree. It was as if the lightning had struck *into* the ground. Two of the young men ran toward where the bolt had hit, toward the plume of smoke that was coming up from the ground. They stopped and called to Ghost Elk to come to them.

Ghost Elk ran to them and could hardly believe what he saw. Below the stark, open plain where they stood was a broad low-land, filled with trees—oak, ash, cedar, hackberry, cottonwood, willow. A small, clear creek ran through the lowland toward the great river they would eventually come to call the Smokey River because of the muddy clouds in its heavy waters. In the bends of the little creek there were open meadows, perfect for the women's fields, and near the river there were long, narrow ponds, almost certainly full of fish and clams. Not far from them, a gigantic, shattered oak tree smoldered where the lightning had blown it open.

Ghost Elk understood. This was the sign. This was the gift of the Thunderers. It was the confusing way of Coyote. The Rain

Bird had died, and the old fire. His hope and courage had died. His people had nothing but despair. And once everything of the old way, the old village, had gone, the Thunderers had given everything back to them—new fire, new hope, new courage, a new home. In dying, the Rain Bird had brought them the rain and given them the new fire, the fire that would become the ancestral fire of this new Nehawka village. Fire had come from, of all places, the rain.

This day was like the stories of Coyote—that fire should come to them from the least likely source, water; and life from death. That's the way Coyote works. Ghost Elk should have known. Only in surrender is there triumph.

In the next days the travelers built lodges and hunted food, of which there was plenty in the woods and waters of the hollow they had found. They found an abundance of wood and plums and berries. Although they planted their corn and squash very late in the season, they harvested more than enough food to take them through the winter, and more than enough seeds to plant the next year. The ponds along the Smokey River were full of crayfish and clams and arrowhead tubers and cattails. Turtles basked on every log along the creek, and so they called it Turtle Creek, and their new village was Turtle Creek village, and they came to be known as the Turtle Creek Nehawka.

Ghost Elk told his people that summer that he was going to wrap the fire shell, the skin of the Rain Bird, and some of the first harvest of blue corn in the white coyote skin his brother Snake had given him. He told them that he was going to hang the packet on one of the supports of his new lodge to remind him and his family and his people of their old home and their long journey and the wonderful gift this new home was. He painted that support, the one furthest from the door of the lodge, with blue mud from a deposit he found not far from the new village. The post represented Wind, one of the four Thunderers, the color of the Rain Bird, and it became the home of the new Sacred Bundle.

And the Rain-Fire Bundle became the new soul of the new Nehawka village on Turtle Creek.

By way of respect toward the Thunderers and by way of compensating for the use of the lodge post and by way of thanking all the Thunderers for the Nehawkas' new home, the new Sacred Bundle was to be known, Ghost Elk told his people, as the Rain-Fire Bundle, and he, Ghost Elk, would be its Keeper. And his new son, born that harvest season in the new village, the first one of his people to be born in the new land, would follow him as the Keeper of the Rain-Fire Bundle.

Just as the Rain-Fire Bundle had brought them here, Ghost Elk told them, it would keep the people whole.

That winter Ghost Elk, Lame Bear, and two other elders in the Turtle Creek village decided that they would know that year in the winter count as "the Winter the People Came Home."

ABOUT THE AUTHOR

▼ ▲ ▼

ROGER WELSCH was full professor of English and anthropology at the University of Nebraska until 1988, when he left the academic world to become a writer, living on a small farm near Dannebrog, Nebraska. He is currently an essayist for CBS's *Sunday Morning* with Charles Kuralt, and columnist for *Natural History* magazine and seventeen other magazines and newspapers. *Touching the Fire* is his sixteenth book, second collection of fiction. Roger has maintained a long and close association with the Omaha Tribe of Nebraska; he was adopted into the tribe in 1967 and was given the name Tenuga Gahi, "Bull Buffalo Chief."